THE KING'S OUTLAWS
HIGHLAND
BEAST

Bestselling & Multi-Award Winning Author
AMY JARECKI

PUBLISHER'S NOTE: This is a work of fiction. Names, characters, places, and incidents either are the product of the author's imagination or are used fictitiously. Any resemblance to actual persons, living or dead, business establishments, events, or locales is entirely coincidental.

Copyright © 2020, Amy Jarecki

Edited by: Scott Moreland

Book Cover Design by: Dar Albert

Published by Oliver-Heber Books

0 9 8 7 6 5 4 3 2 1

❧ I ❧

THE HIGHLANDS OF SCOTLAND, 5TH
AUGUST 1308

"Ye are too ill to weather a voyage," said Rhona of Clan MacDougall, standing on the Dunstaffnage pier, wringing her hands, still unable to believe all was lost.

Her Granduncle Alexander leaned heavily on his cane, its staff carved with the MacDougall rampant lions beneath a raven's head handle. "'Tis either I go now, or I'll be hanging from my own gallows come dawn. I say, I prefer the first option, my wee dearie."

Though uttered with a hint of jest, his words cut like daggers. The elderly gentleman was the esteemed Lord of Lorn, yet he was fleeing his home like a felon. "Please, at the least I ought to go with ye. I'm a healer. I can help."

"Nay, lass. The knowledge that you are here to do my bidding brings my mind peace. Ye are such a strong, stalwart gel. I only regret my son is unable to stand before Robert the Bruce in your stead. Forgive me for the terrible burden I have placed upon your shoulders."

Rhona exhaled with a sharp breath, her world all but crumbling about her feet. "I will perform my duty and consider it no burden at all."

"If anyone should desire to follow, the Lord Warden in Carlisle will ken my whereabouts."

"The Lord Warden," she repeated, committing that tidbit of information to memory.

At one time, she'd believed the might of her clan to be the greatest in Scotland, but after the death of King Edward I, military support from the English had waned, especially in the Highlands. The self-proclaimed king of Scots had taken advantage of England's change of power and marched northward, hell-bent on ruining the Lord of Lorn. Moreover, Alexander MacDougall was too old and frail to lead his army. In his stead, he'd sent his son, John, into the narrow Pass of Brander to fend off the rogue's attack. John was capable if not formidable. Nonetheless, the MacDougall forces had been trapped by the Black Douglas and his archers bearing down from the north while the Bruce and his knights attacked from the south. The surviving soldiers had already fled to England with John. Now, the Lord of Lorn himself trembled with weakness as he climbed into a galley, manned by only a dozen faithful guardsmen.

As the soldiers took up their oars, Lorn pulled a missive from inside his doublet and held it out. "Give this to Robert the Bruce."

Rhona took the letter and examined the seal with her granduncle's crest. "You've written to him?"

"I'm beaten, lass. Dunstaffnage is his, and that wee letter is my last attempt to ensure some of my lands will remain." As the *birlinn* drifted away from the pier, Lorn, ashen and pale, sank onto a bench. "Take care of my sister. Your grandmother thinks she is invincible but she needs you now more than ever."

Rhona blinked against the tears stinging her eyes. She was not about to cry. Not now, not when the townsfolk would be looking to her for leadership. Throwing her shoulders back, she raised the missive and waved it high above her head. "I will as I always care for Gran, m'lord."

Watching the patriarch of her family sail away, she

stood as rigid as a statue, drawing upon every vestige of strength. Refusing to allow herself to break down and cry, Rhona still could not believe the devastation that had befallen her clan. Worse, what tyranny lay ahead?

As the square sail picked up the wind and took the boat farther into the Firth of Lorn, Bram, Dunstaffnage's elderly sergeant-at-arms and the only Mac-Dougall soldier remaining at the castle, tapped her elbow. "Mistress, we'd best go inside and join the others. 'Tis no' safe to remain here."

"Is anywhere safe given these perilous times?" she asked, waving one last time as Lorn's *birlinn* grew smaller.

Bram offered his arm and together they ambled up the climb from the dock and crossed the drawbridge. Not able to smile, she gave the sergeant a nudge. "Look at we pair, holding the castle, a cripple and a soldier who should be enjoying the respite of retirement, albeit a capable soldier, all the same."

"Ye're hardly a cripple in anyone's eyes. Besides, ye move around far better than most." In truth, Bram was a tad lame himself due to rheumatism in his knees. Though Rhona didn't exactly know his age, his skin was etched with deep lines and his hair had been silver for years. "I am duty bound until I draw my last breath, of that ye must have no fear."

"Ye are a good man, though the coming days will be a trial for us all."

"That they will, mistress."

Together they crossed beneath the guardhouse and made their way through the outer bailey to the stairs leading to the castle's inner gate. Rhona's left shoe had a platform of two inches to compensate for the shorter leg, though steps always made her sway like a ship on the open sea. While they climbed, Bram's grunt didn't escape her notice.

"'Tisn't the season for rheumatism," she said, glancing to his knees.

"At my age, the accursed ailment doesn't give a fig about the season."

"Have ye been using my salve?"

"Aye, though not of late."

At the top of the stairs, Rhona stopped in the archway. "Whyever not?"

"I'm afeard the pot is empty."

"Silly fellow, ye should have told me sooner. I shall see to it I bring ye another at my first opportunity."

"My thanks." He inclined his head toward the great hall, from which came dissonant rumbles. "Are ye ready for this?"

Rhona clutched her granduncle's missive to her chest and glanced over her shoulder. From this vantage point, she had a sweeping view of the little village dotted with thatch-roofed cottages, and the winding road between them leading to the town square. Beyond lay the wood and the trail up the mountain pass. She did not spot horses or Robert the Bruce's army, but she knew in her bones they would be here anon. "We'd best haste."

As they pushed through the grand oak doors, all heads turned their way and the noise abated to a hum— at least long enough for Rhona to take a deep breath. While she moved into the hall, the clansmen and women swarmed around her, everyone talking at once.

"Did His Lordship sail away safely?"

"Has the Bruce's army arrived?"

"We're all doomed!"

"He'll starve us out."

"Nay, he'll work us to death and raise the rents."

"And then we'll starve."

"If the bastard doesn't cut our throats first!"

"Enough!" Rhona shouted, stomping the shoe with the wooden sole and making a loud boom resound clear to the rafters. "You cannot be certain what the devil is planning until he arrives. Mark me, ye'll do yourselves no good whatsoever if ye carry on with your predictions of ruin."

In truth, Rhona worried every bit as much about their fate as her clansmen and women did, but if she dared reveal her fears, there might be anarchy. Someone could incite a riot or dream up a harebrained scheme to march out the gates and meet the Bruce armed with nothing but pitchforks and spades.

Cook stepped forward, wiping his meaty palms on his apron. "A time ago the messenger said the army was marching from Loch Awe and should be here within the hour. Where the blazes are they? The waiting is what has us all tied in knots."

Just as he spoke the words, the ram's horn sounded from the direction of the guardhouse. Every muscle in Rhona's body stiffened as she met the concerned gazes of the folk she considered kin.

"There's no need to fret. Not a one of ye has raised a hand against the Bruce or his army. And all of you are crofters, or tradesmen, or servants of the chambers. Each and every one of ye is necessary to the running and provisioning of this keep."

"Ye sound as if ye approve of the murderer," growled Master Tailor.

Rhona's face burned as she looked the man in the eyes. "The Lord of Lorn told me to undertake whatever must be done to ensure the safety of clan and kin. I assure ye, I will *never* look to that man as my sovereign— not until Lorn himself pledges his fealty. We all ken the story of how Robert the Bruce killed our cousin, John Comyn. And in a *kirk* of all places." She panned her gaze across the faces of the others. "Make no bones about it, I am determined to survive these perilous times and to have every last soul in this chamber endure alongside me."

She took in a deep breath to calm her trembling hands while the thud from countless footsteps resounded from the courtyard. Turning, she faced the door with Bram standing beside her.

The time was nigh. In the next moments, their lives would be changed forever. Their fates decided by a man Rhona's granduncle hated to the depths of his soul.

The blackened-iron latch rattled.

Rhona tensed, her heartbeat thundering in her ears.

The hinges screeched loudly enough to be heard all the way to the cottage in the village that Rhona shared with her grandmother.

Dear God.

As the door swung open, nothing could have prepared her to meet the deadly stare of Arthur Campbell.

Arthur. Campbell.

It wasn't Robert the Bruce whose broad shoulders filled the doorway as he marched into the hall. No. Rhona stared into the black and soulless eyes of the one man she cared to never again see.

Bloodied, a helm tucked in the crook of one elbow, he wore a surcoat atop his mail, covered with so much dirt and splattered blood, she could not make out the coat of arms. His weapons clanged as he strode forward, flanked by a bevy of grisly soldiers. His eyes, as piercing as a golden eagle's, widened as recognition filled them. The man's Adam's apple bobbed as he shifted his gaze to Bram. "His Grace, Robert the Bruce has laid claim to this fortress for the Kingdom of Scotland. We require an audience with the Lord of Lorn forthwith."

Though the man sounded as cold as his heart, Rhona bucked up her nerve and stepped forward to assert her authority. "His Lordship is not here."

Arthur's lips disappeared into a thin line while those eyes shifted her way. "Where might we find him?"

No matter how disarming this man's gaze, Rhona

refused to allow the cur to affect her. She had been a foolish child once, thinking herself in love with the dark and handsome man from the neighboring clan, but she'd learned of his true nature after he'd disappeared without a word, as if the love they'd shared had been nothing but a tryst. After an entire summer of secret meetings and stolen kisses, Arthur had not even bothered to write.

"Once word came of the Bruce's *massacre* at the Pass of Brander, His Lordship had no alternative but to rise from his sickbed and flee." Rhona held up the missive and glanced to the clansmen and women behind her. The souls gathered deserved to know what it contained, no matter how much it sickened her to utter it. "My granduncle asked me to deliver this to the Bruce. 'Tis a letter acknowledging the defeat of Clan MacDougall and granting the *king* Dunstaffnage and her surrounds."

While gasps echoed throughout the hall, it nearly cut Rhona to the quick to refer to the man as king, and she crossed her fingers behind her back for good measure.

Arthur inclined his head to a formidable knight wearing full armor, who stepped forward and removed his helm. "I am Robert Bruce, king of Scots, and I come in peace." He said nothing as he panned his gaze across the hall. "I ken the MacDougall of all clans question my right to rule, and I'll tell ye here and now, I did slay John Comyn, kin of the MacDougall, at Greyfriars Kirk, but only after he betrayed me to Edward the Longshanks. Only after he testified, naming me as a traitor so that he could be king. Let it be known I did not kill him in cold blood. It was he who struck first, though I was the man who struck last. The church has absolved me of sin, and now I ask the same of you."

Rhona did not believe a word.

The Bruce handed his helm to Arthur and spread his gauntlet-clad hands. "I desire peace throughout the

Kingdom of Scotland, but hear me now, I will condemn any man who destroys what I, my lords, and knights are trying to build. Right here and now I give you my solemn oath, Scotland will be free from the yoke of tyranny. We must send the usurpers along our borders back from whence they came. We *will* be successful. We *will* again be a sovereign nation, ruled by one king and not a man sitting on a throne in London; a foreign king who cares nothing for Scotland's subjects. Moreover, we need strong men and women like yourselves to support our cause."

With the man's every word, Rhona's skin grew hotter. Aye, he spoke well, like a nobleman ought, but how could he believe a few words uttered might erase all the damage done? Her hand shook as she held out the missive.

The Bruce didn't smile but gave a sharp nod as he took it. "My thanks, *ah*..."

"Mistress Rhona," said Bram. "Lorn's grandniece, and nearest relative in the hall as his sister is infirm. Might I add the lady speaks for His Lordship in his stead."

"I see."

As the man opened the letter and read, Rhona chanced a glance at Arthur, then immediately shifted her gaze away. Good heavens, he'd caught her glimpse. And how dare he stare? Having the Campbell man in her presence was almost as unsavory as hosting the king. It was apt the pair of them had cast their lots together.

His Grace refolded the letter and looked to Cook. "My men will take their respite here for the night and will require food and drink. I hereby appoint Sir Arthur Campbell as constable of Dunstaffnage. He will be responsible..."

Holy everlasting perdition, Rhona didn't hear another word.

Arthur was to be constable? That meant he would not be marching with the Bruce's army. That meant he'd be nearby. *Indefinitely.* Her stomach roiled with thousands of butterflies, or horseflies, she wasn't sure which.

Sir Arthur. When had he earned his spurs?

Could things grow worse?

ARTHUR OUGHT TO BE LISTENING TO THE KING'S oration, but presently he stood utterly dumbstruck. He, the knight who marched beside Robert the Bruce and had taken the Pass of Brander wielding his sword as if driven by Satan, was completely gobsmacked. He'd fought for the king, he'd killed for the king, and he had pledged his life to the king. If anyone dared raise a hand against the man who had climbed from the depths of tyranny to challenge the greatest army in all of Christendom, Arthur would be the first to sacrifice himself to save his sovereign.

But at the moment, it was all he could do to keep his mouth from dropping open and his chin hitting his mail-clad, blood-spattered chest. True, he'd expected to see Rhona MacDougall at some stage. Just not today. And definitely not standing in the Lord of Lorn's stead. In truth, Arthur had expected a fight at Dunstaffnage's gates. He'd expected the unsavory task of escorting the elderly Lord of Lorn to the pit prison beneath the donjon.

Aye, he knew of the prison. He'd visited Dunstaffnage a handful of times in his youth—always for fetes and Highland games and, though his father held the seat of Lord of Garmoran less than twenty miles to the east, Arthur had never been to the fortress upon an invitation from Lorn. In truth, the Campbells and the MacDougalls were not exactly allies.

But that's not what presently occupied his thoughts. By the gods, Rhona was more beautiful now than he remembered. And the lass had become so self-assured. Though she wore a matron's veil, wisps of striking white hair framed her creamy complexion. Vibrant blue eyes were enhanced and fringed by utterly white lashes. In all his travels, Arthur had never met anyone with white hair such as hers. The color was as unique as the lass. Though clearly, she'd come into her own, facing the king of Scots like a Highland princess born to rule.

Mistress Rhona, Arthur reminded himself. When he'd received word that she had married, the news had cut him to the quick. But where was her husband and why was she at the head of the clan? Had Rhona's spouse been one of the MacDougall soldiers in the Pass of Brander who'd fled with John? Arthur prayed the man hadn't been one of the fallen. Fortunately for clan and kin, once the MacDougall had realized they were outnumbered and outsmarted, they had tucked tail and fled. The casualties were not numbered as Rhona had indicated with her ill-begotten use of the term *massacre*.

Regardless of what had happened in battle, Rhona was bitter, to be sure. From the moment their gazes had met, there had been a blaze burning behind those blues —eyes he still adored, though he had no right to do so.

I must reassure her of Robert's plans.

While the king's oration continued, Arthur stood at attention, rigid and unmoving, though every fiber in his body ached. Two nights had passed since he'd last slept. They'd marched, sailed, and fought like demons. And yet, the Bruce had not stopped for rest. Once the battle was won, they'd headed straight for Dunstaffnage. The king had won the right to claim this western fortress and it opened the door for the army to march northward and secure the Highlands for Scotland once and for all.

Exhausted and covered with filth, Arthur studied

Rhona. What must she think of him? His face was splattered with so much blood and mud, it was a wonder the lady had recognized him. Did she blame him for Lorn's demise?

Of course she does.

"With that, I bid ye all a good eve," boomed the king. "I foresee a prosperous future for us all."

As a cacophony of voices filled the hall with everyone asking questions at once, Arthur moved to Rhona's side. "'Tis good to see ye, mistress."

"Sir Arthur," she said with a slight curtsey, her gaze trailing to his filthy surcoat. "I see ye've earned your spurs."

He glanced downward; the silver spurs buckled to his heels were covered with mud. "I was knighted at the king's coronation."

The corners of her lips tightened, as if he'd just uttered a curse.

He brushed his hand down the Bruce's royal shield embroidered on his surcoat, the dried blood sloughing off and doing nothing to make him appear more presentable. "I ken ye must be out of sorts with all that has transpired, but allow me to assure you, we intend for peace to come to these lands. I give ye my word, no harm will befall you or—"

"You have already inflicted enough harm. Even seven years past, ye were unable to keep your word. Your assurances mean nothing to me," she said, her voice filled with malice.

Rendered speechless by the mere wisp of a woman, Arthur stood rooted to the floor with his mouth agape as he watched her march out the door.

Aye, it was he who'd missed their meeting all those years ago. He was but a fool lad of eighteen summers, and she two years younger. His elder brother had informed his father about Arthur's dalliance with the lass. That very day, he'd been sent away to study and become a squire in St. Andrews. But before he left, into his brother's care he'd entrusted a missive containing an apology for Rhona. It had cut deeply when she had never replied.

And though the woman would always hold a place in his heart, any chances he'd had to win the lass had been smote by her marriage. He'd only been gone two years when his brother wrote, saying she'd taken the holy vows of matrimony. But that didn't stop Arthur's dreams or the longing. Not even after so much time had passed.

❧ 2 ❧

Unable to withstand the stifling air in the great hall a moment longer, Rhona pushed out the door, fully intending to head straight home. Except as she made her way across the courtyard, the smoke belching out the chimney of the bathhouse caught her eye. Against her better judgment, she found herself standing at the rear of the building, directly behind the damper. Completely hidden from view of the towers and courtyard, only someone straight above on the wall-walk might see her and, presently, there wasn't a soldier in sight.

Within the blink of an eye, she slid the damper closed and headed on her way. Rhona might have a bit of a limp, but she was definitely stepping lighter. In fact, she almost skipped to the cottage where Gran had moved years ago after the death of her husband, Sir William. And the little cottage had become the woman's haven, which she repeatedly refused to leave. Even after her brother, the Lord of Lorn, had insisted Gran move to the castle, she stood her ground like a stubborn mule. That had been about the time Rhona's husband had died. After only a year of marriage, he'd been gored by a stag in a hunting accident, leaving her

13

pregnant and with little coin. Unfortunately, she later lost the babe as well.

Granduncle Alexander had stepped in and insisted Rhona move in with his sister, and that had been the beginning of her tenure as the clan's healer. Aye, over Rhona's formative years, the old woman had taught her a great deal about the healing arts and even midwifery, but once Gran's hip had grown too painful for her to walk overmuch, Rhona had taken to tending the sick and infirm on her own.

"There ye are," said Gran, looking up from her needlework with a forlorn sigh. "Is it done?"

After closing the door, Rhona removed her cloak and hung it on the peg beside the door. "Aye, did ye see the Bruce and his men march through the village?"

"Heard them, smelled them as well."

Rhona chuckled to herself. At least those toads wouldn't be languishing in warm baths this night.

"And what of my brother?" Gran asked. "Is he away?"

"Aye, set sail only moments afore the king's arrival."

The old woman reached for her shears and thrust them above her head. "Och, do not refer to that man as king!"

Rhona gave the elderly woman's cheek a kiss. "I feel the same, though after hearing him talk, I believe he will not stop until the kingdom is once again a sovereign nation and all the English lords have gone home."

With a scrunch of her nose that made her face look as weathered as a prune, Gran snipped her thread as if it were a vile insect. "And what then? Robert the Bruce is a warmonger. I wager he will not rest until he meets someone who is more devious and more conniving than he."

"I'm afeared ye may be right."

Gran tossed her shears into her basket. "I *am* right."

"But what can we do to fight back?" Rhona moved to the hearth and stirred the pottage suspended over the fire, hanging from an iron hook. "He has cast out the Lord of Lorn, for heaven's sake. I never thought anyone would cross your brother."

"Nor did I. Though there isn't much we can do now since we have no army behind us."

She tasted the concoction and added a pinch of salt, though only a pinch because it was a dear commodity in the Highlands. "Nay, though we might make things a wee bit uncomfortable for the new constable."

"Constable?"

"Aye, the Bruce appointed Arthur Campbell to the post."

Gran drummed her fingers against her lips. "Arthur? Garmoran's younger son?"

"The one and the same." Rhona replaced the ladle and slid onto the bench at the table. "He's been knighted; Sir Arthur, they're calling him now."

"Hmm He's a mite more congenial than his elder brother, if my memory serves. Did ye not fancy him for a time?"

Throwing her head back, she laughed. "Perhaps when I was too young and too naive for my own good."

"Is Sir Arthur married?"

"I rather doubt it, what with following the Bruce about the kingdom. And he looked like a savage brute for certain. Word is that up until they won at Loudoun Hill, they'd been hiding in caves and the like." Rhona took an apple from the wooden bowl in the center of the table and polished it on her kirtle. "The Bruce's army arrived covered with the filth of battle, the swine. I closed the bathhouse furnace damper on my way out. I ken it will not be much of an inconvenience, but at least none of them will be enjoying warm water this night."

"There's a good lass. I kent ye weren't my granddaughter for naught." Gran looked to the rafters and tapped her lips, a clear sign she was scheming. "Mayhap we can lace their ale with a tincture of nightshade."

"Ye're awful!" Rhona scoffed. Though she did not want Sir Arthur and his men to occupy the castle, she didn't care to murder them, either. In her estimation, there had been enough bloodshed and it needed to stop. She was in the trade of healing souls, not harming them. Nonetheless, she didn't see anything wrong with sending a wee message or two to let them know they weren't welcome.

"Oh?" asked Gran. "Tell that to my poor cousin, John Comyn, slain by Robert the Bruce's hand...in a house of God, no less."

"Humph. Yet the Bruce has gained quite a following." Rhona bit into her apple and rolled her eyes as tartness filled her mouth. "With luck, the wars will be over soon and Lorn will be granted leave to return from England."

"Let us pray it is so. Scotland has been so torn by war over the years, I doubt ye remember a time when we were at peace."

"Peace—the self-proclaimed king spoke of peace in the great hall." Rhona took another bite and licked her lips. "I wonder if he truly believes it or if he was simply blowing steam."

Before the elderly lady could reply, someone pounded on the door. "Mistress Rhona, 'tis Fingal, he's been injured!"

"Oh, my heavens, it must be Sara." Gran scooted to the edge of her chair. "Did Fingal not fight with John?"

"Aye, as did most able men in the village." Rhona hopped up and hastened to open the door, finding Sara wringing her hands, her eyes filled with worry. "What has happened?"

"Ye must come straightaway. Lord John left Fingal for dead. He's in a bad way—shot with an arrow."

"I'll fetch my basket," said Rhona, slinging her cloak about her shoulders and taking her medicine bundle from the shelf. "Come, there's not a moment to spare."

Sara, showing with child, led the way through the village. "I pleaded with him not to go. I had a bad feeling about it all along."

"Aye, but what kind of man would your husband have been had he remained behind? He's stronger than an ox, and Lorn ordered all men of fighting age to march."

"And look where it led us. The only men remaining are children and the elderly. The rest have fled."

"At least Fingal has returned to ye. Thanks be to God he lives."

Sara stopped outside the door of her little cottage and clasped her hands over her heart. "He's in a bad way."

"Oh dear." Rhona squeezed her friend's hand and looked her in the eye. "Ye ken if anyone can set him to rights, it is I. Let us not delay."

The cottage consisted of a single room and, inside, five wee children stood at their father's bedside. "Will Da survive?" asked Gregor, the eldest who was ten years of age.

"Of course he will." Rhona ushered the little ones aside as she moved next to the man. His face was ashen, the arrow's shaft still protruding from his shoulder. "Did ye walk all the way from the pass skewered like that?"

"Aye," Fingal grunted as if the single word took a great deal of effort.

She didn't doubt the smithy's fortitude. He was a beast of a man, built like a bull with arms as thick as tree trunks. "Well, I say if ye were strong enough to find home's hearth, ye're strong enough to survive a wee bit of pain." Rhona made quick work of examining the wound. Fingal's skin was cold and clammy to the touch, his shirt soaked with blood and caked with dirt. He was knocking on death's door for certain. She turned to Sara. "I need cloths to staunch the bleeding. Send the children outside."

"But I want to stay," said Gregor, standing tall with his fists clenched at his sides.

"Do as I say," Rhona clipped in a firm tone indicating she would entertain no argument. If the extraction did not go well and the man bled out, she did not want the wee ones watching. "Ye are the eldest and the others must look to ye for strength. Your mother will fetch ye soon enough."

While the wee ones took their leave, Rhona placed an iron poker in the fire, then fished the shears out of her basket. "We'd best cut away your shirt."

"'Tis my best," Fingal croaked, his eyes rolling back.

"I fear it is no longer." Rhona made a single cut from the V in the neckline to make it easy for Sara to repair, and then she exposed the shaft. Aye, the arrow was lodged deep. Before she tried to pull it out, she checked the poker, noting the tip was starting to glow red, then picked up a wooden spoon and moved back to the bedside. "Clamp this between your teeth."

The Highlander blanched. "Mayhap we ought to leave it be till morn."

"Aye? Sleep all night with a pointy bit of lead in your shoulder? Do ye want to dance with the devil? I reckon it has been inside ye long enough." Rhona gently placed the spoon's handle in Fingal's mouth, then turned to Sara. "Stand at the ready with a cloth. As soon as the arrowhead is out, cover the wound and push with all your might."

Sara gripped the bit of linen, her knuckles white. "Yes, mistress."

Rhona tugged on the arrow as gently as possible, earning an ear-splitting shriek from the patient. If she didn't pull it out quickly, he'd suffer far too much.

"There's only one way to ensure it comes out true," she said, planting her foot on the top of his shoulder. "Forgive me!" she grunted as she gnashed her teeth and yanked with all her strength.

With Fingal's thrashing and high-pitched cries, the arrow gave way, making Rhona stumble backward and crash to her backside. "Now, Sara! Press firmly!"

Fingal kicked his legs, his head shifting from side to side as his wife bore down with the cloth, but it was instantly saturated with blood. "Hold still, else ye'll bleed out."

Rhona grasped another cloth. "Move aside!" As she'd feared, there was too much blood, and by the look of Fingal's face, he had none to spare. "Another. Quickly."

Sara pushed in. "I'm ready."

"Hold it firm until I return with the poker."

"What?" Fingal squawked, his voice as shrill as a woman's.

"Do ye want to live or die?" Rhona dashed to the fire and examined the tip of the poker, now glowing red. "On the count of three, pull away the cloth."

"Must ye?" Sara asked.

"Do ye want a father for your wee bairns?"

The matron pursed her lips and gave a single nod.

"One, two, three!"

As Sara snapped the cloth away, Rhona lunged in with both hands, stabbing the tip of the poker into the wound. Bellowing like a steer in the castrating pen, Fingal thrashed, arching off the bed and smacking Rhona across the face. Reeling away, she tightened her grip on the iron rod to prevent it from flying across the chamber.

"'Tis done," she said, rehanging the poker on the nail beside the hearth.

Fingal lay on the bed, barely conscious, and breathing as if he'd just run a footrace.

"Will he recover?" asked his wife.

Giving a nod, Rhona took a chair and placed it beside the bed of her patient. "If he survives the night, I reckon he'll have come through the worst of it." She inclined her head to the pitcher and bowl. "I'll see to it the fever remains at bay. Ye'd best go tend to your wee ones."

AS WAS HIS CUSTOM, ARTHUR ROSE WITH THE CALL from the first cock just before dawn. He stretched and made his way to the washstand, using the ewer to fill the bowl. He splashed his face and beneath his arms with the bracing water. A soldier oft bathed in chilly lochs and the like, but one day soon he intended to enjoy a warm bath.

Last eve, his men had suffered the chilly water in the bathhouse. Arthur spoke to the soldier he'd assigned to starting the fires and the man had sworn he hadn't left the bathhouse until the bricks of peat were smoldering, but the fellow hadn't opened the bloody damper. The bathhouse not only filled with smoke, the water was as frigid as Loch Etive. Rather than endure the smoky chamber, Arthur had gone down to the loch, stripped bare, and dove in, lingering only long enough to wash away the filth of battle.

When the door to his bedchamber cracked opened, Clyde popped his head in. The old manservant had been Arthur's closest confidant since his first year in St. Andrews. "Will ye be donning your armor this morn, sir?" Clyde may have been born in England, but after the atrocities of the Massacre of Berwick, he'd left his roots and pledged his services to the Scottish sect of the Hospitallers Order of St. John. The man was too old to fight and it was no secret the wars had taken their toll. At one time, he'd even fallen into the depths of melancholy. When Arthur was a fledgling squire, he'd found Clyde at his lowest, having succumbed to the evils of drink. But that had been the beginning of their bond. Arthur had nursed the man back to health in that time he somehow gave him new purpose. In turn, Clyde became a mentor, imparting valuable instruction, not on weapons and the like, but on how to navigate the competitive and often political Order. And after Arthur had been knighted, Clyde followed, pledging his fealty and acting as a manservant, though the elderly gentleman was so much more.

"I will," he replied, pulling on and tying his braies and then tugging his chausses over them. "Will ye find Bram and ask him to meet me in the hall?"

Clyde held up a clean shirt, which Arthur took and pulled over his head. "Certainly."

"Is all well this morn?"

"Thus far." The manservant raised a jerkin. "As usual, ye are the first knight to rouse."

"And so it should be." Arthur shrugged into the quilted garment and tied the front laces. "I've a great task in front of me, bringing peace of mind to the locals."

"Their trust will be hard-won I reckon."

"Aye, the lot of them have been led to believe the Bruce is a monster. It is up to me to shift their opinions."

"I'm glad the task has been assigned to you and no' me. I'm too old to take on the likes of Clan Mac-Dougall." Clyde gestured to the coat of mail draped over a chair. "Are ye ready for that beastly set of armor?"

Arthur chuckled. "I've been wearing it near every day for three years. Without the additional six stone, I feel as if I'm floating."

"Just do not go trying to float in a chilly loch with it on your back, sir."

After he was properly dressed, complete with a pristine surcoat belted atop his mail, Arthur headed to the great hall to break his fast, not surprised to see the guard Bram arrive shortly thereafter.

"Ye asked to see me, sir?"

"Aye." Arthur gestured to the bench across. "Have a seat and a bite to eat."

Though the man looked a tad surprised to be asked to dine at the high table, Arthur cared not a whit. He needed to talk and this was the best time for it. "I ken it isn't easy for ye or the local folk to accept the new rule."

"Nay." Bram took a bowl of porridge from a servant. "I'd be lying if I said otherwise."

"Understood. But tell me, of the people who remain —the tradesmen, the crofters, the clergy, and the like— what are their fears? Their deepest concerns?"

The sergeant-at-arms took up his spoon and pointed it at the rampant lion on Arthur's surcoat. "To begin with, everyone is worried about suffering an increase in rents. And I reckon they need someone who will listen to them—ye ken? Really pay attention as if their worries truly mattered."

With his eating knife, Arthur stabbed a brown sausage sitting on a trencher in front of him. "Did Lorn not hear supplications?"

"I suppose he heard them, true enough." Bram filled his mouth with a bite of oats, and by the knit of his wiry brows, he was not inclined to explain further.

Arthur had spent years at his father's side and he understood there were oft disagreements between master and serf. The problem was the lower man usually received the brunt of any decisions made. "I will endeavor to be fair."

"That is all I ask of any man."

"What other concerns have they?"

"At the moment 'tis summer, and there is food

aplenty. But the harvest will be upon us soon, and I'll wager ye ken as well as I, too much rain or not enough can bring famine."

"Famine for us all, mind ye."

"Mayhap, but I reckon the crofters suffer most. Believe me, Lorn never starved in lean years, though plenty of others suffered."

Arthur reached for a pitcher and filled his cup with mead. "Let us pray the harvest is good. And let it be known I give my oath there will be many hands to bring it in."

Bram raised his cup. "*Sláinte mhath.*"

"*Sláinte mhath,*" Arthur echoed the Gaelic toast of good health. "I want ye to ride out on sorties with me and my men. Starting this morn."

One of the sergeant-at-arms' eyebrows arched. "A peacekeeping venture?"

In truth, Arthur chose the man to be amongst the king's soldiers as a show of solidarity. With Lorn's army gone, Bram was the only fellow he could rely on. "Of sorts. And the sooner I start, the better."

"I'VE CATTLE THAT NEED TO BE TAKEN TO MARKET and the lot of ye have had the passes blocked for months. A man can't step out of his home for fear of having his heart pierced by one of the Bruce's arrows," said a drover, sitting atop an old nag, standing on knobby knees with her grey-muzzled head stooped forward.

"I see." Arthur tapped his heels and looked out over the paddock dotted with a handful of fat heifers and steers. "Ye can safely take them to Crieff now."

"What of the Black Douglas? His archers are in the hills, ready to fire upon any poor soul who happens past."

Arthur knew full well James Douglas and his men were heading north with the king, but he also knew better than to reveal too much about the Bruce's plans. Still, he needed to earn the locals' trust and whether they knew it or not, they also needed to earn his. "'Tis my understanding Douglas has moved on, but I'll write ye a letter of safe passage should ye come into any trouble."

"I'd feel better if ye sent along a man-at-arms or two as well. I'm no' as spry as I once was, I'll have ye know."

Arthur scratched beneath his helm. Until his recruiting efforts stepped up, he didn't have many men to spare. Early this morn, the king had marched northward, taking three-quarters of the army's numbers. Nonetheless, he needed to earn favor in the eyes of the locals as well—as long as they didn't try to take advantage. "Very well, I'll write the letter and assign a guardsman to drive the cattle with you. In payment, I'll need two heifers for Dunstaffnage's larder."

The man's eyes bulged. "Two? Ye'll ruin me."

"Do ye want to drive your cattle or not?" Arthur eyed the man with a hard stare, making it clear he wasn't to be trifled with. "This once, I'll accept one beast, but as soon as ye return, I'll expect your rents paid in full."

"I kent it, ye're raising my rents and driving me out."

"I do not recall mentioning anything about raising rents. As a matter of fact, I've heard this same question from a number of others today, and I assure ye, I will not charge a penny more than Lorn. I'm certain whatever you agreed upon with His Lordship is fair."

"Och, 'tis hardly reasonable, sir, barely enough remains to feed my kin."

Arthur leveled his gaze with the man. "Know this, I've a fortress to run, and I intend to do so as expediently as possible. Since rents appear to be quite a bone of contention, I will review the ledgers with my cleric as soon as I am able."

Bram cleared his throat. "I'll wager that's fair."

The drover gave a nod, though by the set of his mouth, he appeared to have the taste of sour apples on his tongue.

"When do ye intend to drive your livestock to market?" Arthur asked, steering the conversation away from the bloody rents.

"Friday next, if the pass is safe."

"Very well, I'll ensure you have a signed letter and a guardsman first thing Friday next." Arthur picked up his reins and tapped his heels against his horse's sides as he bowed his head. "Good day."

Bram rode in beside him. "Where to next, sir?"

This crofter having been the last of a dozen visits, Arthur had had enough. "Back to Dunstaffnage. I reckon today's work was a good start, but I intend to continue with these peacekeeping sorties three times every sennight." At a trot, he led the men past the chapel and into the village of cottages nestled in the foreground of the fortress. "In order to gain trust, these good people need to see us frequently."

"Perhaps they'll stop complaining," Bram mumbled.

"In time."

Ahead, Rhona came out of a cottage, clutching the handle of a basket. She was followed by another matron while a passel of children darted out and swarmed around her skirts. With a tired smile, she patted their cheeks and bid them good day before starting down the path.

Arthur's heart may have skipped a beat or two, but he pretended not to notice, glanced to his men, and signaled to the fortress gates. "Ride on. I'll join ye anon."

Turning his mount, he reined the horse beside the lass. "Good morrow, Mistress Rhona."

She rubbed a hand across her forehead and looked up with reddened eyes. "Is it? I hardly noticed."

"Ye look overtired. Are ye unwell?"

She stopped, gripping the basket while a furrow formed between her white eyebrows. "Forgive me for not seeming my best, sir," she said rather curtly, as if they had not once been sweethearts. "I've been up all night with a man shot in the shoulder by one of the Black Douglas' arrows. And I'll have ye know, Fingal is a father with five children, not to mention he and his wife have another bairn on the way. He's also our smithy, and he'll not be able to work for sennights, thanks to ye and your king."

It seemed mending fences with the crofters wasn't the only area where he needed to smooth out damages done. Arthur dismounted, noting the contents of her basket were stoppered pots, bottles, and rolled bandages. "Allow me to give ye a ride home."

"No, thank you," she said, marching away with the once-familiar hitch to her step. The lass may have been born with one leg shorter than the other, but she had never allowed her lameness to slow her down. She also seemed to be as spirited now as she had been at sixteen summers.

Leading his horse, Arthur kept pace. "Are ye a healer now?"

Rhona's shoulder ticked up, still so very reticent. "I do what I can."

"And the smithy, Fingal. How is he faring?"

"'Tis too early to tell. If the wound doesn't fester, he most likely will survive. Only time will determine his fate."

"I shall see to it his wife receives the food she needs to feed her family until he is able to resume his duties."

Rhona stopped outside a cottage, its thatched roof the worse for wear, the door askew. "I suppose that is the least ye can do. Am I now expected to shower ye with thanks?"

Arthur tightly clamped his lips together. Of all the folk living nearby the castle, it was this woman's favor he desired most, but he abhorred insincerity and didn't expect it from Rhona MacDougall. "I did not ask for thanks."

"Nay, but you marched through the castle gates and announced ye were claiming the keep for Robert the Bruce."

"I did. I'll not deny taking Dunstaffnage was a much-needed victory for Scotland's king."

"Aye?"

Arthur gave a resolute nod. "Aye. He desires unity and peace above all else."

"Try telling that to Fingal and his poor wife."

"I regret that a man with wee bairns has been injured. But this is war, and in war men who take up arms run the risk of injury. Ye ken as well as I some soldiers die, and on both sides."

Rhona glanced to the door. "If there's nothing else, I'm tired and would like to take my rest."

"Of course, madam." Arthur bowed. "I would like to have a word with your husband if he's in."

"I'm afraid that isn't possible."

"Is he away?" Good Lord, Arthur prayed the man wasn't one of those who fled with the Lord of Lorn.

The lass's pale gaze slid up to his. Her eyes were full of emotion and anguish and something upon which Arthur could not put his finger. "Ivor is deceased."

As his jaw dropped, the lass slipped inside without another word and closed the door.

He stood for a moment, gripping his horse's reins in his fist. When had her husband passed? Had he been a casualty of the war?

3

The next morning, Rhona's first stop was Sara and Fingal's cottage. At the smithy's bedside, she pressed her palm against Fingal's forehead. He wasn't burning with fever, but he didn't feel cool to the touch either. "I care not if there's work to do, ye must stay abed until I'm certain your wound will not turn putrid."

"She's right," Sara added, hovering and wringing her hands. "Besides, we ought to fare well with the food Sir Arthur delivered this morn."

Rhona looked to the enormous basket on the table filled with bread, a whole ham, a sack of oats, apples, and more. She'd assumed it had come from the castle since Arthur had promised to do so. Perhaps he had learned the importance of keeping one's word during his time of training to become a knight. "I'll wager he had one of the soldiers deliver it," she said, raising her chin.

"Nay, the man himself knocked on the door just after dawn." Sara's brow furrowed. "I feel a wee bit awkward accepting such a generous gift, especially from one of Robert the Bruce's knights. Only days ago, my husband fought to keep them from storming the castle and sending Lorn on his way."

"But they're here now, are they not?" Fingal thrust

his finger toward the basket. "We'll take every morsel and eat it. The Lord of Lorn and his son have left us to the wolves. We've not but to have care for our own."

"What are ye saying?" asked Sara. "Ye took an arrow for naught?"

"I'm saying I took an arrow and lost." The beefy blacksmith shifted against the pillows on the narrow bed. "The battle was a travesty to behold. As soon as the archers attacked from the high ground, ye should have seen Lord John turn tail and run. He left me bleeding in the glen. I ken when to lick my wounds and when I'm beat. It doesn't mean I'll be kissing Arthur Campbell's arse. As soon as I rise from this bed, I'll keep my head down, tend to my affairs, and see to it there's food on the table and clothing on our backs."

Rhona exchanged woeful glances with Sara. Of course, with most of Lorn's army sailing for England, MacDougall clan and kin had naught to do but to bear what may come. "See to it ye stay abed. And drink your willow bark tea to keep the fever at bay." She slipped her medicine basket into the crook of her arm. "I'll return on the morrow, but send Gregor for me at once if he should take a turn for the worse."

Sara walked her to the door. "Thank ye ever so much. I'll see to it he rests."

Rhona glanced back to Fingal, fearing he would try to rise too soon. Surely, he was talking blather. At least she hoped he was. She pulled a small vial from her basket. "This tincture is very potent and ye must keep it somewhere the children will not reach it. If your man grows restless, put a drop in his beer. He'll sleep like a bairn."

"What is it?"

"Essence of henbane. I never add more than a teaspoon to a vial of water for fear of having someone use too much. Only a drop, ye ken?"

"Very well, a drop in his beer." Sara glanced over her shoulder. "Mayhap I ought to give it to him now."

"If ye can manage to wait until after the noon hour, 'tis best; then he'll sleep until morn, which would be a boon once he starts acting like a sore-headed curmudgeon as they all do." Rhona patted her friend's shoulder. "Ye'll ken when it is time."

With that, Rhona bid Sara goodbye and headed across the drawbridge to Dunstaffnage to deliver a pot of salve for Bram's rheumatism. With luck, the new constable would be out on a sortie and she'd miss him altogether. In fact, she'd prefer to avoid him for the rest of her days.

As she was about to stride beneath the portcullis, two guards crossed their pikes, blocking her path. "Halt. What business have ye in the castle?"

Good heavens, never in all her days had Rhona been questioned at the gate. She was not only the healer, she was the grandniece of the Lord of Lorn. Everyone about these parts knew her. Welcomed her as well.

But then again, she did not recognize one of the faces snarling down at her.

Flaring her nostrils, she squared her shoulders and tipped up her chin for good measure. "I'm merely bringing a salve for Bram, the sergeant-at-arms." Her gaze darted between the two as she dug into her basket and held up the pot. "My word, the lot of ye have driven off anyone who might raise a hand against the Bruce's army. Moreover, these gates are here to protect the people of the village, nay to keep them out."

"Mistress Rhona is right," said Bram, stepping into the archway. Evidently, his status had held even though only days ago he had served the Lord of Lorn. "Stand down, men."

As the pikes uncrossed, Rhona hastened forward. "Did Sir Arthur order the guards to be so brash?"

"The soldiers report directly to Donal Ramsey, Sir Arthur's lieutenant."

"Well, ye must say something to him about having the guards acquaint themselves with the local folk. I'm nay accustomed to being stopped by pikes. Those curs acted as if a wee crippled lass were capable of mounting an insurrection." She held the pot of salve out. "This is for your rheumatism."

"Och, ye are an angel of mercy." He took it and inclined his head toward the kitchens. "Come, have a wee cup of cider with me. The brew master has just finished a batch."

Rhona licked her lips. "Mm. That sounds delicious."

Bram led her into the brewhouse, which had a rough-hewn table in the center. "Where's the master brewer?" she asked, sliding onto one of the two benches.

The old sergeant picked up a wooden cup and opened the tap on one of the casks. "I'll wager he and the others have gone to the hall for their nooning."

"Just as well," Rhona said, noting a tapped barrel of wine and another of ale. Beside them was a quarter-cask of vinegar used for cleaning. "This gives me a chance to ask how things are faring without ye feeling as if ye must suppress your true opinion."

Holding two frothing cups, Bram moved to the opposite side of the table and sat. "I've heard that tone afore. What's on your mind, lass?"

"My mind?" she asked, taking one of the cups. "What is on everyone's mind of late? My granduncle is gone and our lands are now claimed by Robert the Bruce. Moreover, *his* man is the dreaded constable, now lording it over us all."

As he took a drink, the guard regarded her with a bit of scrutiny deepening the etched lines at the corners of his eyes. "If my memory serves, ye were once quite fond of Sir Arthur."

"Och, must you and Gran have memories hewn of iron? That was long ago and well before he was knighted, let alone took up arms for Bruce." She sipped the cider, the delicious tartness making her swill another. "I saw ye riding with the sortie yesterday. What vile things is our constable up to? Raising the rents as everyone feared? Or worse? I wouldn't be surprised if Sir Arthur laid claim to all the livestock just to see us starve come winter."

Bram swiped the froth from his beard and moustache. "In truth, he has promised not to increase the rents, and the livestock he sequestered is less than that which Lorn claimed for himself."

"That would be right." Rhona snorted. "He's attempting to win everyone's favor afore he cuts them off."

"Mayhap, but I doubt it." Bram looked her in the eye. The man was one of the few Rhona trusted implicitly. His judgment was sound as well. "After what I've observed, I reckon the constable truly desires to bring peace to all of Argyll."

She shifted uneasily. Perhaps his reasoning wasn't quite as sound as usual on this matter. Perhaps he was wishing too much for an end to the fighting. "Peace? Sir Arthur is a knight, trained in all manner of weapons, not to mention he's supporting a man who's a known warmonger."

Bram chuckled. "Then ye'd best pray for clan and kin. Ye ken the Lord of Lorn is too ill to attempt to take Dunstaffnage back. He's entrusted the keep to the new king and sailed to England where he intends to live out his days—or at least wait out the duration of this war."

"And what of you? Do ye intend to continue your service as a sergeant-at-arms?"

"I reckon so—at least until my knees will no longer allow me to climb the winding stairs to the wall-walk."

"And the others—Cook, the servants, and the like? Are they staying?"

"Aye."

The door cracked open and a soldier popped his head inside. "There ye are, Bram. Did ye no' hear the ram's horn? The guard has changed and ye're needed atop the west tower."

"Och, these walls are as thick as battlements." The sergeant-at-arms stood. "My thanks for the salve, mistress. Have a bonny afternoon."

"You as well." Rhona stood, collecting both cups. "I'll rinse these afore I go."

It took not a moment to wash up. On the way out, the tapped barrels of ale and wine caught her eye. She bit her bottom lip as she nudged the lid of one, making it move. Perhaps she ought to make just a wee bit of mischief before she took her leave.

Her interest piqued, she sidled to the door, pushed it open a fraction of an inch, and peered out. Seeing and hearing nothing, Rhona dashed back to the quarter-cask of vinegar, pulled out the cork and poured half in the ale and the other half in the wine. She carefully re-placed the stopper, then slipped out with a wee spring in her step.

She wasn't about to sit idle while Sir Arthur assumed control of Dunstaffnage with his army, bullying folk when they tried to cross through the gates. Mayhap Bram and Fingal had endured a gutful of war, but Rhona wasn't finished with it. Moreover, she'd not forget how Arthur Campbell had discarded her as if she were nothing but an alehouse wench. Even after all these years, his jilting caused her heart to tighten like a fist.

Anyway, a wee bit of vinegar never hurt a soul.

On her way toward the gate, Rhona made a slight detour to the rear of the bathhouse and closed the damper just for good measure. If it weren't for her lameness, she would have skipped the rest of the way home, but it was good enough to settle for a longer than normal stride.

Until a gap-toothed guard stepped into her path, leaning on a pike as if it were a post. Why was it every man within these walls saw fit to carry an eight-foot pole with an iron spear at one end? "What have ye in the basket, bonny lass?"

Heat flared up the back of her neck. The man was about as polite and as alluring as a toad. "My name is Mistress Rhona, and I would prefer it if ye referred to me thus."

"Filled with importance, are ye?" He pinched a lock of hair that had escaped her veil and tugged—not terribly hard, but not in a friendly way either. "I've never seen the likes of white hair afore. Are ye a witch?"

Rhona batted the swine's hand away. "I most certainly am not. I am a healer and have been tending the souls within and without this castle for years."

"A healer, aye?" The mongrel hooked his fingers on the collar of his shirt. "In that case, I've a terrible—"

"What are ye on about, soldier? Have ye not someplace to be?" Sir Arthur stepped between them. Towering over the guard, he planted his fists on his hips. "Move along and let it be known I'll not stand for anyone heckling Mistress Rhona. Moreover, if I ever again see you being discourteous to her or any other woman, I will lock ye in the pit and throw away the key."

"Sorry, sir." The guard scratched his flank. "I thought she might have a look at my rash, is all. It is causing me consternation, I'll say."

Sir Arthur arched an eyebrow her way. "Have ye a salve for a rash?"

Pursing her lips, she looked the buffoon from head to toe. He was so covered with hair, even his neck was unshorn, giving her no clue as to how the affliction presented. "Is it burning, itchy, dry?"

"Itchy and dry."

After fishing in her basket, she pulled out a pot of feverfew ointment. "Apply this day and night. It ought to come good in a fortnight unless ye're sleeping on a pallet filled with fleas and midges."

The man took it and scratched the back of his neck. "My thanks."

"You have what ye need, now move along, soldier." Arthur waited until the guard ducked into the stairwell and started upward. "He seemed a bit overly familiar. My apologies."

Rhona tucked her basket in the crook of her elbow and headed for the gate. "No apology necessary."

To her chagrin, Arthur followed. "Would ye have a moment?"

"Are ye needing something, sir?" she asked over her shoulder.

"Aye. I'd like a word."

Rhona stubbed her toe on a cobblestone and stumbled, though she straightened and continued forward as if she weren't as clumsy as a drunken sparrow. "I believe we had a *word* yesterday."

"A wee bit of one that was cut rather short, I'd say."

She sped her pace. "I see no reason for us to speak overlong. After all, ye made yourself clear years ago. Or should I say scarce?"

"Ye ken I didn't plan to go to St. Andrews."

"Hmm," she said noncommittally as he walked with her beneath the gate's archway. "What was it ye wished to say?"

"Would ye mind stepping into the hall? The day's cider is delicious; it would be nice to have a wee chat over a cup."

"Bram has already shared the cider with me, thank you." Good heavens, would the man leave her be? She cast a forlorn glance toward the village. "I'm afraid Gran needs me."

The big knight bowed and gestured along the cobbled path. "Very well, I'll walk with ye."

Groaning, Rhona rolled her gaze toward the heavens. "Have ye not something more important with which to occupy your time?"

"Not presently." Arthur stroked his fingers down his beard while he drew in a heavy breath. "I...*ah*...realize it isn't easy for any kin of the MacDougall to readily accept me or my men. But it is important to me to earn their respect. Ye ken? I want the tensions to ease and folk to continue on with their lives without fear."

She stopped and craned her neck to study his face. He'd marched into Dunstaffnage and taken over like a tyrant. What was he doing? Trying to butter everyone up with talk of easing tensions? By the candid stare in his eyes, he did not appear to have gone mad. In fact, he appeared serious, and far too fetching, blast him. Rhona quickly shifted her gaze, but only managed to stare at the center of his very broad, mail-clad chest. "Mayhap if ye did not wear a coat of arms everywhere ye went, it might help."

"Understood. Perhaps if I wear my mail only when there is a danger, such as when we ride out on sorties."

"If ye must." She turned and started away.

"What else? What would Lorn do?"

"Lorn had the trust of the people by his centuries-old inherited right to the land."

"Come, Mistress Rhona, we are friends, are we not?"

For the love of Moses, now he'd returned with a knighthood, he wished to let bygones be bygones? "You and I are most definitely *not* friends."

"Unfortunate, 'tis yet another problem I must remedy," he mumbled as if he were scribing a missive in his head.

None too soon, they arrived at the cottage door. "If ye desire to weave your way into anyone's good graces, it goes without saying ye should feed them."

He stepped far too close while a smile lit up his features—straight, white teeth, those dark eyes shining and far more alluring than they ought to be. He, too, captured a lock of her hair. But rather than pull it as the guard had done, he wrapped it around his finger and drew it to his nose. His eyes grew so dark and hungry, one would have thought he'd just sampled a fragrance from heaven. "Mayhap a feast."

"See?" she said, unable to bat his hand away as she'd done to the guard. In truth, her knees had suddenly started to wobble and her mouth had gone dry. It was reminiscent of being off on one of their secret rendezvous from years past where she darted into his arms and reveled in the excitement of a kiss.

Rhona forced herself to stop staring. Neither of them was a child without a care. Arthur had not only become a man, he'd become braw beyond imagination. And she? She was a widow who looked after her grandmother as well as any ailing townsfolk. "'Tis not so difficult once ye put your mind to it." It took every ounce of willpower in her body to turn her back and pull down on the latch. "Good day."

As soon as Rhona slipped inside and shut the door, Gran looked up from her knitting. "Whatever has happened? Ye look as if ye've seen a ghost."

The woman was too perceptive and oft pried overmuch. Rhona affected an unflappable expression as she moved to the pot of rabbit pottage simmering above the fire. As she neared, a smile spread across her lips. "Let us just say the soldiers' drink might be a tad off for their evening meal. I added a wee bit of vinegar to their wine and ale."

❧ 4 ❧

If they hadn't been sweethearts, Arthur would have thought Rhona wanted nothing to do with him. In truth, after she'd shut the door of her cottage in his face, *twice now*, he was fairly certain her feelings toward him had soured considerably. He couldn't deny that one of the reasons for accepting this post was because of her. For the past seven years he'd dreamed about returning to Argyll where he'd be able to see the lass now and again, even though he knew she'd wed. Over and over, he'd tried to convince himself that just being close to Rhona MacDougall would be enough. He'd even expected her to have a brood of wee ones about her skirts, though Bram had told him she had not a one.

That she was widowed had buoyed his hopes of rekindling their romance. Except the woman seemed hardly able to bring herself to look him in the eye.

"What has ye so long in the face?" asked Donal, Arthur's lieutenant and second in command.

Arthur blinked repeatedly, then looked along the length of the high table where they had gathered for the evening meal. "Is there nothing to drink? And where is the food?" He cast his gaze out to the hall. "Nearly all the men have assembled."

"How about I go to the kitchens and find out?"

Arthur flagged Bram. "I'll ask the sergeant to do so." God's bones, if he sent Donal to the kitchens, someone might end up bloodied. The man was a boon on the battlefield because he was built like a stone wall and fought like a demon, but he had no business meddling with anything that did not concern fighting, or training to fight.

"Aye, sir?" asked Bram, grunting as he lumbered up the three stairs to the dais.

"Have ye injured yourself, sergeant?"

"Nay. I've a wee bit of rheumatism is all. I went without Mistress Rhona's salve a few days too long."

The mention of the lady's name hit Arthur low and deep. "The healer's salve works wonders, does it?"

"Aye. She has a talent for certain."

"That she does," Arthur agreed, though his thoughts had turned to stolen kisses and how supple she'd once been when in his arms. "Ah...please pay a visit to the kitchens and find out what's holding up the meal."

"Straightaway, sir."

"Please?" asked Donal.

Arthur gave the lieutenant a sidewise glance. "I reckon a wee bit of civility is required at the moment. Especially with Lorn's former man."

"If it were up to me, I would have rounded everyone up and thrown them in the pit."

"That's why the Bruce did not see fit to make ye constable. Hell, aside from Bram, there aren't but servants and tradesmen remaining." Arthur pulled his *sgian dubh* from its scabbard and set into cleaning his fingernails. "I'd like to plan a feast."

"Och, and now ye're intending to kick up your heels?" Donal asked with a snort.

"Watch yourself." Arthur leveled his knife at the lieutenant's nose. "Your tone borders on sedition."

"Sorry, sir. That was no' my intention." The lieutenant grew red in the face. "I reckon we've already missed Lammas Day. The next feast is no' until Michaelmas."

"I ken, but we mustn't wait that long. I want the villagers to warm to us straightaway."

Donal pounded his fist into his palm. "They need to respect us."

"Agreed, though thumping them with our might may not endear us to their hearts."

"So it is love ye're wanting? I never thought I'd see the day."

"Wheesht, and pull in your bloody head." Arthur looked toward the kitchen doors and saw no one. "Believe me, offenses will be dealt with and dispatched just as they always are. But would it not be better to have a friendly conversation with the smithy or the tailor when visiting them for service, or do ye prefer to suffer their sidewise glances and thin-lipped, monosyllabic chat?"

"I do no' mind it when a man holds his tongue."

Angus held up his knife. "I want the men to attempt to be friendlier—with the local folk, of course. They ought to come to know them so when they do pay a visit to the castle, they recognize their faces. And the best way I ken how to do that is to break bread. And mayhap we stop wearing armor on market days."

"No armor?" Donal's eyes bugged out. "With all due respect, sir. A sennight away from the front lines of war and ye're talking about good manners and parading about without a coat of mail. God's bones, ye're the one who taught me a soldier must always wear his armor or he goes soft."

"I'm not saying we do without it, especially when we're out and about on sorties and the like. Lord kens we could face an insurrection sooner than later. I'm just suggesting when the lads go to market, they leave their armor with their squires to be polished. Of course, the men on duty will be dressed in full tilt."

Batting his hand through the air, the lieutenant shook his head. "Next ye'll be turning a wee feast into a bout of Highland games."

Arthur re-sheathed his *sgian dubh*. "Games, aye?" He liked the idea. "We could invite my kin, as Lorn did afore the wars."

"I cannot believe ye just said that...*er*...sir."

"Nay, 'tis brilliant. There's nothing like a wee bit o' sport to kindle friendship."

"Or feuds."

"Wheesht. Bless it, Donal, I've been tasked with bringing all of Argyll into the king's good graces. If ye do not want to put forth an effort, ye should have marched northward with the Bruce."

The lieutenant opened his mouth, but rather than speak, he pointed to Bram, who was marching through the aisle of tables with a cup in his hand. Moreover, Cook and the brew master were on his flanks and there wasn't a trencher of food between them.

This time, the sergeant didn't even grimace as he ascended the steps. "It seems we have a prankster in our midst, sir."

Arthur regarded the grim expressions on all three of the men's faces. Damnation, a stone sank to the pit of his stomach and roiled with the bile. "Oh?"

"'Tis off." Bram placed the cup on the board. "Someone has tampered with the ale and the wine only tapped today—tasted fine then as well."

"Poison?" Arthur asked, peering dubiously at the frothing cup.

The master brewer shook his head. "Nay, else we'd have a funeral to plan—*mine*. I reckon 'tis only vinegar, but it still rendered both barrels undrinkable. I poured meself a dram of ale afore the meal as I always do, and spewed it across the floor. Mark me, I take pride in me brew, and there was nothing amiss with the ale when we took our nooning. It was from the same tap, mind ye."

"I can attest to that," said Cook. "The kitchen stewards tapped the casks themselves. Ye ought to ken the wine has been laced with vinegar as well."

"Both barrels stand beside each other in the brewhouse," Bram added. "After Mistress Rhona brought my salve, she joined me there for a spot of cider. The barrels were tapped and sitting side by side then."

"Did nothing appear amiss at that time?" asked Arthur, recalling Rhona had mentioned having a cup of cider with the sergeant.

"Nay, sir. But I was there for the cider, not the ale or wine."

"Did anyone else pay a visit to the brewhouse after the barrels were tapped?"

"Not that I saw," the brew master replied. "Though I did no' ken Bram brought the healer in there until he told me."

Cook stepped forward, rubbing his round belly. "I reckon ye ought to post a guard outside the brewhouse when the fellas take their nooning."

"Aye, or lock the door," Bram agreed.

Donal stood, pressing his knuckles into the board. "We ought to round up all loyal to Lorn and lock them in the pillory for a fortnight."

"I beg your pardon? Your methods are completely unwarranted and careless. If it has escaped your notice, all three men standing before us served His Lordship." Arthur unsheathed his dirk and rapped the hilt on the table. "Silence in the hall!"

"Silence!" bellowed Donal loud enough to shake the timbers.

As the noise ebbed, Arthur moved to the center of the stairs and affected a wide stance, his fists on his hips. Before he spoke, he panned his gaze across the chamber, meeting the hard stares of several of his soldiers. "I've just received word none of us will enjoy a drink this eve on account of a jester tainting both the ale and wine casks with vinegar."

A low rumble filled the hall, and a soldier within the masses stood. "Did ye ken the damper on the bath-house was closed again as well?"

A tic twitched beside Arthur's eye. "I did not."

"'Tis vinegar now but wait until the culprit grows bolder," Donal groused.

"He could poison us all!" hollered someone from the crowd.

"Silence!" Arthur shouted, holding out his palms. "Let it be known that such trickery will not be toler-ated. I hereby make it my personal task to apprehend this culprit. Be forewarned, should this guile and devi-ousness continue, anyone caught will be severely pun-ished. *Severely!*"

"Hang him by his cods!" shouted a soldier.

"A noose around his neck would suffice!"

Arthur raised his hands again, demanding silence. "And henceforth let it be known, I will reward a purse of coin to anyone who comes forward with news of this scoundrel."

With the applause, Arthur turned to Cook. "Ye'd best feed them, else they'll be looking for blood."

"Straightaway, sir. At least me mutton hasn't been tampered with."

As Bram started for the stairs, Arthur grasped his elbow. "Tell me true, who might our trickster be?"

The sergeant-at-arms frowned, his eyes giving away no hint of deviousness. "I've no idea, unless it is a servant."

"I thought that a possibility as well."

"I'll make some inquiries. But—"

"Aye?"

Bram cringed a bit, running his fingers down his

grey beard. "Do ye reckon it could be one of *your* men, perchance?"

"What would be the motive?" asked Donal with an edge to his voice.

"Mayhap they're no' fond of anyone allied with Clan MacDougall. Mayhap they want the lot of the towns-folk cast off their lands—there's plenty of clansmen and women worried at the moment."

Unrest and undue worry were exactly what Arthur was trying to prevent, and why Donal's tactics were not advisable. "I assure ye that will not happen. If this skull-duggery continues, the cur will eventually misstep, and then we will deal with him accordingly."

AFTER RHONA RETURNED FROM MAKING HER ROUNDS, tending to the ailments of the folk in the village, Gran was not in her usual spot in her chair beside the hearth. Odd. With the elderly woman's hip ailment, she didn't step out often. Rhona headed for the little chamber where they shared a bed. "Gran?"

No, she wasn't there either, nor had her grand-mother mentioned anything this morn when they broke their fast. Noting Gran's walking stick was not by the door, Rhona hastened outside and around to the rear garden where they grew their herbs. Down near the hedgerow of feverfew, a shock of white hair reflected the sun.

There she was, the silly old woman, out of doors without her head covered. Aye, though her grandmoth-er's hair appeared well and truly grey, it had been white all her life, just as Rhona's was now. They both knew better than to spend much time in the sun without a veil or head covering, especially today of all days when there were but a few puffy clouds in the sky.

"Whatever are ye doing out here?" Rhona asked,

pulling the veil from her own head. "Ye'll burn something awful."

Gran glanced back and grinned. "Ah, I was wondering when ye would return," she said as if Rhona hadn't spoken at all. Was the old woman beginning to grow feeble-minded?

Rhona carefully situated her veil atop her grandmother's crown, ensuring it extended a bit over the forehead to protect her face. "Ye ken ye shouldn't be out here with a bare head. Are ye feeling unwell?"

"Never better." Gran gestured to a basket overfull with feverfew cuttings. "Did ye hear? There's going to be a fete—three days it will last with Highland games and a *ceilidh*."

"Aye, I'd heard and I assumed 'tis one of Sir Arthur's ploys to win our favor."

"That may very well be, lass, but a fete is a fete and an opportunity to earn a bit of coin. I care not if Sir Arthur announced the event or nay. The folk in the village will be stocking up on remedies in preparation for winter."

"Agreed, we must take care of our own, though I'm not in favor of a celebration of any sort. We ought not grow overly familiar with the constable or the soldiers. Who truly kens what they're planning for us all? Aye, they say they wish for peace, but your brother was driven from his lands when he should have been idling his time away in front of his hearth."

Gran reached for her walking stick. "We do what we can, lass. And ye just laced their ale and wine with vinegar—though *I* would have used something stronger —mayhap something to loosen the bowels."

"At least vinegar is harmless. I truly do not want anyone to suffer, even if he is not welcome." Rhona helped the old woman stand, then picked up the basket. "Are ye planning to make a cough tincture with the feverfew?"

"Aye, to sell at the fete."

"I reckon by setting up a stall to peddle our remedies, we'll be playing straight into Sir Arthur's plan."

"I don't mind as long as we're the ones to profit. When better to make a bit o' coin than setting up a wee market stall at a Highland gathering? People will be coming from miles about. Mind ye, we'll be concocting a salve from those cuttings as well. The midges are biting, ye ken."

Rhona noted Gran's use of the term "we," which meant Rhona would be brewing the salve and the tincture, and would be expected to set up a wee table to peddle their remedies. She huffed out a sigh. "I ken."

❀ 5 ❀

Standing beside his horse with reins in hand, Arthur addressed yet another farmer who was worried about the coming months and his ability to feed his family. "There will be a market day during the fete," Arthur said. "Bring your sheep. I'm certain they will sell."

The crofter frowned and scratched a full beard that hung down to the center of his chest. "Do ye reckon anyone will come?"

"Aye, people will be flocking to Dunstaffnage in droves, mark me. Even the Lord of Garmoran. I'll wager ye'll have so many orders for mutton, ye'll nay be able to fill them all."

"Ye reckon so?" The man's eyes brightened a bit. "I'll give it some thought."

Arthur patted the fellow on the shoulder. "On top of that, ye have my word the castle's cook will place a good-sized order for Dunstaffnage's larder."

The man gave a gap-toothed grin. "Ye ken ye are a difficult man to ignore."

"I can attest to that," Donal agreed, sitting atop his horse in a line with a dozen other soldiers out for the day's sortie.

Arthur made his goodbyes and mounted his steed.

"Where to now?" asked Bram.

"I thought we'd pay a visit to Connel—ensure the folk across Loch Etive are invited to the fete as well."

"If ye ask me, I still believe 'tis too soon to be making merry with MacDougalls," said Donal, moving his horse into formation at Arthur's flank. "'Tis likely a row will break out."

"Perhaps, but I intend for friendships to be forged. There's a reason I've set the date a fortnight hence. The king's men will all have coin in their sporrans."

"If the crofters pay their rents," said Donal, ever the naysayer.

Bram trotted his mount to the other flank, completing the diamond formation. "Oh, ye of little faith."

Over his shoulder, Arthur gave the old sergeant a nod. There were already funds enough to pay the soldiers, but he wasn't about to utter such a thing. Though he trusted his men, when it came to coin, one must never reveal sums on hand or lack thereof.

As their leader, he had taken to riding at the point of the retinue's formation. When he faced forward, the hairs on the back of his neck stood on end. Tightening his grip on his reins, Arthur looked up to the heavily wooded bluff—nothing seemed amiss. Though leaves rustled, an eerie quiet swelled through the air as if the birds of the forest had all been silenced. Within a heartbeat, he reached for the hilt of his sword.

But his fingers only managed to brush the handle's leather. He heard the hiss first, but there was no time to react as an arrow slammed into his chest, hurtling him backward, his horse rearing with the sudden jerk of the reins. Grunting, Arthur tried to straighten as he grappled in vain to pull the shaft free from the links of his mail. All around him, deadly arrows shot through the air. "Take cover!" he bellowed, his eyes rolling back as he dug in his heels and drove his mount toward the trees.

Gnashing his teeth, he forced away the knives of pain. Blood seeped through the fingers of his gauntleted gloves.

My blood.

"'Tis an ambush!" shouted a soldier.

Hissing arrows continued to whip past while the earth spun.

"The archers are on the ridge!" bellowed Donal, pointing toward the slope. "We can ride around their flank and head them off."

"Do not let them escape," Arthur commanded, intending to follow. But with a sickly whinny, his horse reared for a second time. The beast thrashed his head, rising upward while Arthur pushed his heels down and held fast—until the stallion twisted and jolted. Unable to maintain his grip, Arthur sailed backward. The thud of his body hitting the earth was the last thing he heard before everything went black.

"MISTRESS!" BRAM'S FRANTIC SHOUT RESOUNDED through the timbers before he kicked open the door and lumbered inside, carrying an unconscious soldier over his shoulder. The old soldier's face was drawn, his knees bent as he staggered forward, clearly suffering beneath the weight of his burden.

"Good heavens, what has happened?" she asked, hastening to the back room for the supplies to make up a pallet near the hearth. This was not the first time the old sergeant-at-arms had hauled a wounded man into the cottage. And this one looked to be in a bad way, with droplets of blood splashing onto the floor.

"Our sortie was ambushed by archers lying in wait atop the ridge on the road to Connel," Bram explained while Rhona returned and spread a feather mattress on the floor. "The constable took bolt from a crossbow in the chest. And when his horse was hit, the beast reared and threw the poor fellow."

"'Twas bound to happen," said Gran, sitting on the edge of her chair.

"Constable, did ye say?" Rhona asked, ignoring her sudden rapid heartbeat while she shook out a linen sheet and draped it over the mattress. "Why the devil did ye not take him to the castle?"

Bram grimaced as he kneeled and carefully laid Sir Arthur onto his back. "There's no' a healer at the castle."

Gran grabbed the armrests of her chair and craned her neck. "Ye mean to say ye brought the Bruce's man into *this* cottage of all places?"

"Aye, he happens to be the fella giving me orders at the moment, m'lady." Bram looked to Rhona. "Can ye stop the bleeding?"

"I'll need ye to help me remove his mail. I won't ken how badly he's injured until I see the size of the hole. Did ye pull out the entire arrow or just break the shaft?"

"Got the whole arrow with one tug. I reckon the knight would no' be breathing if he hadn't been wearing armor." Bram tugged Sir Arthur to his haunches, making the man's head loll forward. "Hold him steady, and I'll pull off his hauberk."

"How long do ye reckon he'll be here?" asked Gran, clearly irritated at the inconvenience, and not sounding as if she cared a whit about the knight's wellbeing.

"No longer than absolutely necessary." Rhona kneeled beside the pallet while the sergeant-at-arms hefted the heavy mail over Sir Arthur's head. Before the man fell backward, she quickly placed a hand behind his neck and another at his flank to help ease him down.

The front of his quilted jerkin was soaked with blood. "Give me the shears."

Gran held up a set. "Be careful, else ye might end up stabbing him in the heart." She snorted. "Since the arrow didn't manage to finish the job."

Bram retrieved them. "Och, ye have no' lost your sense of humor, m'lady."

Rhona made quick work of cutting away the garments and baring Sir Arthur's chest. "Bring me the stack of cloths from the shelf, please. He's still bleeding."

Bram complied and Rhona applied a cloth, holding pressure. "Do ye ken how much blood he has lost?"

"Plenty. He bled like a spigot after I pulled out the arrow."

Rhona lifted the cloth and examined the wound. It wasn't terribly large—no more than a half inch in diameter, but an enormous bruise encircled it. "By the stars, he was lucky."

"Hit by an arrow from a crossbow and ye reckon 'tis luck?" Gran sat back and picked up her knitting. "Mayhap I suppose it might be a bit o' luck if the good Lord sees fit to send him to his judgment day."

"Nay, this is not a mortal wound, else he'd already be dead. In truth, I'm surprised he hasn't regained his senses." Rhona took a fresh cloth and pressed it atop Arthur's chest, and then she looked to Bram. "He was thrown from his mount, did ye say?"

"Aye."

"What happened to his helm?"

Squinting, the sergeant-at-arms tapped his temple. "Come to think on it, he did no' have it on when I pulled the arrow out of his chest."

Rhona slid her fingers beneath Arthur's neck and moved them upward until she found a knot nearly the size of her fist. "Now I ken why he's dreaming with the fairies. When he wakes, he'll have a miserable ache of his head."

"The question is not when," said Gran, her needles clicking. "'Tis if."

Rhona ignored the woman. Though she was displeased with Sir Arthur and his army's presence, she couldn't imagine losing him. She inclined her head to the sergeant-at-arms. "I need two pillows from the bedchamber."

Bram placed the mail on the bench. "I'll fetch them."

"Not my pillows!" sniped Gran.

"Enough," Rhona scolded. "I intend to take care of Sir Arthur no matter who he is. Ye ken I've never been fond of losing patients, especially when they're under my roof."

"*Our* roof, mind ye."

Bram returned and helped Rhona prop up the wounded man. "What else do ye need, mistress?"

Rocking back on her haunches, Rhona regarded the elderly soldier's stooped shoulders. "I'll wager ye are tired. Why not go home? There's little to do now aside from dressing the wound and keeping him comfortable."

"Very well, then." The sergeant-at-arms straightened. "But if ye should need anything, send wee Gregor to fetch me."

"My thanks."

Bram looked to Gran and winked. "See to it ye do not poison the poor blighter, m'lady."

The old woman's eyes popped as if she'd been affronted. "Me?"

Laughing, the sergeant-at-arms slipped out the door.

"That man has a great deal of gall," Gran said, using her walking stick to hoist herself out of the chair. Grunting all the way, she lumbered across the floor and stood over the pallet. "Och, the constable is quite braw for a man aligned with the enemy, is he not?"

Rhona gulped. Ever since she'd cut away Sir Arthur's shirt, she'd been trying not to notice the thick bands of muscle across his chest and abdomen. Or the soft purse of his lips, or the way his dark lashes fanned his cheeks in slumber. For heaven's sake, the man was knocking on death's door!

Moreover, her grandmother was uncannily perceptive and the last thing Rhona wanted was for the matriarch of the clan to think she was smitten. She carefully dabbed the cloth around the wound. "He was brought here to be healed, not to be ogled."

"I daresay with a form as well-muscled as his, 'tis near impossible not to give the knight a once-over or two." Gran leaned forward on her cane and studied Sir Arthur's face. "I reckon he is pleasing to the eye, though the black beard gives him a wee bit o' venom—makes him look like a Bruce man for certain."

Rhona could have laughed. Fingal had a black beard, as did Bram before it turned grey, but that didn't matter. "There ye are. Sir Arthur is far from perfect."

"Aye, far from it." Gran sighed. "Though he's not the same lad who left for St. Andrews years ago."

"How did ye ken he'd gone to St. Andrews?"

"He's a local fellow, why should I not know?"

"On account of him being a Campbell. And he's from Loch Awe—twenty miles away, mind ye."

"Aye, but he's not just any Campbell. He's the son of the Lord of Garmoran."

"Second son."

"True." Gran ambled back to her chair, groaning as she sat. "Though in these perilous times, 'tis not unusual for the second in line to inherit. I watched him from afar, especially after ye started batting your eyelashes at the lad when ye were sixteen summers."

Not caring to remember all the eyelash-batting

she'd done, Rhona stood and set to work spreading a blanket over Sir Arthur. At least when he was covered, she would not be distracted by his well-muscled form or his inordinately hairy chest, especially with her grandmother doing plenty of inappropriate ogling. "The past is over and I'm no longer a silly child. At the moment, this Highlander is in my care and I aim to see to it he's up and out of our cottage as soon as practicable."

❧ 6 ❧

Arthur drew in a deep breath and, as his ribs expanded, he jolted as if a knife had been driven into his chest. His reaction made the ache more intense, complemented by throbbing agony in his head. He struggled to open his eyes, only to have them roll back and flutter closed. But not before he'd looked up. What had he seen? Dim light, the shimmering outline of a woman.

Or an angel.

Fragrance enveloped him as a cloth was removed from his forehead and replaced with a cooler one. He knew the fragrance. Nay, the overtone of clove hadn't been what stirred his blood. A honey-sweet scent had roused him, as alluring as a hedgerow of roses.

Rhona.

He wasn't in his chamber at the castle, was he?

Dim light and the outline of a woman? I ken in my bones 'tis her.

Arthur's heart skipped a beat as he forced his eyes open. "Mistress Rhona?" he whispered, his mouth dry, his lips chapped.

"Ye're awake?" The woman leaned over him and studied his eyes, her long white tresses falling forward and framing the face he'd dreamed about near every night for the past seven years. "How are ye feeling?"

"Uh..." He tried to sit up but with one finger, she urged him back down. "My brain is near bursting out of my skull and I feel as if I've returned from the trenches of a losing battle."

"I reckon that about sums it up. Do ye remember what happened?"

Arthur closed his eyes. "I led the retinue straight into an ambush. My horse reared. The rest is a blank. How did I come to be here?"

"Bram brought you to the cottage—carried you inside draped over his shoulder, mind ye."

"Why did he not take me to the castle?"

"I asked the same. He said there was no healer at Dunstaffnage."

Arthur smiled to himself. If he were to choose to be under anyone's care, it would be Rhona's. "I smell cloves," he said, wishing he could tell her he'd recognize her scent anywhere, any day, no matter how much she tried to mask it.

"That would be the oil of avens I've applied to the wound on your chest."

Ah, yes, now he recalled. He'd been skewered in the chest with a bolt from a crossbow. The strike alone had nearly unseated him. He glanced downward; his torso was bare, aside from a bandage wrapped around it. Farther down, there was a blanket folded over at his waist. "Where is my armor?"

"On the bench. Bram removed it to allow me to tend ye."

"And your grandmother? Is she here?"

"Aye." Rhona inclined her head toward a closed door. "She headed for bed hours ago."

"And you? Have ye slept?"

"Nay, sir. I've been doing all I can to ensure the fever remains at bay."

He gingerly ran his fingers over his abdomen, relieved his skin was cool to the touch. "It seems to have worked. I do not feel feverish."

"Which is why I haven't slept, though 'tis a bit early yet."

He grasped her hand. "I must thank ye."

"I'm a healer. No thanks is necessary, though I do appreciate—"

When she didn't finish, Arthur gently squeezed her lithe fingers. "What do ye appreciate, lass?"

She slid her hand away and rubbed her fingers on her skirts as if attempting to wipe away the sensation of his touch. "Payment."

The single-word answer curtly issued, cut more deeply than Arthur cared to admit. How changed this woman was from years gone by. He missed the happy, carefree gel he'd known. What had happened in the span of time since they had been a pair of fledgling lovers?

"Naturally," he whispered. He would see to it she was handsomely paid. As long as he was constable, he would see to it Mistress Rhona wanted for naught.

"Are ye hungry?" she asked.

His stomach churned at the mention of food. "Not especially, though I've a thirst."

Rhona stood and headed toward a cupboard where she pulled a pot from the shelf. "I've a tea that will help with stomach upset."

"How did ye ken I'm a bit queasy?"

"'Tis common after a blow to the head." She used a spoon to ladle some powder from the pot into a cup, then filled it with water from the kettle hanging above the fire, and then added something else he couldn't make out. "Ye'd best not try to rise for a time."

Arthur pushed up to his elbows, but the effort sapped him. "Och, I cannot be a burden to ye and your grandmother."

The lass moved to the pallet and kneeled beside him. "Believe me, I'd like to see ye up and about sooner than later, but not until ye are set to rights. And when it comes to healing, I'm the constable in this cottage." She held up the spoon. "Open your mouth."

Arthur pushed up with his elbows, then reached for it.

"Nay, nay." She drew the spoon away from his grasp. "Ye mustn't tax yourself. Now open."

"What is it?"

"A wee bit of honey with ground nettle and dandelion leaves."

Feeling a bit silly, he let her feed him. "Mm, 'tis good."

"Ye sound surprised," she said, tempting him with another spoonful.

"I am surprised. I do not recollect a remedy ever tasting pleasant."

"Hmm," she mused as he swallowed another. "I've also added a drop of henbane to help ye sleep."

"Henbane? Are ye trying to kill me?"

"'Tis just a drop. It won't do ye in but will ensure ye get the rest ye need."

Arthur licked his dry lips. "I've slept enough."

"Nay. Injuries heal best when the afflicted slumber. And I think we both can agree ye must recover with haste."

Well, she seemed to ken what she was on about, and presently, he hadn't a mind to move, not with his head pounding as if he was being bludgeoned from the inside. Arthur resigned to let her feed him at least this once. "I was wondering..."

She stilled the spoon in the air. "Hmm?"

"What happened to your husband?"

Sighing, Rhona moved the spoon to his mouth while a bit of color flushed her pale cheeks. "'Twas a hunting incident. He thought he'd felled the stag when he approached. However, the animal was but wounded and gored him straight through the heart with a point of his antler."

Arthur couldn't imagine—well, he knew what it felt like to be nearly skewered through the heart by an arrow, but to be the one left behind and alone must have been devastating. "I'm so very sorry. Ye were widowed far too young."

"Nineteen years of age, if ye must know—married only a year. I then lost his unborn not long after." Her pale eyes misted before she blinked and glanced away. "If only the bairn had survived, my husband would have left a legacy."

"Ye mean to say ye lost your husband and then your babe? My word, how devastating for ye." Arthur brushed the back of her hand with his finger. "It seems all the fighting has made a great many widows in the past score of years."

Rhona started to rise, but he caught her wrist, ever so slender in his meaty grip. For a fleeting moment, she looked at him the way she once did—light blue eyes fanned by inordinately thick, white lashes and filled will longing. With her next blink, the expression vanished. "I've said too much."

"Nay." Arthur swirled his fingers around her wrist. "You have had a difficult time of it. Of that I can see for certain. Yet..."

A pink tongue slipped to the corner of her mouth as he hesitated.

"Yet you have acquired an inner strength ye did not have at sixteen years of age."

She gave his hand a wee squeeze. "I was but a child. Ye mustn't think of me in that way. I'm now a woman grown and I care for a great many souls about these parts. Healing was not the vocation I had planned, but now it suits me quite well."

"Agreed, ye are far more complex, more mature and,

I never would have believed it possible, but you are even lovelier now than before. Och, lass, I've never forgotten one single minute we shared." Closing his eyes, he drew her fingers to his lips and kissed them, praying his simple gesture imparted the slightest modicum of how deeply he cared for this woman.

As Rhona drew her hand away, she balled her fist and drew it against her midriff while the hint of longing returned to her eyes. "Ye should not have done that."

No matter how much she fought it, the woman still had feelings for him. He could read it upon her face. She hadn't pulled away. She could have slapped him or scolded him with a wicked tongue. But she had not.

The corner of his mouth ticked up. "Forgive me, though I'll never say I am sorry for kissing your hand, lass."

She rose and turned away from him. "Ye'd best sleep now."

It seemed Sir Arthur but closed his eyes and he'd drifted into slumber. Rhona wasn't surprised in the slightest. A few drops of henbane were enough to make a horse drowsy. Too much could kill a man, which was why she always administered it herself and never left a vial with even a single drop of the essence in the care of a patient, aside from leaving a bit with Sara for Fingal, but she knew she could trust Sara not to abuse it.

To her chagrin, the back of Rhona's hand still tingled from his kiss. She had even tried to rub the sensation away, but to no avail. Why, after all this time, did this Highlander still make her insides take to flight as if she were still young at heart and ever so foolish?

She didn't want to like him. In truth, she wished her granduncle had let her sail to England with him.

Or did she?

Rhona had lived in the shadow of Dunstaffnage Castle all her life. The folk eking out a living on the surrounding lands were her kin and in her care. How could she have left them behind?

Her gaze trailed to Sir Arthur. Even though he had joined with Robert the Bruce, the man still held a claim on her heart like none other. Aye, her husband, Ivor, had been a good man, a kind man, and she had learned to love him, she supposed. The marriage had been arranged by her granduncle and she hardly knew Ivor when they wed. Nonetheless, had he lived, she would have been content. After all, stability and contentment were all any woman could hope for.

Alas, it wasn't meant to be. At three and twenty, she had now been a widow for four years and, in that time, had enriched and perfected the healing skills she'd learned from Gran when she was a lass.

"I suppose I ought to have a look at your wound," Rhona said, though she knew he would be asleep for hours to come. She kneeled beside the knight and pulled away the dressing. Angry and red, the injury seeped a bit, but thus far, there was no pus and the flesh around the laceration was cool to the touch.

Bram had not been wrong when he'd said Sir Arthur had been lucky. Had he not been wearing a coat of mail, the arrow would have pierced his heart and the knight would not have drawn another breath.

If only Ivor had donned armor when he'd set out on the hunt that fateful morn.

Sighing, Rhona took a clean cloth to fashion a new bandage but stilled her hands when Sir Arthur emitted a soft murmur. "Och, Rhona, if only I could hold you in my arms forever," he mumbled in his stupor.

Her breath caught as she studied his ruggedly alluring face. Had he meant what he'd said? He'd never forgotten a single moment they'd shared?

Truly?

Rhona had not forgotten either. As if their romance had only been a summer ago, she remembered every meeting, every kiss. She'd once yearned to marry the man unconscious on the pallet in the main chamber of the wee cottage. Aye, he'd hurt her something awful when he disappeared from Argyll without a word. The thought of standing alone and abandoned, still made her heart ache.

But by the saints, Gran hadn't been wrong when she'd said he was braw. Beneath the black curls on his chest and abdomen was a masculine form at its finest. Sir Arthur's shoulders were broader now and he had not an ounce of fat covering the ripples of sinew. By the gods, the sight of him took her breath away—fanned the flames of the desire smoldering deep and low in her core. A flame she thought extinguished long ago.

Forcing herself to stop staring, she reapplied a swath of avens oil and replaced the dressing. In truth, the lump on Sir Arthur's head worried Rhona more than the wound on his chest. The next few days would be crucial to his recovery.

By the time she'd placed a new cloth on the Highlander's forehead, she could barely keep her eyes open. Perhaps if she rested her head for a few moments, she'd be ready to face the morn. Indeed, she'd spent many sleepless nights at the bedside of the infirm and she ought to be accustomed to it by now. But somehow, she never truly grew used to going without sleep...

RHONA WAS PRODDED AWAKE BY THE UNFORGIVING point of Gran's walking stick. "Why the devil did you not come to bed if ye were tired?"

Good Lord, her backside was flush against Sir Arthur's hip—a very sturdy hip indeed. How had she managed to sidle up beside the man? Rhona quickly shifted away as she wiped a bit of spittle from the corner of her mouth. "I only meant to close my eyes for a moment."

"Well, need I say 'tis a good thing I found ye and not one of the townsfolk. You would have been marked a jezebel for certain."

"Heaven forbid," Rhona mumbled under her breath as she roused herself and stood. "I'll stir the fire and set the pot to boiling for some oats."

Gran lumbered to her chair. "There's a good lass. I've grown so feeble, I do not ken what I'd do without ye."

After adding a brick of peat to the fire, Rhona used the poker to stir the cinders. "At least ye have no need to worry about that."

"How did the constable fare through the night?"

"He slept well." Rhona bit her bottom lip. Gran's comment about being labeled a jezebel stopped her from mentioning the fact that Sir Arthur had awakened. For the first time in years, he had made her feel wanted...*desirable*. He'd kissed her hand and had imparted a world of emotion when he'd closed his eyes and furrowed his brow. It seemed as if he truly did oft think of her and their time together.

Except Rhona knew it wasn't so. If the Highlander truly thought so fondly of their summer of stolen kisses, then he would not have gone off to St. Andrews without a word. And must she remind herself he had stayed away for seven long years?

She replaced the fire poker on its nail beside the hearth and picked up the bucket. "I'll fetch some water from the well. I won't be but a moment."

Outside, the cool air provided relief, clearing Rhona's head. Following the path to the well at the rear garden, she told herself never to allow Sir Arthur to kiss her hand again. That chivalrous gesture had sent her heart into ridiculous palpitations. He might be charming but he was not for the likes of her.

Let him make eyes at some other maid who is more suited to his politics.

With the upcoming fete, she had no doubt that lassies would come in from across Argyll. One of them was bound to catch his eye. But as Rhona put the pail's handle on the hook and lowered it to the water, her stomach twisted in knots.

Seeing Arthur Campbell with another woman would be difficult to bear—very difficult indeed.

❧ 7 ❧

"Ye are a mutton-headed Highlander for certain," said Lady Mary. "Ye ought to be paying heed to my granddaughter, nay defying her."

Arthur's shoulders shook as he restrained his laughter and spooned a bite of porridge into his mouth. It had been a long time since he'd received a tongue-lashing from a matronly woman, and Rhona's grandmother spewed bile as sour as unripe grapes. "I beg your pardon, m'lady, but the first lesson a soldier must learn is to push himself at every turn."

"When Bram brought ye here last eve, ye were on death's door. Ye should be on your back and nowhere else, listening to Mistress Rhona's every word."

He took another bite. "I promise I'll go back to my pallet as soon as I've finished eating. Will that suffice?"

Lady Mary picked up a ewer of milk and poured it over her porridge. "I suppose it must do, given ye are already sitting up. But if ye fall face-forward into your bowl, do not blame me."

"I'd never dream of placing such blame on anyone's shoulders except my own, especially when it comes to falling on my face."

Rhona climbed onto the bench across from him and picked up her spoon. "The blow to your head was more severe than ye think. Over the next few days, it will be imperative not to jostle yourself overmuch—no horseback riding, no sparring, and definitely no dancing."

"Ye wound me." Arthur regarded her with a gape-mouthed expression. "No dancing?"

"What have ye been up to behind Dunstaffnage's curtain walls?" asked Lady Mary. "Carousing with wenches and kicking up your heels?"

"Aye," he teased. "Have ye not seen the wagonloads of wenches rolling through the village every eve?"

Groaning, Rhona cast her gaze to the rough-hewn rafters above. "Wheesht, the pair of ye."

Arthur exchanged glances with the elderly woman, whose eyes were full of mischief, as well as a hint of malice. He supposed that since her brother was Lord of Lorn, she had more reason than anyone to be unhappy with his new posting of constable. He then regarded Rhona. As soon as their gazes met, she shifted her eyes downward. A bit of color flooded her cheeks as if looking him in the eye rendered the lass a wee bit bashful.

The mere thought of having such an effect on her buoyed his spirits. Did Mistress Rhona still harbor a modicum of affection for him? Arthur intended to find out—perhaps when Lady Mary wasn't listening to their every word, the old battleax.

"In truth, there hasn't been time for dancing," he said, as if there had not just been hundreds of unspoken words expressed between all three of them. "Not for ages. I think the last time I danced was with Angus Og MacDonald's wife when the Bruce was holding court on the Isle of Islay months before the Battle of Loudoun Hill." Arthur waggled his eyebrows at Lady Mary. "And there wasn't a buxom wench in sight at the time, either."

The elderly lady sucked in her cheeks, making her look positively cadaverous. "Ye are a brazen lad."

"Forgive me if I have injured your sensibilities." He scooped a spoonful of porridge, fully aware that Rhona's grandmother was enjoying their banter. "However, I do hope ye will see fit to pronounce me fully cured and able to engage in the most rigorous of reels the night of the *ceilidh* at the upcoming fete."

"I'd heard about your games. 'Tis to be in a fortnight, aye?" asked Lady Mary.

"Twelve days hence, to be exact." Arthur looked to Rhona. "What say you, mistress?"

Rhona again met his gaze with a fleeting intensity, then quickly looked to her bowl. "Only time will tell. I see ye've regained your appetite. 'Tis a good sign."

"And will you be attending the *ceilidh*?" Arthur hedged.

"It is unlikely."

"Whyever not?" asked the lassie's grandmama.

"I'll most likely be tending someone's bedside. That is the way of things." Rhona thrust her spoon toward Arthur's pallet. "Ye've been sitting up quite long enough. To bed with ye."

Just as he swung his leg over the bench, there came a pounding from outside. "Sir Arthur, we've captured the murdering bastards!" The deep bellow undoubtedly belonged to Donal.

"Oh, my heavens," said Rhona as she hastened to open the door while Arthur pushed to his feet, the effort making his head reel enough to force him to steady himself by placing his palm on the table.

Donal gave the lass a nod before he swept inside, muddy boots and all. "Sir, it took an entire night of riding, but we caught the bastards who set the ambush."

"Mind your vulgar tongue, soldier," Arthur said, clenching both fists. "There are ladies present."

The lieutenant removed his helm, revealing a thicket of unkempt hair. "Forgive me." He bowed in the direction of the two women and cleared his throat.

"The miscreants who set the ambush have been apprehended, sir."

"I am glad to hear it."

"What are their names?" asked Mistress Rhona.

"A beefy cur named Auley, and his five sons."

"Auley of Dunbeg?" Rhona shot a panicked glance to her grandmother. "His youngest has not yet seen fifteen summers."

"Aye?" asked Donal. "The lout should have thought about that afore he unleashed his crossbows on the king's retinue."

"The king?" Lady Mary groaned under her breath.

Donal seemed not to hear, or at least he ignored the grandmother's comment. "The men are preparing the gallows. Ye'll need—"

"Gallows?" asked Rhona, her voice stricken. "Auley is a fine man, none more loyal to the Lord of Lorn. Surely ye're not planning to hang them?"

"Have ye another suggestion?" Donal raised his thick eyebrows as if in disbelief. "They nearly killed the constable."

"A moment." Arthur spread his palms, looking from the ladies to his man. No matter how much he agreed with Donal, the treatment of the outlaws needed to be handled with the civility of a court of law, and since Arthur was the constable and therefore the magistrate, he would be the one to hear their pleas and sentence them accordingly. "They will require due process. We must first determine who fired the arrows."

"The bloody lot of them, that's who." Donal skirted toward the door. "I'd best return to the castle and oversee the hanging."

"Nay. There will be no hanging until I have had the opportunity to hear their supplications."

"And then ye'll hang them?" Rhona thrust her fists onto her hips. "All six? Even Ricky, the youngest?"

"Do not put words into my mouth, woman," Arthur

said while from outside the cottage rose a great deal of shouting.

"The townsfolk are up in arms," said Donal.

"Then there's not a moment to spare." Arthur's head swam as he stooped to retrieve his mail, but there was no chance he would allow any discomfort to show. He'd been coddled on his sickbed long enough. "Thank you for your kindness, ladies, but I must hasten to dispel the crowd."

"Did ye not pay attention to a word I said?" Rhona stepped in front of the path to the door. "Ye ought to be in your bed. Ye may not die from the arrow to the chest, but the blow to your skull is far more perilous."

"I understand," he said while Donal helped him don his mail. "But a man's duty must sometimes come before his healer's wise advice. Moreover, if the people of the village believe me to be knocking on death's door, they will be more inclined to revolt."

"He's most likely right there," said Lady Mary.

Rhona thrust her finger at his chest. "If ye walk out that door, I will not be held accountable for your death."

Arthur grasped her hand and kissed her knuckles. "Stay here with your grandmother. I ken where to find you, should I grow worse. My thanks for all ye have done. I am truly in your debt." He removed a purse of coins from his belt and placed it in her palm. "This is not enough by half but should sustain ye until I am able to return with more."

AFTER ARTHUR TOOK HIS LEAVE, RHONA STOOD IN the doorway and watched while the crowd followed him straight through the castle gates. Groaning, she stepped back inside and emptied the contents of the purse into her palm. "Oh, my."

"How much is there?" asked Gran from her chair.

"'Tis all gold and silver—not a copper among them. I'll wager there's enough here to feed us for a year."

"'Tis the devil's coin. Ye ought to give it back."

Rhona slid the money into the pouch and tightened the leather drawstrings. "I disagree. I told him I expected payment, and he heeded my request. These coins are far more useful in our coffers than in Sir Arthur's."

"Very well, if ye put it like that. I'm just glad he's gone, the insolent cur."

Rhona added the pouch to the pot they kept on the shelf. "I though ye were enjoying yourself with your dear cynicism."

"Och, I reckon he enjoyed our banter more than me. I do believe the man nearly burst out with laughter more than once."

"I only hope he will be fine. I was serious about his head. He should not be up."

Gran picked up her embroidery and tugged on the needle. "I say, if Sir Arthur is planning to hang Auley and his sons, he deserves to succumb to that blow to the head."

"Good Lord, the thought of losing the swine farmer is awful. But 'tis another reason I didn't try too terribly hard to stand in his way. Mind ye, if matters had been left up to Donal, the men would have had no trial and would already be heading for the gallows."

"You and I ken Auley is as hotheaded a man as has ever lived, but he was only doing my brother's bidding. And you were right when ye said there was not a more loyal soul in all of Argyll."

"Aye, but what has me worried is that Lorn surrendered. He fled to England and told the rest of us to stand down."

Gran pulled the needle through the linen. "Mayhap Auley did not receive my brother's directive. He's most likely been holing up in the hills. And I'll wager he was ordered to hold the ridge at Connel. He's probably been there ever since the battle at the Pass of Brander."

Rhona groaned. "And now it appears as if he's going to pay with his life and the lives of his sons."

After tying off her thread, Gran reached for her shears. "Ye ken as well as I, had the tides been changed and he had set an ambush for the Lord of Lorn, the lot of them would have been led to the gallows, no matter their character."

"How can ye say that?"

"I'm not saying 'tis right, but it is the way of things." Gran held up the scissors, a single eyebrow arching as it did when she was scheming. "However, there might be a way..."

"Oh, no. What are ye scheming now?"

"Sir Arthur still fancies ye."

"Pshaw." Rhona batted her hand through the air. "And I reckon your eyesight is waning."

"I ken what I'm on about, lass. Ye ought to march up to the castle and tell the new constable to grant Auley and his sons a pardon."

"A great deal of good that will do."

"It cannot do any harm, now can it? And whilst ye're there, ye might lace the ale with hemlock rather than vinegar."

"Ye are awful! Next I'll be the one climbing the gallows' steps."

"Not as long as Sir Arthur remains constable."

"Yet another reason I shouldn't poison their ale with hemlock." Rhona picked up her basket. "I'm away. I must check on Fingal, and meanwhile, do not go dreaming up any harebrained ideas about poisoning the soldiers at the fete."

"Me? I'm more worried about Auley's fate at the moment."

So was Rhona. "Heaven help him and those lads.

They do not deserve to die," she said, slipping out the door and hastening for Sara and Fingal's cottage.

Think. What can I do? What can I say to Arthur to convince him to be lenient?

As she approached the tiny abode, the sounds of shouting, crying, and just plain sniveling practically rattled the thatch on the roof. Rhona knocked, but judging by the racket coming from within, no one heard. She cracked open the door. "Sara? 'Tis me."

"Me ma's no' here," shouted Gregor, standing in the center of the chamber with the babe on one hip, the toddler on the other, both of whom were wailing as if the world had ended. In fact, not one of the children was silent.

"Is everything well?" she asked, sliding inside.

"This one has wet all over everything, and the other bonked her head on the table and has a knot the size of a pebble coming up." Gregor shot a heated glance to the second and third eldest. "And that pair doesn't reckon they need to take orders from the likes of me even though Da said I was in charge of this miserable lot."

Deciding the bump to the temple was more critical than the wet babe, Rhona took the toddler from the harried boy, which instantly stopped the child's wailing. "Ye have a sore head, do ye, wee Maggie?"

The little girl nodded while her bottom lip jutted out.

"Well then, allow me to have a peek." Rhona gently brushed aside the girl's hair, finding a small bump with a bruise starting to form. "I see ye are being very brave."

"I want Mummie."

"Of course ye do. But your big brother, Gregor, is looking after ye at the moment. If I kiss your head, I'll make it feel better, ye ken?"

Maggie gave a woeful nod and Rhona applied a practiced healer's magical kiss to the child's temple.

"Better?" she asked.

The lass squirmed. "Down."

After setting Maggie on her feet and watching her run off to play, Rhona turned to the thunderstruck lad. "Let us see what we can do about changing the swaddling, shall we?"

Gregor inclined his head to a basket. "The linens are there. Came in off the line this morn."

She spread a sheet of linen on the bed before she took the bairn from the lad. "Where are your parents? Your da ought to still be abed."

"They went to the castle to watch the hanging."

Rhona unwrapped the soiled swaddling and cast it aside, then placed the babe atop the clean cloth. "Well, they'll be sorely disappointed. Sir Arthur intends to hear the prisoners' pleas afore he passes judgment."

"That's no' what me da said. He reckons they're going to stretch Auley of Dunbeg's neck, and his lads' as well."

Rhona made quick work of wrapping the babe up tightly, then lifted the child into her arms. "Goodness, no!"

"But Da said that's what's to be done with anyone who defies the new king or his men. He says Robert the Bruce is a tyrant."

"Does he now? So your da is well acquainted with the king?"

The lad's toe turned inward. "Aye."

"And he kens the king's wishes?"

Gregor stood a bit straighter as if he knew what he was on about. "Aye. Da even said Lorn would hang them for setting an ambush. He said Auley doesn't ken when to hold his temper and now they're all going to die."

"I don't think—"

"Da also said if the new constable doesn't send them to the gallows, everyone from miles about will reckon he's milk-livered."

"My, your father is full of opinions, is he not?" Rhona placed the infant in the cradle and headed for the door. "Stay here with your siblings and do try to keep them from harming themselves."

Gregor followed. "Where are ye off to?"

"To stop a hanging."

"But me da said—"

Rhona didn't wait to hear what other vile words Fingal had said in front of his children. As far as she was concerned, the man had uttered more than enough for innocent ears. Sir Arthur might put all six of them to death. Heaven's stars, he'd be wiping out the legacy of an entire family!

Outside, black clouds hung low, drizzling a misty rain. Rhona clutched her veil tightly at her throat and tried to run across the drawbridge and through the gates. She hated running because it made her clumsy and moreover, with the rain, she slipped and stumbled over the cobblestones. After the guards let her pass, without crossing their pikes this time, she stopped under the archway to the outer courtyard. Clapping a hand to her chest, she fought to catch her breath before proceeding into the inner bailey.

A sizeable crowd had gathered, shouting jeers and taunts—some for mercy and others for justice. Never in her life had she seen a people so divided. Clearly, some had already moved on and accepted the new constable as their magistrate.

Sir Arthur climbed onto the gallows' platform, none too steadily while the telltale sign of blood seeped through his surcoat, proving he'd been shot in the chest. Obviously, by his pallor, Rhona had been right that the knight needed to be abed.

"This never would have happened if Lorn were still lord and master of Dunstaffnage and Argyll to boot!" shouted Fingal in his resounding bass.

Arthur held up his palms, requesting silence. "Wheesht."

"They attacked the king's men and will pay for their crimes!" shouted Donal, standing behind the constable on the platform.

Sir Arthur thrust his finger beneath the lieutenant's nose and, though Rhona couldn't hear exactly what was said, it was clear by the way Donal stepped back, he had been curtly reprimanded. And the man-at-arms was no small soldier. He was almost as fierce and intimidating as Arthur.

"Silence!" Arthur bellowed to the crowd, looking so angry it appeared as if fire were about to shoot from his eyes. "There will be no hanging this day. I will hear the prisoners' testimonies and then will decide what is to be done. The king's men are not barbarians. Scotland is under new rule—not lenient but also not tyrannical as with the English king. I give ye all my oath, justice will prevail. Now go home to your hearths, the lot of ye."

As the townsfolk began to disperse, Rhona surged ahead, making her way to the gallows where Arthur was descending the steps. "Sir, ye are in no condition to hold court," she said, both because it was true and also to purchase time for Auley and his sons. "I implore ye to rest."

After reaching the cobblestones, Arthur swayed on his feet while he narrowed his gaze at her, his lips disappearing into a thin line. "I've nay time to lie abed. I have been charged with keeping order in this shire, and I intend to do so swiftly."

"Then I implore ye to allow me to stand by."

The knight closed his eyes, while a pinch formed between his brows. Rhona had seen this before. He most likely had swelling inside his skull causing a great deal of pain, let alone dizziness and slower reflexes. Presently, he appeared to have symptoms of all three.

"The duty I must perform is not meant for a lady's ears."

"Ye have no idea the things a healer hears near every day." She placed her hand on his arm and squeezed. "I must caution ye, it is possible for ye to lose consciousness again—at any moment. Ye absolutely mustn't strain yourself."

A tic twitched beside his eye. "As I said, my post requires swift action and I am no milksop to be cosseted by a healer."

"Then allow me to remain in the hall. I assure ye, I am not a fragile maiden."

"My orders were—"

"She may have a point, sir." Bram stepped between them. "Just as a precaution, of course. I ken I would feel better knowing Mistress Rhona is on hand should ye take a turn for the worse."

The braw knight pressed the heels of his hands against his temples. "I am on the mend and shall not have a relapse of any sort. However, since Mistress Rhona has willingly volunteered her time, and if there are no subjects who need her healing arts at the moment, I will allow it." He thrust his finger at her nose. "However, there will be no interrupting. No pleading on behalf of the accused. In fact, I require complete silence from your quarter."

Rhona's jaw dropped before she gave a curt nod. "Very well, but let it be known that there is no one more loyal to Clan MacDougall than Auley of Dunbeg. I ken in my heart of hearts he would never fire upon ye in cold blood. He would not!"

Arthur leveled a hard gaze upon her. "Interesting ye should attest to his character, madam, given the hole in my chest."

... ...

❧ 8 ❧

Grinding his molars to stay the pounding in his head, Arthur headed for the great hall. "Bring the prisoners and let them stand before me in irons."

Bless it, he had told Rhona to remain at home with her grandmother. There was a reason he didn't want the woman within earshot of the proceedings. Acting magistrate was an ugly business, especially when passing judgment over a bevy of men who had attacked his very own retinue. Be they MacDougall kin or nay, they had defied the laws of the kingdom and must be punished. Moreover, the punishment must suit the crime, and, if it did not, he would become the laughingstock of Argyll, not to mention word would eventually reach Robert the Bruce and Arthur would doubtlessly be relieved of his post and disgraced.

Not only did his head feel as if it were about to burst, it was all he could do to keep down his breakfast of oats and stand upright. God's stones, even the floor beneath his feet seemed to be spinning. Not that he'd admit it to a soul, especially to the healer who'd just insisted he ought to be abed.

He focused ahead and marched directly to the table on the dais. Stifling a groan, he placed his palms flat on

AMY JARECKI

the board to steady himself, doing his best to appear fearsome and in command.

Donal moved beside him and stood at his shoulder. "If it were up to me, the culprits would be swinging by their necks at the moment."

Arthur gripped the back of the man's hand across the top of his knuckles, where it was sure to cause pain, and squeezed. Sinew and bone crunched beneath his fingers as he looked the soldier in the eye and lowered his voice to a growl. "Here me clearly; I will tolerate no insubordination within my ranks. You may fight like a Spartan on the battlefield, but if ye cannot learn to hold your tongue and carry out your orders without expressing your unbidden opinion, I'll be throwing your arse into the pit alongside these varlets. Am I understood?"

Donal blinked, his eyes watering, his face growing red. "Aye, sir."

Arthur strengthened his grip a tad more. "The king's position is still precarious at best. Our victory in the Pass of Brander was a boon, indeed. But there are many who would still prefer to see Robert meet his end than to watch him march his army into Stirling and Edinburgh and end the English occupation once and for all. Think it through, soldier. We must not only hold this castle on behalf of the kingdom, we must win the favor of the clansmen and women who till the land, who provide the woolens, the food, and the goods we need to survive. I ken we are within our rights to take our due, but then, how many more ambushes will we encounter?"

Scowling, the lieutenant bared his teeth. "Ye may never win their favor."

"Not from all, I'm certain of that. But I aim to win half. Once that's done, I'll set my sights on three-quarters. After that, I reckon these hearings will be few and far between." Arthur released his grip. "And mark me, no matter the outcome, this day's proceedings will do nothing to improve the acceptance of my jurisdiction or the king's favor."

Donal rubbed his hand. "I'd rather be a soldier. I'm nay gifted with political maneuvering."

In truth, Arthur wouldn't mind being in his lieutenant's shoes at the moment. Even though he was the son of the Lord of Garmoran and had been raised to be a leader and trained by the Knights Hospitaller in St. Andrews, this business was unpalatable. Did anyone ever grow accustomed to sentencing men to their deaths?

At the far end of the hall, the guards led the prisoners forward. A brick of a man, Auley was unmistakable as their leader, flanked by what appeared to be his two eldest sons. The swine farmer from Dunbeg was broad-shouldered like a smith, with greasy black hair hanging in unkempt waves. Regardless of where his loyalties lay, Arthur had seen Auley's type many times— tough as iron nails, set in his ways, and determined to be right.

As the men moved forward, he motioned to a servant. "I'm parched."

"Mead, sir?"

"Please."

No sooner had Arthur taken his seat at the high table when Rhona appeared on the gallery with Bram beside her. Damn, if only she were a soldier, she would have obeyed his order to remain at home. His duty would be far easier to perform without being under *her* watchful eye.

The procession stopped in front of the dais and the prisoners were instructed to queue across the front of the platform as a goblet was placed in front of Arthur. He sipped while he examined the faces of those who tried not only to murder him, but who attempted to kill the men in his retinue. To incite anarchy. To defy the rightful king of Scotland.

As Arthur looked each man in the eye, he tried to see past their rough-hewn and ragged clothing, their filth, the cuts and bruises on their hands and faces that he suspected had been incurred after their capture.

Arthur set his goblet down and looked to Donal. "Lieutenant, are these the men who set an ambush on the road to Connel and fired an arrow into my chest with intent to fell me like a stag?"

"Aye, sir."

"And what proof have ye of their guilt?"

Donal's black eyebrows shot up as if he did not expect to be questioned. "As soon as I determined they were firing from the ridge, we made chase."

"Did they fire upon ye at that time?"

"We took a circuitous route, though I fail to see what that has to do with their guilt, sir."

Arthur glanced up to Rhona, who was leaning out over the rail and wringing her hands. "I am merely gathering the facts so that I may make a sound judgment. Please answer my question, lieutenant. Did these men fire at you whilst ye were pursuing them?"

"By the time we reached the bastards, they were fleeing with their backs to us."

"Were they on horseback?"

"On foot, sir."

Arthur sipped his mead, buying some time to gather his thoughts. "I was hit in the chest with a bolt from a crossbow. Were these men in possession of such weapons?"

"Aye, sir."

"All of them were equipped with crossbows?"

"We removed crossbows from those two." Donal pointed to the shortest—a lad whose beard had not yet come in, and another who looked to be on the precipice of manhood. "The others carried longbows. All had knives of varying size. The leader carried a sword—rusted, mind ye."

"And where are these weapons?"

"Under lock and key in the guardhouse."

Arthur glanced up to Rhona. Aye, she was leaning out over the rail, hanging on his every word. "When ye came upon these men, did they try to fight?"

"No' exactly. They fled. We were forced to chase them down."

"Whilst ye were on horseback?"

"Ye ken we were on horseback, sir."

"I'm just trying to gather the facts. Was there a struggle?"

Donal pointed to the pig farmer. "Auley drew his sword. The others wielded knives and dirks."

Thank God there was some attempt to fight. "Was anyone injured?"

"Nay, aside from a few cuts and bruises."

"Very well." Arthur reverted his attention to the prisoners while the walls around him seemed to spin. He again sipped the mead, forcing himself not to let his eyes shift to Rhona again. On one side, he had Donal and the men who had loyally marched and bled on Scotland's battlefields for the king. On the other, the only woman he had ever loved. This very day he might ruin any chance, no matter how remote, of winning her favor. "Auley of Dunbeg, I remember ye from the Highland games in the foreground of this very fortress, in the spring of the year of our Lord thirteen hundred and one. Ye won the stone put that year. Do ye recall?"

The man snorted. "Aye, and ye're the wet-eared younger son of Garmoran, though I do no' remember ye winning any purse of note."

"I wcn the footrace, truth be told; however, I would not expect ye to remember so long ago." That summer also happened to be before Arthur grew into a man. Before he was sent away to study to become a knight.

Moreover, Auley was a good ten to fifteen years his senior.

The pig farmer had a touch of grey in his beard and a disrespectful glint in his eye as he tipped up his chin. "Ye always were a slippery whelp."

Arthur slammed his fist on the table, making a boom resound throughout the hall. "Mind ye, I hold your life in my hands and I'll nay stand for a modicum of disrespect."

"Aye, and why this sham?" Auley threw his thumb over his shoulder in the direction of the courtyard. "Ye ken ye will send the lot of us to the gallows."

"I'm the one asking the questions, and you will hold your tongue unless ye'd like Lieutenant Ramsey to sever it from your gob." Arthur rose and started to pace, but when his head swam, he decided standing in place was wiser. "Tell me, why were you lying in wait? It was as if ye kent we were coming."

"We had no idea—just we knew ye'd come sooner or later." The man ran his hand over his unkempt beard. "The Lord of Lorn ordered us to hold the ridge ages ago—said if we saw anyone wearing the royal coat of arms on his surcoat, we were to open fire. I tell ye true, no one came to relieve us. His Lordship sent not a soul to tell us to stand down."

"I knew it," said Rhona up on the gallery.

Arthur gave her a scowl before he continued. "Tell me, which one of you fired the bolt that hit me in the chest?"

"I did," said Auley without hesitation, while all five of his sons looked his way, every one of them tight-lipped.

"But ye were not found with one of the crossbows."

"That is because I gave the weapon to young Ricky to carry. Back home I fell off a ladder and injured my back. He was helping to lighten my load."

"Yet ye carried a sword? And though you were injured, ye led your brood of sons up to the ridge where ye lay in wait—far longer than any *reasonable* man would have done. Then you held the ridge until my retinue rounded the bend like easy marks."

Arthur stood while his vision blurred and his head throbbed. He paused a moment and blinked to gain his focus, and then he moved across from Ricky and looked down. From atop the dais' platform, the lad appeared even younger than Arthur had first thought. "Did ye fire the crossbow, son?"

Ricky squared his shoulders, his jaw taking on the hard line of defiance. "I'm nay your son."

"Answer the question," Arthur demanded, his tone hard. He'd faced many an obstinate soldier over the years, and this whelp gave him no pause.

The boy shook his head, though by the red flush of his complexion, Arthur suspected he had fired the bolt. "I'll wager ye are a fine marksman," he pressed, appealing to Ricky's pride.

The lad said nothing.

"I'll wager ye can fell a deer at a hundred paces."

"Farther." Taking the bait, Ricky thumped his chest. "I have the keenest eyesight in all of Argyll."

"Wheesht, lad," barked Auley.

Arthur had his proof, but regardless of the hammering in his head, he continued to draw out the interrogation, systematically questioning each of Auley's sons. Not a one was willing to talk at first, but as he found points of pride and convictions of politics, he was able to gather the facts. In the end, Auley was bellowing about his loyalty to the Lord of Lorn, who had not been particularly kind, but who had allowed him to eke by after a particularly bad winter when all but one of their sows had succumbed to a swine blight that had affected many pig breeders four years past. All of them had also obeyed John of Lorn's order to hold the ridge and to give their lives to defend Clan MacDougall's honor. Every last one of them had fired arrows from their lookout on the road to Connel. By the grace of God, the only projectile hitting its mark had been the bolt lodged in Arthur's chest.

Which had been fired by the boy.

By rights, Donal was correct. They lot of them should face the gallows.

About to pronounce the sentence, Arthur made the mistake of looking to the gallery. During the drawn-out duration of the trial, he'd sensed Rhona's presence. Her veil had fallen back, exposing her halo of white hair, making her appear as righteous as the archangel Zadkiel, God's messenger of freedom, benevolence, mercy, and forgiveness.

His jaw twitched. *They're all guilty.*

Rhona pressed her palms together and raised praying fingers to her lips. Hell, she might as well sprout a pair of wings.

With the kingdom at war, there's nowhere I can send the youth to pay his penance.

Arthur also could not allow these men to walk free. A year or two in the pit would either kill them or turn them into raving lunatics. Moreover, someone must pay in blood, else no one in all of Scotland would respect Arthur's authority.

A beam of sunlight from a window across the hall settled on Rhona, turning her into a heavenly vision. Hell, the wings would have been enough.

Before he did something completely daft like dropping to his knees and pleading to her for forgiveness, Arthur tore his gaze away. Every prisoner down below stood with his head bent, remorse written on their brows, except for that of Auley.

The father scowled, his eyes narrowed, his stance bold and assured, as if he were waiting for a chance to dirk Arthur in the back and finish what they'd started.

Arthur didn't flinch. "Do ye confess to firing the bolt with intent to send me to my grave?"

Auley crossed his arms. "Afore ye began this sham, I did and I do so now. Me sons are innocent."

"Hogwash," grumbled Donal.

"Very well." Arthur ignored his lieutenant and motioned to the cleric who had been recording the proceedings. After the man's quill stilled, Arthur continued, "Auley of Dunbeg, at dawn on the morrow, ye will be taken to the gallows and hung by the neck until ye are dead."

Above, Rhona gasped. The light had moved on, thank God.

"As for the rest of you," Arthur continued. "Ye shall be guests of Dunstaffnage's gaol and subject to daily torture until ye repent, accepting Robert the Bruce as your king, accepting his scepter as the law of Scotland." He looked to Donal and gestured toward the door. "Remove this rabble from my sight."

The lieutenant opened his mouth, but before the man said a word, Arthur eyed him. "And keep your opinions to yourself." He raised his voice and panned his gaze across the faces of the guards. "That goes for all of ye. As long as I am constable of Dunstaffnage, my word is final."

While the now silent crowd filed out of the great hall, Arthur allowed himself to breathe—and again glance up to the gallery. Rhona was gone, a fact that made his head throb more and the ache in his chest stretch. No matter how he'd handled the situation, she wouldn't approve, for certain. In fact, he should have insisted Bram escort her home rather than allow her to attend. But at least she had not attempted to intervene.

At least that's what Arthur thought until she met him in the passageway between the great hall and the donjon where he had taken over the lord's chambers. The lass blocked his path with her arms crossed—as if she thought herself able to stop him. He frowned and planted his fists on his hips, affecting a stance of a man who would accept no argument.

"Ye are weaving on your feet," she snapped in an accusing tone.

"I am fine."

"Ha! How quickly you forget it was I who sat up with ye all night whilst ye lay unconscious."

"I have not forgotten." Dropping his fists, Arthur took a step farther along the passageway, though the lass refused to move aside. "If it pleases ye, mistress, I plan to rest anon."

"It does not please me. Nothing ye do pleases me." With her scowl, Rhona's white eyebrows pinched together. "Why did ye sentence Auley to hang and not the others? I saw it in your eyes. Ye ken Ricky's the one who fired the bolt that struck ye. Why did ye not send the lad to the gallows?"

Arthur gaped down at her face—flushed with anger, her eyes filled with disapproval. Wasn't having the youngest spared what she wanted? Most likely, she would have preferred him to kiss Auley's arse whilst the braggart marched out the door. "Auley is their father, the leader, the man who gave the order to attack. It was my impression that Ricky would not have pulled the crossbow's trigger had he not been coerced into doing so by his da."

"But ye sentenced the lads to daily torture until they repent."

"Aye, and they will be more than able to repent on the morrow."

"Ye ken they will not. They'll hang on until they're on death's door, and then it will be too late. Your sentence was worse than hanging. 'Tis a *prolonged* death." Rhona jabbed her finger into the wound on Arthur's chest, making him suck in a gasp. "Mark me, *constable*, not a one of those lads will be alive in six months' time."

He shifted his eyes to the archway above. Was there no pleasing this woman? "So ye would have preferred it if I had sent the lot of them to the gallows?"

"Nay!"

"God on the cross, ye are a confounding female." Arthur pounded his fist against the wall. "What then? What in the name of all that is holy would ye have had me do?"

Rhona gave his shoulder a shove as she stepped aside. "Ye're not well enough to think clearly. Go on with ye and ignore my warning, but do not expect me to sit by your sickbed ever again."

Good God, she was as adept at avoiding his questions as any woman he had ever met. Worse, in her eyes he was a fool and there wasn't a damned thing he could do about it.

❧ 9 ❧

Behind the bathhouse, Rhona carefully peered around the corner before she stepped out and started for the gate.

"Mistress!" Bram called, moving toward her from across the courtyard. "I'm surprised to see ye are still here."

Rhona glanced over her shoulder to the bathhouse. Had he seen her? She'd been ever so careful. "I remained for a time to have a word with the constable after the hearing," she replied, affecting the dutiful air of a healer who would never dream of closing a damper. "Tell me, how do ye feel about the sentence?"

"It could have been a great deal worse."

"How so? Rarely has a man survived day upon day of torture."

Bram gave a grim nod. "Perhaps if they repent and accept Robert the Bruce's reign, they will be spared undue misery."

"That's exactly what Sir Arthur said." Stopping, Rhona leaned into the old sergeant-at-arms. "Those lads stood up for the Lord of Lorn at a time when His Lordship is too weak and frail to fight. I cannot believe ye have so easily forgotten he was your lord and master not so long ago."

88

Bram's gaze shifted from side to side before he moved his lips nearer her ear and lowered his voice. "I will never forget my service to Lorn. But, mind ye, mistress, he surrendered this keep and the lot of us with it. Robert the Bruce is gaining favor throughout the kingdom and, I for one would like to keep my head attached to my neck. Furthermore, the Bruce may have slain Lorn's cousin John Comyn in Greyfriars Kirk, but only after the earl betrayed his trust. Ye ken the truth of the matter. The two men had entered into an agreement and though Comyn did not physically stab Bruce in the back, he did so by betraying the king's trust. Did ye ken Longshanks arrested him in London and if it weren't for the Earl of Gloucester's help, Robert would have faced the same fate as William Wallace?"

In truth, aside from the king's claims in the great hall, Rhona had only heard her granduncle's point of view, accusing the Bruce of being a cold-blooded murderer. "Who told ye this? Sir Arthur?"

"Nay, nor have any of his men. After the incident at Greyfriars Kirk, Lorn sent me with a missive for the Earl of Lennox, to solicit his support."

Rhona drummed her fingers on her chin. "And Lennox did not give it?"

"He did not, though he went to great lengths to explain why."

"I see. Did ye take his side?"

"Och, lassie, I am but a poor soldier. I must take the side of the man who employs me."

"If ye had a choice? On which side would ye stand?"

Bram released a long breath. "Though it may no' please ye to hear it, on account of loyalty to your kin, I must admit, I am weary of war. I thought it was an abomination when Edward the Longshanks made a puppet of King John Balliol and laid the borders of Scotland to fire and sword. I fear now that King Edward is dead, his son will be as tyrannical, if no' more so." Bram brushed a rough knuckle across Rhona's cheek. "Scotland is a sovereign nation. Her sons and daughters deserve to be free from tyranny."

Rhona took a step away. "I don't disagree with ye there, but as ye said, it is not easy for me to set aside my convictions. And at the moment, there are five men in the pit who were fighting for my granduncle's honor for naught."

With her head reeling with all that Bram had confessed, she gave a brusque curtsey and hastened out the gate. Bless it, she was confused. Never in all her days did she ever think she might doubt the guidance of her granduncle, but Bram had sounded so ridiculously reasonable, even if it seemed as if the sergeant-at-arms was able to change sides as if he were but a banner blowing in the wind.

I definitely cannot.

Even though Arthur, who was clearly unwell and who had snubbed her directive to rest, had presided over the trial for Auley and his sons with efficiency and judicial fairness, giving the accused a chance to talk, she was furious with him. Though she couldn't allay the fact that the man had carried out his duties with magnificence. Sir Arthur had been completely in control, leaving no stone unturned. Blast her traitorous heart, she'd found him impressive and imposing. However, his solution was no solution at all.

Rhona had no illusions either. The entire time she'd stood upon the gallery, she had been unable to think of an outcome that would save the lads from Dunbeg as well as avoid making Sir Arthur the laughingstock of the shire of Argyll. Of course, if it were up to her, she would prefer the latter. She'd prefer for Robert the Bruce to ride to Dunstaffnage and send Sir Arthur as far away as possible—on crusade to the Holy Land, perchance, so she would never again gaze upon such masculine magnificence.

Sir Arthur could be as braw and commanding as he wanted to be in the Holy Land. If he went on crusade, Rhona could forget about him—forget about the way his eyes shone, or the black curls of hair on his well-muscled chest, or the way he looked at her—the same way he did all those years ago. Moreover, she could deny herself and the traitorous way her knees grew unsteady and her breath caught when those black eyes gazed upon her with longing. Rhona wanted none of it. Not a lick. Not one single heart palpitation.

Having completely worked herself into a lather, she marched into the cottage. "Gran, that miserable, godless man not only convicted Auley to hang at dawn, he's sentenced those poor lads to daily torture until they repent and accept Robert the Bruce as their king."

Stooped over the hearth, the elderly woman straightened and turned with a ladle in her hand. "Lord, nay. I'd rather face the gallows than to have my life slowly snuffed by spending my days in my brother's torture chamber."

Rhona removed her cloak and hung it on the peg. "I said the same to Sir Arthur, though my words fell on deaf ears."

"I feared as much as soon as Donal came in here with the news. I cannot see what ye ever saw in that man. He's a power-hungry Campbell, exactly like his ruthless father, forever at odds with Clan MacDougall."

"If only I could do something!" Rhona stamped her foot. "Auley marched into the Pass of Brander for your brother. In good faith. Aye, he attacked Arthur, but I believe he did so because of his loyalty to Lorn, not loyalty to any king."

"The pig farmer and his sons ought to have followed Lorn to England with Lord John and the rest of the army."

"But England, Gran. Leave their homes? Whatever is there for them?"

"Their lord and master, that's what. Mark me, my brother is biding his time. Sooner or later, Robert the Bruce will either drive the English out of Scotland or Edward II will drive Robert the Bruce to his grave. Once it is settled, the Lord of Lorn will rise again."

"Do ye mean he will bow to the Bruce should he be victorious?"

"Think on it, child. My brother is a powerful man but he's not daft. He will eat crow and bow to anyone who will honor his title as well as his lands." Gran tapped her finger to her lips. "But that does not mean we twiddle our thumbs and sit idle while one of our own climbs the gallows' stairs. Ye are right that Auley was merely carrying out my brother's orders. Hmm...I wonder..."

"What?"

"When I was a wee lass, there was a hidden tunnel from the firth of the castle leading to the prison. 'Twas a dank, spider-infested passageway, but my siblings and I used it to spirit away from the keep—ye ken I've always said 'tis ever so dull to grow up under the thumb of a lord."

"Is the tunnel still there?"

"I have no idea. My father had it sealed off after my sister eloped with a minstrel."

Goodness, Gran had never told her about such a scandal. Rhona didn't even know her grandmother had a sister. Perhaps at some other time, she might question her further about it, but presently she needed to know more about this tunnel. "Tell me, exactly where along the shore might one find this *sealed* passageway?"

AFTER GRAN HAD GONE TO BED, RHONA TOOK THE leather purse of coins Sir Arthur had given her and placed it into a satchel along with a small tinderbox containing flax tow and flint. She slid her *sgian dubh* into her boot and took a lantern with a tallow candle inside, draping the handle over her elbow. She wouldn't light it yet—not until she was absolutely positive she had found the wall.

Having lived all her life in the shadows of Dunstaffnage's looming fortress, she knew every inch of the surrounding coast. She'd played on the stony beach as a young girl; she'd even engaged in a daring rendezvous with Sir Arthur there once, and spent an eve watching an astonishing sunset in his arms.

Who knew the man would turn out to be a heartless beast? And Rhona did not give a fig if Sir Arthur was bound by some sacred oath to uphold the laws of the land. Robert the Bruce had defied the laws of God Almighty when he dirked John Comyn in the nave of a church, of all places. Aye, he had been pardoned by the bishops, yet it was those very men who had insisted he hasten for Scone to be crowned king.

With all the skullduggery afoot, I believe I am within my rights to bend a few rules of my own.

After Gran had told Rhona there had once been a tunnel leading from the castle to the lake, an image from her youth flashed through her mind. She must have seen no more than five summers when she'd been playing hide-and-go-seek with some of the children from the village. An older boy who was a bit of a bully was the seeker, and Rhona most definitely did not want him to find her for fear of receiving a wallop on the head. She had wormed her way into a clump of vines overhanging the embankment and had inched inside until she came against a stone wall of sorts. At the time, she hadn't given the wall a second thought, but as soon as Gran mentioned it, Rhona knew her childhood hiding place—where the boy had *not* found her—was the sealed entrance to the pit prison. After eighteen years, the memory of it was dim at best. Except something had crumbled when she'd leaned against it.

Carrying the satchel across her shoulder, Rhona slipped out of the cottage. From the woodshed, she grabbed the old pickaxe with a blade on one side and a spike on the other, then hastened to the bay in Loch Etive where the fishing boats were moored. Sitting on the shore was a wee skiff that had been owned by one of the men who'd fallen in battle last spring. He had no kin and the boat had sat unused for months. She placed her things into the hull and shoved it into the surf. Though she tried to jump in quickly, her boots and skirts still ended up doused and she cursed her clumsiness beneath her breath.

There wasn't a soul in sight as Rhona picked up the oars and headed for the promontory that marked the transition from Loch Etive to the Firth of Lorn. To avoid being spotted by a night guardsman, she rowed the boat close to the shore where she would be concealed by the bluff. Low clouds hung above, making it difficult to see much of anything. Though, if she couldn't see but a few feet ahead, neither could the men posted atop the wall-walk.

By the time she rounded the headland and pointed the skiff into the firth, her arms burned. Rhona hadn't rowed a boat in ages and working against the slapping surf and wind made it all the more difficult. But she wasn't about to stop. Gripping the handles tighter, she bore down and dragged the oars through the water with long, strenuous strokes until the wee boat arrived at the spot from her memory.

Though she couldn't see the castle above the bluff, in her mind's eye, if she had a ladder allowing her to climb up and pop her head above the ridge, she'd be directly below the donjon, where, above stairs, Sir Arthur lived in the opulent chambers once occupied by her granduncle. Even Gran had lived in those rooms before she married her knight. Below the donjon was the pit prison where the vilest of criminals were housed along-side the torture chamber. Where Auley and his sons were imprisoned.

Rhona rowed the boat toward the shore, running it onto the sandbank. She crawled to the bow and hopped over the side, still unable to avoid dousing her boots and hem. She slipped over the seaweed-encrusted stones until she planted a very soggy foot on dry ground. Negotiating the rocky beach was nowhere near as easy at night, and Rhona was forced to slow her pace else she'd risk turning an ankle, especially the one on the shorter leg. The wooden-soled boot always slipped more on rocks and twisted awkwardly. She was far surer-footed on her right where she wore a boot with a sturdy leather sole that flexed enough to mold to the craggy stones.

Though visibility was shrouded by night, Rhona didn't want to light her lantern any sooner than neces-sary. Behind the embankment, guards patrolling the wall-walk might not be able to see her or the lamp's candle, but they might see the outline of a glow radi-ating above the bluff. When she reached the ridge, she knew she had to be close. Just as she had remembered, vines draped downward from the top of the hill, their leaves rustling with a slight breeze. But at night, they didn't look like the verdant green climbers from her childhood. Darkness made them look like gnarled black snakes, twisting toward the stones below. It seemed haunted, as if banshees, spiders, and all manner of evil lurked there, bidding her to turn back now or face her doom.

Gulping, Rhona clenched her fists. She had never been a shrinking violet and she wasn't about to start now.

I must find it.

Cringing and holding her breath, she slid her arm

inside the vines and met only with gnarled woody branches and dead leaves. The slapping surf and the mounting howl of the wind grew more acute as she stretched her fingers farther. Above, an owl hooted, making her crouch and her heart roar in her ears. An unbidden whimper slipped past her lips and she glanced over each shoulder, only to find herself alone, the sea looking like an abyss of ink.

Rhona's fingers trembled. In fact, everything trembled as she squeezed her eyes shut and forced herself to step into the creeping vines. She'd done it in daylight when she was a child. As a woman fully grown, she ought to be strong enough to summon the courage to venture inside at night. The leaves rustled and brushed her shoulders, making her skin feel as if it were crawling with spiders. Clenching her teeth, she forced herself to move deeper, until her fingers met with cool, damp earth.

"Curses!" she whispered.

When she tried to step to the side, the vines had grown so thick, they refused to let her squeeze through the foliage. She had no choice but to back out and try again.

It took two more miserably frightening attempts, but her fingers finally met with stone.

I kent it was here!

Rhona placed her satchel and lantern aside and used the blade of the axe to cut away the vines, purchasing enough room to access the wall. Only after she'd exposed a section about as wide as her shoulders, did she lower the axe to the ground, lean on it and suck in a number of reviving breaths. Goodness, she was already spent, and yet she had a stone wall to knock down.

But first she needed to see exactly what she was in for.

She placed the flax tow on a large rock and shielded the bundle from the wind with her cloak. Taking her *sgian dubh* and flint, she struck the knife several times before she got a spark. Cupping her hands around the fluff, she protected the tiny flame until it grew enough to ignite the lantern's wick.

The light transformed the vines from frightening snake-like creepers into the harmless plants she'd remembered. Farther in, the mortar was solid where she'd exposed the wall, but to the right where the earth encroached, moisture had seeped through and damaged some of the masonry. With her hands, Rhona was able to pull away one of the stones, revealing a black cavern beyond. She used the pick to hammer out four more boulders, making enough room for her to crawl inside. It was a tight squeeze and Auley wouldn't fit for certain, but he and his sons were a great deal stronger. Besides, they hadn't exhausted themselves by rowing a skiff and chopping away vines.

Holding up her lamp, she peered through the passageway, thick with spiderwebs as Gran had said.

I hate spiders!

Rhona mightn't be a shrinking violet, but chopping at snake-like vines and now traversing through a dark tunnel filled with sticky cobwebs was almost enough to shatter her resolve. Nonetheless, she'd come this far, and if she weren't successful, a MacDougall clansman would die on the morrow. Moreover, his sons would be doomed as well. And she must not allow such a thing to happen.

She summoned her courage and, with sweeping brushes of the pickaxe, she surged forward through what seemed to be an endless passage to hell.

As she rounded a bend, a faint light glowed ahead. She placed the lantern on the floor and left it where its flame wouldn't be seen. Immediately around the corner, she was met with a rusty grill barring the exit. Only a foot from the wall, it appeared to be designed to give the illusion of being completely walled off. On her toes, she sidled up to the gate, and peered out. Directly across, was the prison with faint forms of sleeping bodies on the floor. Farther up, a ring of keys hung on the wall.

Rhona dared to lean against the bars and look to the source of the light. Just as she spotted a guard sitting in a chair with his back against the wall and his feet propped atop a half-cask, the grill shifted and creaked.

The guard's head snapped up as if he'd been roused from slumber. Rhona pulled back and pressed herself against the wall where she wouldn't be seen.

"Auley? What the devil are ye up to?" the guard asked, his footfalls slapping the stone floor.

For the second time this eve, Rhona's heart thundered in her ears. Would he find her?

A loud bang came from beyond—a door. Rhona held her breath as if doing so would make her quieter.

"Is all well, soldier?" asked a man.

"Aye, these poor blighters are sound asleep." The footsteps sounded again, though this time moving away. "I'm in sore need of a visit to the privy. Ye mind spelling me for a bit?"

"Och, I've been on guard duty since the noon hour. Those bastards aren't going anywhere, and I've an appointment with me pallet."

After some shuffling and another loud boom, an eerie silence swelled through the cavern.

Unable to believe her luck, Rhona again peered out to the guard's station to verify he had truly stepped out.

Indeed, he'd left his station. Moving quickly, Rhona grasped the bars and gave the gate a good shake. Iron screeched and creaked the hinges, clearly loose. It didn't take as much effort as chipping away the stones in the wall, to use the pickaxe to unseat the grill from the wall, thanking the good Lord that salt from the sea and the damp air ate away at metal over the years.

"Who's there?" asked a spooked voice from within the cell.

"'Tis a friendly ghost," Rhona whispered, hastening to retrieve the keys and release the padlock while Auley and his sons stirred. "Come. We've little time."

"Mistress Rhona?" asked Ricky, rubbing the sleep from his eyes.

"Wheesht. I was never here, ye ken?" She pushed the pickaxe into Auley's hands and headed for the tunnel. "Haste!"

"How the blazes did ye spirit in here?" he asked.

At the bend, Rhona picked up the lantern. "It seems my grandmother kens even more about the castle than I do."

With no time to worry about the spiderwebs, she tugged the hood of her cloak low on her brow and surged forward. "There's a skiff at the end of the tunnel," she explained. "Take it and sail along the shore until ye reach Dunollie—the keep is only about three miles to the south, ye ken. Moored along the shore, you ought to find one or two of Lorn's *birlinns*." She crossed herself, praying the boats were still there where they'd always been kept at anchor. "As ye may be aware, my granduncle is hiding in England. Sail into the Firth of Solway until you reach the mouth of the River Eden and then make your way to Carlisle. The Lord Warden will help ye find His Lordship."

"I cannot believe ye are here," said Auley. "I'd already made me peace with God."

"With luck, God will grant ye many more years." When the lantern's light reflected on the hole at the end of the tunnel, she stood aside. "I cleared away enough rubble to slip in, but ye'll need to make it larger to get out."

The older man's teeth glistened with his grin, the whites of his eyes round. "I'll make quick work of it." He beckoned his sons. "Come, lads."

"Thank ye, mistress," said Ricky, grasping her hands and kissing them. "Will ye marry me?"

"I reckon ye should be helping your da find His Lordship rather than proposing to an old widow." She took the satchel from her shoulder and gave it to the boy. "Do not lose this. The contents will help on your journey."

"Ye're no' old," said one of the sons, though Rhona couldn't make out which.

It took but a few swings of the pickaxe to make a hole large enough for Auley to fit through. It was a good thing because the thunderous echo of a man's bellow boomed through the passageway as if it were Satan himself.

❧ 10 ❧

"The prisoners have escaped!"

Startled awake from a deep sleep, Arthur's eyes flashed open while Donal marched into the chamber, carrying a torch.

Throwing aside the coverlet, Arthur swung his legs over the edge of the bed, the rapid motion making his head swim. "What bloody prisoners?" he asked, as he reached for his shirt, finding it impossible to believe Auley and his sons were cunning enough to mount an escape from the confines of the prison.

"The only bastards in the pit," said the lieutenant as reality hit Arthur in the gut with the force of a fist.

"Good God, we have a traitor in our ranks for certain." He marched to the washstand and splashed his face. Damnation, if only the ache in his skull would be gone. "Tell me what happened."

"Someone from the outside broke in through an old tunnel that had been walled off."

"Did the varlets overtake the guard?" Arthur asked, wiping his face with the drying cloth.

"Nay, the miserable fiend stepped away to use the privy. He said the bastards were asleep and quiet as mice afore he stepped out. The cell was locked, the keys on the wall, far out of reach. Moreover, he swears he hadn't heard a bloody sound all night."

Arthur made quick work of donning a brechan and fastening his belt. "Your guardsman left five murderers unattended?"

"Aye. Mark me, the bastard will pay with a pound of flesh."

"I'd expect no less," Arthur said, grabbing his sword. "Have the men made pursuit? They could not have gone far."

Donal waved his torch in the direction of the firth. "All I ken is once the guard returned from the privy, he hollered for help and chased them through the tunnel. But by the time he reached the shore, Auley and his brood were nowhere to be seen. I've dispatched three sorties in pursuit. But 'tis a moonless night. A man can hardly see but a few feet ahead of his nose."

Arthur belted on his weapons, threw his cloak about his shoulders, and headed for the door. "I want to see this escape tunnel. Are any of the guards acting suspiciously? Is anyone missing, including the servants? What leads have ye as to the culprits? Where is Bram?"

"Here, sir." The old sergeant-at-arms stepped out of the stairwell. "All of the servants are accounted for."

"Aye, that would be right," groused Donal, his voice filled with distrust. "I'll wager the lot of them slipped out of their beds to lend a hand. No man alone would have been able to knock down a wall."

Though Bram shot the lieutenant a scathing glance, he said nothing.

Arthur kept mum as well. No one in his estimation had acted suspiciously of late. Bram himself had ridden along with the sortie that had been attacked by Auley. And thus far, the sergeant-at-arms had been a valuable resource, encouraging the servants to put any differences they might have felt behind them and accept the

Bruce's kingship, as well as the new constable's authority.

Mystified, he led the way down the winding steps to the pit prison.

Beyond the guard's station, Donal strode toward a rusted old grill off its hinges and waved his torch. At first it appeared there was nothing but a wall behind the gate, but further in, there appeared to be more. "This is the tunnel."

Arthur examined the wall where the gate had hung. Not only had the hinges broken away from the wall, the stone holes where they had been mounted were worn. He picked up one of the broken pieces and slid it into the hole from whence it had fallen, noticing a fair bit of give. "This gate would have posed no barrier for a child, let alone a grown man."

"Aye, but the bloody thing was walled off." Donal beckoned them into the tunnel. "There should have been no need for the gate."

"It seems ye are mistaken on that point," said Arthur as they followed the snaking cavern filled with spiderwebs and dripping water.

By the time they stepped out onto the shore of the Firth of Lorn, the sky had turned cobalt with the promise of dawn. For a brief moment, a memory sparked at the back of Arthur's mind—one of happier times and a winsome lass in his arms. Rhona had looked at him with such adoration in those sky-blue eyes. If only she would see fit to gaze upon him fondly again.

"The varlets chopped away the vines as if they kent exactly where to find the tunnel," said Donal, waving the torch and setting alight a few dead leaves, which Bram quickly snuffed with a swipe of his dirk.

Snapping back to the matter at hand, Arthur examined the debris around the entry. "Moisture had seeped through the mortar. Again, it would not have been difficult to make this hole." He straightened and turned to the sergeant-at-arms. "Who about these lands is kin with Auley? Where is his wife? Are there other children —lassies, perchance?"

"The man only had sons," Bram explained. "His wife died some years back. But near everyone in Argyll kens they could call on him for the best swine in the Highlands."

"We ought to bring everyone within five miles in for questioning. Line them up and take a horsewhip to them," said Donal. "Mayhap let the lot of the curs spend a fortnight in the prison—stretch a few on the rack."

"Oh, aye?" barked Bram, crossing his arms. "That would do a great deal to instill trust in the king, would it not? For the love of Moses, ye are an ignoramus. Most of the folk who live here cannot afford to quarrel with Sir Arthur or the Bruce. Their days are filled with the need to survive and feed their families—stay warm, pay their rents, and keep the peace. Lorn himself told us to heed the new rule."

Donal tipped up his bearded chin. "Is that so?"

"Wheesht, both of ye," said Arthur as he spotted a smooth spot on the shore, as if a small boat had rested there recently. He scrutinized the evidence. Clearly the stones around the slip had been disturbed, but there wasn't a bloody discernable footprint. "They escaped in a skiff. Call in the sentries and send out a fleet of *birlinns*. With six large men in a tiny boat, they won't travel far."

"Straightaway, sir," said Donal.

Arthur looked to Bram. "I want to find out who's closing that damned damper. I'll wager whoever the culprit is also kens something about the curs who abetted Auley in his escape. Have ye any ideas?"

"None, sir. And the last time it was closed, the lot of

us were with you. If you recall, ye had summoned us to the hall—right after ye had passed sentence on the prisoners."

"Fie," Arthur cursed while a wave of dizziness swept over him. "Go fetch Rhona and if she balks, tell her I'm in need of a healer. And if she still refuses, throw the lass over your shoulder and carry her all the way to my solar. That woman kens everyone within a ten-mile radius of the castle. If anyone has an inkling who might be our Judas, it is she."

BEFORE HE HEADED ABOVE STAIRS, ARTHUR ASKED A servant to bring up a trencher of food along with a ewer of cider. It was just on dawn. Rhona most likely would not have eaten and he wanted to do anything he could to see to her comfort. Aye, she'd been angry with him when she left yesterday, and he hadn't been able to stop thinking about it.

Why had such a divide grown between them? If he had been free to marry her all those years ago, she would have moved to Innis Chonnel Castle and stayed with his kin while Arthur studied with the Knights Hospitaller. The woman's life might have been far easier had she been wedded into his family with servants aplenty. Perhaps she'd have even been more willing to accept Robert as king.

But it was not to be. At the time, Arthur's father had chastised him for falling in love with a MacDougall. As a second son, he was expected to join the Order of St. John and become a Hospitaller knight and monk. Though he could live with the strict oaths of poverty and obedience, the notion of taking a vow of chastity had never sat well with him.

It had been a boon two years past when Bishop

Lamberton had approached Arthur with the news that Robert the Bruce was headed for Scone to be crowned king of Scots. His Grace needed loyal knights and Arthur was one of the few squires ready for the task. On the same night the crown had been placed on the Bruce's head, in his first act as king, Arthur was knighted into the Order of the Thistle with eleven others, including James Douglas and Robbie Boyd.

And now the king had placed Arthur in charge of Dunstaffnage, the most important fortress in the Highlands. Bloody oath, there was no chance Arthur was going to allow some swine farmer to subvert his authority and make him look the fool.

Not long after he set foot in his solar, the food arrived, though Rhona was yet to make an appearance. Arthur popped a grape into his mouth and slid into his seat at the head of the table. He rubbed his temples, fully aware he could have done with more sleep. The bruise from the crossbow bolt had spread, turning his chest purple, and it ached like the devil. On top of that, it still hurt to breathe, not that he'd complain about it to anyone, especially the healer.

When the door opened, he sprang to his feet all too exuberantly. After taking a moment to blink and steady the swimming of his head, he strode forward. "Mistress Rhona," he said, grasping her hand and kissing it. Holy hellfire and damnation, she smelled like a sea of wildflowers laced with honey. Her scent instantly calmed him and he lingered with his lips caressing her soft skin a bit longer than he ought. With a deep sigh, he forced himself to straighten. "Thank ye for coming. I hope I did not disturb your sleep."

"The cock had already crowed," she replied, though there was no mistaking the shadows beneath her eyes.

"Mayhap, but I ken ye did not sleep well the night before." He pulled out a chair. "Please sit. I've ordered some food if ye're hungry."

"My thanks," she said, sliding into the seat and placing her healer's basket on the table.

Arthur poured two cups of cider and set one in front of her, along with a pewter plate. "Help yourself. The grapes are delicious."

"They always have been." She took a clump and popped a piece of fruit into her mouth. "Bram told me you are unwell. I'm not surprised, mind ye."

"I'm better this morn than yesterday." He resumed his seat and helped himself to a bit of bread, slathering it with butter as Rhona did the same. "To be perfectly honest, I didn't think ye'd come if Bram told ye I wanted to ask some questions about Auley's escape."

The knife slipped from her hand and clattered to the floor. It wasn't like her to be clumsy, but what Arthur noticed most was the way her eyes flashed wide —only for a moment, but he'd caught her reaction for certain.

Did she know something? Or was she surprised at the news?

Arthur stooped to retrieve the knife, set it aside, and offered her the handle of his. "Use mine."

Rhona took it, her expression now composed and unruffled. "Bram mentioned the prisoners had broken out of the pit. What makes ye think I can help?"

"You are familiar with near every family from Connel to Dunbeg. And ye are kin to Lorn. I reckon folk are more comfortable talking to you than to the likes of me or my men, and I need to stop this meddler afore things grow worse." He leaned forward and leveled his gaze with hers. "Tell me, who is so vehemently against the king he would dare to thwart me, knowing full well I am within my rights to send him to the gallows?"

Her eyes shifted aside with her shrug. "It is not easy for the clansmen and women to change their loyalties. Not after our men have taken up arms against the

Bruce. Those who have remained in Dunstaffnage need time to grow accustomed to your ways."

"I ken, and that is one reason I was so set on holding the gathering."

"Have you decided to cancel it?"

"Not as of yet." Arthur sipped his cider. She hadn't answered his question and now they were talking about the fete, bless it. He hadn't brought her here for idle chat. "You must have your suspicions as to who's doing all this meddling."

Sitting straighter, she crossed her arms. "What, pray tell, do you mean by *all this meddling*? Has there been more skullduggery than setting Auley and his sons free?"

Arthur rubbed the back of his neck. "The worst of it was the prison break, for certain. And whoever did it kent a great deal about the castle. That passageway had been walled up for years—at least long enough for the mortar to crumble. Moreover, someone has been closing the damper to the bathhouse. And not long ago, a cask of wine and another of ale were tampered with."

"Oh, my." Rhona again looked away while a bit of color spread in her cheeks. "Tampered, aye? Did someone try to poison the men?"

"Let us just say someone tried to let us know we were not welcome."

Without meeting his gaze, she clipped a bite of bread with her teeth. "I am sorry, but I ken of no one who has boasted of putting vi...ah...*poison* in your ale, nor have I heard about the bathhouse damper. And Bram was the first to bring the news of Auley's escape. Where do ye think he went?"

"He and the lads fled in a skiff. I doubt they'll go far in a boat that small. I've sent a fleet of *birlinns* to apprehend them."

"Recently?" she asked, her tone a tad higher in pitch.

"At dawn—after I had been alerted."

Arthur sat back for a moment and watched as Rhona took a drink of cider. Aye, she may have changed a great deal since the days when he had pursued her, but she was still the MacDougall lass to whom he'd given his heart. Nonetheless, something seemed awry, even if she no longer harbored feelings for him. Her reactions were guarded as if she knew far more than she was letting on, as if she believed him to be the enemy.

"Ye ken..." he ventured. "The ale and wine was *poisoned* the same day ye visited the brewhouse with Bram."

Rhona scoffed, dropping her bread onto her plate. "Surely, you do not suspect me for all that has gone wrong? Perhaps I ought to take my leave, or are ye planning to throw me into the pit and torture *me* for the rest of my days?"

"Nay, nay, nay. Not at all. But circumstances as they are, you were the first person who came to mind as someone who might have a clue as to the identity of our culprit. Please do not misunderstand, I truly did ask ye to come here because I need your help." He slid his palm over her hand. "Rhona, do ye not remember how close we once were?"

As her lips parted, she drew in a sharp breath. "A lass never forgets her first kiss." She drew her hand away, her light blue eyes wary. "But I am not the one who ended our wee liaison. Ye vanished."

Pushing her chair away, she stood. "If ye are not in need of a healer, I'd best be on my way and tend to those who are truly ill."

"My head is swimming something awful," he admitted, rising and walking with her to the door.

"Rest and willow bark tea ought to help."

Arthur reached for the latch. "I will keep that in mind, though my position does not seem to afford much time for rest. Especially now that Auley is on the run."

He hesitated for a moment while she raised her chin and smiled—not really a smile, but more of an acknowledgement of his duties. Sadness reflected in her eyes.

He licked his lips, wanting her with every fiber of his body, yet knowing she no longer desired him. Then something in her expression changed. Softened, as if she, too, remembered the intensity of the flame they'd shared.

Unwilling to allow the moment to pass, Arthur cupped her cheek and ever so slowly dipped his chin until their lips met. On a sigh, Rhona opened for him and, in a heartbeat, he deepened the kiss while his fingers slid back and threaded into her silken hair. Their tongues entwined as if they'd never been apart. A surge of longing swelled through him akin to if a levy restraining years of emotion had burst. Pulling the woman into his arms, he savored her, not wanting this kiss to end, his heart thundering while the woman matched his fervor.

Alas, it did end and Rhona suddenly pushed away, her eyes filling with horror. "Nay." She vehemently shook her head. "I am not about to let ye break my heart once more, Arthur Campbell. Never ever try to kiss me again!"

Shouldering past him, she hastened out the door.

Dumbfounded, he stepped into the corridor and watched as she dashed for the stairs, the limp in her gait more obvious than usual. Rhona had always been very self-aware when it came to her shorter leg. It was only when she was truly upset that the hitch in her step was pronounced.

Arthur puzzled. It seemed he piqued her ire at every turn of late. But he'd be damned if he hadn't imagined the woman turning to butter in his arms. She'd kissed him back as well. She might fool herself, but Rhona MacDougall did not fool this knight.

The woman still harbored affection for him and Arthur intended to make her realize it, even if it took the better part of a bloody decade.

❧ II ❧

On her way out, Rhona definitely did not close the damper at the rear of the bathhouse. Her mind whirred with so many conflicting thoughts and not a one made sense.

He kissed me.

Worse, her knees had grown weak and her resolve had crumbled, as if seven years hadn't passed without receiving a word from the man—as if all the war and all the feuding had never happened. When Arthur had walked her to the solar door, her skin had tingled with awareness. He'd stood disconcertingly close, not that they hadn't been close before, but they were alone and, though Rhona didn't understand why, the solar was far more intimate than the cottage with Gran about, or outdoors, or in the great hall, or anywhere they had been together since his return.

Arthur's scent had ensnared her at first—raw, masculine, and feral. With a single inhalation, her pulse had quickened and her body betrayed her with a long-forgotten yearning. And now Arthur was taller, stronger, and ever so virile. When he'd first arrived, Rhona had considered herself immune to him. But now she knew differently.

And the realization terrified her.

True, she'd been caught unawares, having been rushed to the castle by Bram while believing the knight was suffering from the blow to his head—which he admittedly was. Nonetheless, Arthur Campbell had summoned her to ask if *she* knew who had aided in Auley's escape, not because he was feeling poorly. By God's grace, even if Rhona were not the cause of Arthur's consternation, she would never cross one of her own clansmen and reveal his or her identity. Just as Auley would never tell a soul who had broken into the prison and set him free.

I should be angry with the constable because he had Bram escort me to the castle under false pretenses!

It didn't matter that the Highlander's head was sore. She ought to have given him a tincture from her basket, but she was angry enough not to bother. The man could very well have a servant bring him a cup of willow bark tea from the kitchens. Though the tea was not as effective as one of her tinctures, it would still help ease the pain in his thick head.

As Rhona made her way toward the cottage, she bit down on her thumbnail. She couldn't allay the fact that it was entirely possible that Arthur had her summoned to the castle because he suspected her. The man had even mentioned that whoever broke into the tunnel had to have a good knowledge of the castle. Of course, most of the folk living around Dunstaffnage had been here all their lives, which might cast some doubt away from her and Gran. After all, he hadn't outright asked if she'd done it. And thank the stars, he had not. Rhona was a terrible liar. In fact, her cheeks had burned when he'd mentioned she had been at Dunstaffnage when the vinegar was put in the ale and whenever the bathhouse damper had been closed.

She must be more careful in the future. In retrospect, it was probably not the wisest thing she had ever done to chastise him after he'd passed judgment on those poor lads.

I am far too outspoken. I must remember to hold my tongue!

But someone needed to take matters into hand. The only reason Auley had holed up on the ridge was because he didn't know Lorn had surrendered. Aye, Auley could be a bit overbearing at times, but the man had a good heart. And there was no more loyal servant of her granduncle for certain.

Though Rhona's thoughts jumped from one mishap to the next, it seemed every time she blinked, she saw Arthur in her mind's eye. His black, unruly shoulder-length hair as wild as the Highlands. Those dark eyes gazing upon her with the intensity of an arrow darting straight to her heart. The man was rugged, yet chivalrous. As intense as a starved dog, yet as alluring as a blood rose. Bless it, time had not taken away his charm. Whether she wanted to admit it or not, Rhona was every bit as drawn to him now as she had been when she was sixteen years of age.

Being near him was perilous for her soul. How could she trust the man after he'd abandoned her? How could she trust a brute who had been knighted by Robert the Bruce?

Rhona looked to the skies. Aye, she was as loyal to Lorn as Auley, but she wasn't a fool. And times were changing faster than she cared to admit. If the Bruce were to take all of the Highlands, her granduncle would bow to the king of Scots and pledge undying fealty. That was the way of the nobility.

Am I fighting a battle I cannot win?

When she stepped into the cottage, her lips still tingled from Arthur's kiss, curse it all.

Across the chamber, Gran immediately grabbed her cane and stood, waving a missive. "I've been busy whilst ye were at the castle."

"Oh?" Without removing her cloak, Rhona strode forward and held out her hand. "Have ye written to someone? Your brother, perchance?"

Placing the folded vellum with a broken seal in her palm, Gran grinned like a wee imp who'd stolen a plum tart from His Lordship's kitchens. "Nay, I've intercepted a letter written by Robert the Bruce and addressed to the constable."

As Rhona's stomach dropped to her toes, she examined the broken seal, then turned it over. Sure enough, the letter was addressed, *"Only to be opened by Sir Arthur Campbell."*

"How did this come into your hands?" she asked, while a stone sank to the pit of her stomach. She was already under scrutiny and now this?

Gran lumbered to the table and groaned as she lowered herself onto a bench. "Do ye remember Doyle of Balliemore who I nursed back to health after he'd nearly drowned off the Isle of Kerrera?"

It took a moment, but Rhona pulled on a vague memory. "That was years ago."

"Mayhap, but all the same, he called into the cottage on his way to the castle. Said he was carrying a missive for the constable."

"And ye took it from him?"

Gran swayed in place, obviously proud of herself. "Nay, he gave it to me."

"Why would he do that?"

"Because I told him I would take it to Sir Arthur myself, for which he was grateful because he was anxious to be on his way to see his wife and kin."

Rhona turned the missive over in her hands. "And then ye broke the seal and read it?"

"Of course I did. How else am I to learn anything about what that dastard is doing with my brother's lands?"

Rhona's mouth grew dry. If Arthur ever found out

about this missive, she'd be his first suspect for certain. "What does it say?"

Gran flipped her hand through the air. "Read it, dearie."

Sighing, Rhona sat on the bench beside her grandmother and opened the letter. The king requested Arthur to have an army at the ready to sail north with Angus MacDonald and, as a contingency, if the Lord of Islay did not arrive by mid-September, they were to march to the western shore of Loch Ness. Furthermore, the letter went on to stress that Arthur's presence at Dunstaffnage was paramount to maintaining peace in the Highlands and that Arthur must remain there with a force strong enough to deter enemies from possible attack.

As Rhona looked up, Gran plucked the vellum from her fingers. "I'm going to burn it."

"What? Think of Doyle. If this missive is not delivered, will he not be punished?"

"He's an old man now and finished with fighting. He's heading for home's hearth where he aims to live out the rest of his days—far away from the wars, mind ye."

"Still, I reckon I ought to give the letter to Sir Arthur."

"But the seal is broken in half. He'll ken we meddled for certain."

With a groan, Rhona told Gran about her conversation with the constable in his solar—leaving out the last bit where she'd suffered a severe lack of judgment and kissed him. Then she thrust her finger at the missive. "If we tell Sir Arthur that Doyle left the letter with us with the seal already broken, I'll be far less likely to spend the rest of my days in Dunstaffnage's pit."

"Hogwash." Gran ambled to the hearth. "He'll never ken what happened to it. And we do *not* want the constable sending reinforcements to the north."

"But what will happen when Angus MacDonald arrives and Sir Arthur has no conscripts at the ready?"

"Pshaw!" Gran spat as she tossed the vellum onto the coals. "I may not care for the Campbells, but I *detest* the MacDonalds. Our clans have feuded over lands for centuries. If the Lord of Islay sails his *birlinns* to our shores, he will be delayed. Such is the pity."

Rhona watched as the edges of the letter began to curl and burn. She stared at the flames until the entire document was alight. Gran was right. Besides, with Scotland crawling with the Bruce's enemies, this mightn't be the only correspondence from the king to go missing. Moreover, no one would suspect her feeble, bent, old grandmother had intercepted it.

Rhona gulped against a strangling sensation. Perhaps they mightn't suspect Gran, but her neck was in a noose. *I'd best be more careful.*

A SENNIGHT HAD PASSED SINCE ARTHUR HAD SPOKEN to Rhona in his solar. He'd been busy with the details of the fete, which largely had been overseen by his cleric and the castle's steward. Nonetheless, as constable, Arthur was inundated with preparations while continuing to ride out on sorties, as well as working to locate Auley of Dunbeg's whereabouts. Though it seemed the swine farmer had vanished along with a *birlinn* that had gone missing from Dunollie, one of Lorn's lesser keeps three miles south of Dunstaffnage.

The soldiers who had been posted there had not seen a thing, awaking the next morning to find the boat missing. Arthur had brought the two remaining *birlinns* to the pier at Dunstaffnage, as well as added two more guards to Dunollie and ordered them to patrol the tower night and day. Regardless of his efforts, however, he doubted Auley was still in the Highlands. In all probability, the man and his sons most likely were no longer in Scotland.

That's why Arthur had sent Clyde to the borders. The manservant was stealthy and able to blend in with any crowd, Scottish or English. If anyone could locate Auley and his sons' whereabouts, it was he, though only God knew how long it might take or when the old man would return.

But Arthur didn't want to worry about the swine farmer at the moment. It was market day and the fete had begun at last. The canvas tents flapped in the wind while vendors displayed their wares. The air smelled of honeyed crisps, pigeon pies, and freshly shorn wool.

Arthur stopped at the smithy's tent. "Ye're not burning the furnace today, aye, Fingal?"

"I reckoned I'd have a go at selling the rings and baubles I've been making over the years," said the blacksmith as his pregnant wife stepped beneath the canvas, followed by her brood. Sara offered a friendly smile.

"Good day, mistress," Arthur said before glancing over the jewelry on display. He picked up a silver ring with a smooth pink stone in the center. The color of it reminded him of Rhona, though everything beautiful reminded him of the lass. "How much are ye asking for this wee bauble?"

"I put a mark on that one, but I'll sell it to ye for six shillings."

Arthur pulled a silver mark out of his sporran and placed it into Fingal's hand. "'Tis fine workmanship and worth the price."

The coin disappeared into Sara's hand. "Thank ye, sir."

Arthur dropped the ring into his sporran and tightened the leather drawstrings. "And how is that shoulder of yours? Are ye swinging the hammer with ease yet?" Arthur asked. Since Rhona had informed him about

Fingal's injury, he'd discovered the man had an apprentice who had been able to keep the shop running during the smithy's recovery.

Fingal rolled the appendage. "'Tis coming good. My thanks for your help, sir."

"Aye," Sara agreed. "I do no' ken what we would have done without the food ye brought us."

"No thanks are necessary. The village needs a smith who's fit and healthy, as do my soldiers. We may have fought on opposite sides in a battle, but there is no reason why we cannot stand together now."

"Sir?" asked Gregor, the eldest of the five children.

Arthur mussed the lad's hair. "Aye?"

"Would ye be needing a squire?"

"Hmm." That was about the last thing he expected Gregor to ask. "How old are ye?"

The boy puffed out his chest. "I've seen ten summers."

"My, your beard will be coming in soon." Arthur looked to the lad's father. "I reckon your da will need ye to learn his trade, will he not?"

"This lad's been chopping wood to keep the furnace burning," said Fingal. "Though a bit o' time squiring might do him some good."

"I want to be a knight and ride on sorties, just like you," said Gregor.

"I see, but are ye willing to take care of my horse, pick his hooves and brush him?"

Gregor's eyes popped wide. "Aye, sir."

"And what about my armor? It takes hours upon tedious hours to polish the links in my mail, not to mention shining my helm, my spurs, and keeping my tack in good order."

"I'd do anything ye asked of me, sir. Thanks to me da, I already ken how to sharpen blades, even swords."

"I suppose we might be able to come to an arrangement, but ye must attend your chores at home every day afore ye come to the castle. If I receive word that ye're not helping your ma and your da, I'll send ye back with my boot up your backside."

Gregor threw back his shoulders. "I'm the eldest. I always help."

Sara gave a nod. "He's a good lad."

Arthur didn't exactly need a squire, but bringing the smithy's son into the fold might do well to show the villagers his commitment to young and old. "Come to the castle after the games are over and I'll set ye to work. We'll discuss your wages as well."

"Ye mean ye'll pay me?"

"No man works for free, lad."

"Thank ye, I promise I'll be the best squire ye've ever had!"

Arthur gave Gregor's shoulder a pat, then turned to Fingal. "Are ye certain about this?"

With an incline of his head, the smith stepped around his table and together they headed into the crowd and away from the tent. "Och, ye ken ye needn't take Gregor on as a squire. I've plenty to keep him busy."

"I thought you said a bit of squiring would do the lad some good."

"I did. The lad watches ye and the soldiers ride out on sorties every day, 'tis all he talks about—how important ye look on your warhorse clad with the red-and-gold caparison."

"'Tis up to you, of course, but I'm in need of a squire," Arthur said, even though the word "need" was a stretch. "Why not let him have a go?"

"Very well. We'll see how he warms to it."

Arthur gave a cordial bow. "Gregor will be better for it and we'll talk often enough, friend. Ye'd best return to your stall. I'll wager your fine baubles will be a favorite of the folk this day."

"Och, I hope so, sir."

"Will ye be taking part in the games on the morrow?"

Fingal pointed to his shoulder. "Only the footrace. With arms like these, my specialty is the caber toss and the stone put, but Sara forbade me to take part in those —insists I'm no' fully healed as of yet."

"Then listen to her. Women ken best about these matters."

Chuckling, Arthur left the smithy and ambled through the crowd, until across the way, he spotted Rhona and her grandmother beneath a tent, their table filled with salves and tinctures, the scene reminding him of his youth when Rhona once assisted her gran at a similar fete right there in the foreground of Dunstaffnage.

"What remedies have ye this day?" he asked when he stepped up to their table.

As Rhona's gaze met his, the lass turned as red as an apple. Aye, she still had feelings for him, he sensed it clear to his bones. The problem was, she hadn't a clue what she harbored in her heart.

Lady Mary, on the other hand, gave him an eely-eyed glare. "The feverfew is in season. We've a salve for afflictions of the skin and midge bites, and a cough tincture. The soldiers ought to buy it now. We may not have any to spare when the snows bring on winter fever."

Arthur pulled out a handful of coins and dropped them into Lady Mary's palm. "Please have a dozen of each delivered to the castle at your convenience."

The woman nodded, the weathered lines etched around her lips deepening. "We mightn't have any remaining by the end of the day."

"Then I'll send a sentry to fetch them straightaway." Content that he'd assured the old woman of his earnestness, Arthur shifted his attention to Rhona—the only reason he'd stopped at this table, truth be told. "There's a band of minstrels near the bridge. I ken how much you enjoy music. Would ye walk with me?"

"Ah..." The lass looked to her grandmother with clear indecision. Rhona frowned, followed by a toothful, unconvincing grin. "I'm afraid I'm needed here."

Arthur had expected her refusal and was about to put forth an iron-clad argument when Lady Mary flicked her hand his way. "Och, why not go and enjoy the music for a time, lassie? It only takes one of us to tend the stall."

The old woman was full of surprises, which didn't bother Arthur in the slightest. He offered his elbow. "Shall we?"

Rhona placed her delicate fingers in the crux of his arm, her touch making tingles skitter all the way up his neck. "Very well. Only for a wee while, mind ye."

He could have sworn he walked taller as together they strolled through the row of tents. The sound of the music grew livelier, the banter of the people milling around them was gayer. Laughter filled the air with happiness as it did Arthur's chest. No one had coerced Rhona into coming along with him, and that fact alone was enough to set his heart to flight.

With her fingers grasping the crook of Arthur's elbow, Rhona accompanied the knight into a crowd of onlookers surrounding the musicians, composed of a troupe that included a lyre, flute, drum, and a minstrel who danced and sang. Off to one side, a group had started a reel, joining hands while the tailor held forth, bellowing the steps.

"I see Master Tailor is still calling dances," said the knight, clasping a warm palm over the top of Rhona's.

She couldn't help but compare the size of Arthur's hands to hers—his were nearly twice as large, and as rugged as the Highlands with countless white-scarred knicks. And Rhona didn't need to ask where the marks had come from. She'd seen knights before and not a one earned his spurs without being cut with a blade when learning to wield not only a sword but all manner of weapons—or when on a battlefield. "Aye, the tailor does it so his wife will not make him kick up his heels."

"He has the voice for calling dances for certain. I reckon even an old crone who is hard of hearing ought to be able to hear his every word." Arthur gestured to the dancers. "Shall we join them?"

Rhona drew her fingers away from his arm, curling

her toes inside the boot with the platform sole. "Och, nay, ye ken I do not care to dance."

"As I remember, ye are quite light on your feet."

"Then your memory is flawed. 'Tis difficult enough for me to dance in the hall on the hardwood floor. Though out here the sheep keep the grass short, the footing in this paddock is uneven; I'd end up falling on my face for certain."

Arthur said nothing for a moment, his presence beside her making it seem as if she were floating, which was both a delightful change as well as confounding because she most definitely should not be delighted. "I'm surprised not to see the Lord of Garmoran here. Did ye not invite him?"

"Hold a *ceilidh* and Highland games at Dunstaffnage and not invite my da? I'd be disowned." Arthur's chest shook with his chuckle, making the brooch clasping the plaid to his shoulder reflect the sunlight. He was dressed as a Highlander this day in brechan and doublet, looking as magnificent as a seven-point stag. "He and my brother, Niall, will be here for the games on the morrow."

Rhona shook her head in disgust. "Och, Niall."

"What has he done now?"

"Of late, I have no idea. But I recall him to be an arrogant brute who treated ye as if ye were a dog bred to be at his beck and call."

Laughing, Arthur threw his head back. Goodness, his Adam's apple was prominent, his neck unusually long and stately. He wore his black beard cropped shorter than most of the other men, and the style suited him. "'Tis true that Niall used to play the bully as is common with most elder brothers. But I'm taller than he is now. Stronger as well."

"I'll wager he doesn't care for that at all."

Arthur shrugged. "We both have our roles to play.

He's the heir and will inherit Da's lands. I'm the second son and must make my way."

Rhona looked across the grounds to the enormous stone walls of Dunstaffnage, presiding over the festivities. There had never been any question that whoever held the castle was the most powerful man in the Highlands, be it a lord or a knight. "It seems ye've done well for yourself."

He glanced at her out of the corner of his eye. "I am but a soldier, mistress."

"A soldier who has won the trust of the man who has laid claim to the Scottish throne."

His eyebrow arched. "Ye do not approve of Robert the Bruce, do ye?"

"Nay." Rhona turned her attention to the dancers for a time. This was such an unusual state of affairs, her being a MacDougall, keeping company with the king's man as if there were no divide between them. "Tell me, what is it about His Grace that has impressed ye so?"

"A great many things and not a one has anything to do with my posting at Dunstaffnage." Arthur rested his palm on the pommel of his sword. "'Tisn't easy to step forward after two decades of tyranny and backstabbing. But Robert did. He's not perfect, mind ye, but he's not afraid to make a decision and live with it. Neither is he afraid of the English army or the English king. He wants what I want for Scotland, what ye want, I'd reckon, as well."

"Hmm. What, pray tell, do ye think I want?" Rhona asked, unable to hide the sarcasm from her voice.

"Peace. Freedom from fear. Ye many not have seen it overmuch, living under Lorn's protection, but those poor crofters along the borders have been ravaged again and again. Robert will no longer stand for such barbarism. He aims to send the English back across the border once and for all."

"And ye think he'll be successful?"

"I do."

Rhona pondered the strength of Arthur's conviction. She had heard of the oppression along the borders. It even went as far north as Stirling. And though her granduncle had thrown in his lot with Edward the Longshanks and his successor, she'd heard Lorn curse the English throne as well. The knight had been right when he'd said not only she, but those who lived near Dunstaffnage, had been sheltered from the atrocities of the wars—though they'd lost plenty of men. Even Rhona's father had died at the Battle of Falkirk, fighting beside William Wallace, leaving her an orphan when she had only seen thirteen summers.

The lively music drew her from her thoughts. Dancers skipped in a circle, laughing with joined hands. It had grown so raucous, not a single woman still had her head covered. Rhona swayed to the lively tune while Arthur hummed along with the minstrel.

He had a pleasing voice—deeper now that he'd grown older.

The song ended and the crowd applauded and called for more.

Arthur leaned nearer, turning his lips to her ear. "I remember the first time I saw ye."

The sudden fluttering in Rhona's stomach made her draw in a sharp breath. "Oh?" She would never forget either, but she wasn't about to say so.

"'Twasn't far from this very spot, though it took me a time to work up the courage to talk to ye."

She eyed him. "I thought we met in the hall."

"Aye. That would have been about the hour I worked up my nerve."

At the time, Rhona had been on the receiving end of a bit of bullying herself. A few of the local girls her age had insisted she'd never find a match because she was deformed and cursed. "Given the circumstances, I was glad ye did."

"And we danced."

"On the floor in the hall," she said, making a point of not having danced on uneven ground.

"Aye. Ye were as graceful as a swan on the water."

"Mayhap a duck out of water." She chuckled. "I suppose I do waddle a bit."

"Och, nay. I reckon ye sway—and very gracefully at that."

Rhona's cheeks burned as she looked away. Arthur certainly had a way with words, and she mustn't allow him to snare her heart. She wasn't as gullible as she had been seven years past.

As the little band began to play a ballad, Arthur nudged Rhona's arm, making it tingle. "The fishermen are letting their boats for a farthing. What say you we paddle around the wee bay?"

She rubbed away the sensation, chiding herself for the silly tingling. Heaven's stars, she was a woman fully grown. She ought to be impervious to any man's touch. "I really should be heading back to the tent to give Gran a spell."

"So soon?" He tapped a stone with the toe of his boot. "Surely Lady Mary can do without ye for a bit longer."

Rhona took in a deep breath and looked toward the tents. The day was fine and her grandmother always enjoyed idling in the market where she could gossip with her friends.

"Please," he urged. "I promise I won't keep ye overlong."

She tsked her tongue. "Very well, but this does not mean in any way we are starting where we left off. I'm no longer a foolish young lass, ye ken. I'm a widow, for heaven's sakes."

Grinning, he took her hand and pulled her toward the beach where the fishermen had their boats. "Aye, but ye're the bonniest widow I've ever seen."

The ridiculous butterflies in Rhona's stomach took to flight. She was doing her best to try not to be attracted to this man, and then he had to go off and say something like that. "Ye'd best watch yourself. Ye ken the selkies will come steal ye away for telling tall tales."

He winked. "'Tis a good thing I speak the truth, then."

Arthur stopped at the first boat and dropped a farthing into the owner's palm.

"My thanks," said the man. "The boat is yours for the hour, but do not take her out of the bay."

After giving the man a nod, Arthur helped Rhona alight and settle on the bench at the bow before he pushed the skiff into the surf and hopped in, taking up the oars.

Rhona moved her hand over her heart, watching his muscles flex beneath his doublet as he rowed. He planted his feet wide, his plaid hiked up to his knees. As her heart beat out of rhythm, she couldn't help but admire the way he embodied the likeness of a Highland warrior—strong, virile, dangerous. Why was it when they were together, it always seemed as if they'd never been apart? Must she continually remind herself she had been married and widowed and had become the village's healer? They could not pick up where they left off, especially when Arthur had vanished with no explanation whatsoever.

But she was ever so comfortable with this man, even more than she'd ever been with Ivor.

"What are ye thinking?" he asked as if he truly cared as to the contents of the myriad of thoughts ever-swirling in her head.

"Ye were not wrong when ye said ye've grown stronger."

He grinned at that, a devilish grin making renewed awareness flood through her body, even down low in her belly where it had no business flooding. "It has been a long time since I rowed a skiff."

Rhona gulped. The last time she had rowed a skiff, hadn't been all that long ago. In fact, the ache in her arms had only eased a day or two ago. Good Lord, what would Arthur do if he ever discovered she'd been the one behind Auley and his sons' escape?

He must never know.

As the little boat rounded the headland and continued east further into Loch Etive, Rhona grasped the sides of the hull. "The fisherman said we're not supposed to leave the bay."

"We'll only be a moment," he said, running aground on the sandbank of a wee cove. "I've something to show ye."

Arthur pulled the skiff onto dry ground, then offered his hand. "Madam."

Despite herself, Rhona batted her eyelashes. "Ought I trust ye?"

"Need ye ask? I am a knight, ascribed to the orders of chivalry above all else."

She took his hand and let him help her step onto the shore. "What is it you have to show me? Ye'd best make it quick."

He gave her a sidewise glance as he tugged her to a grove where he stopped and gestured to a clump of small, dark rose-colored flowers.

"Water avens!" she said, dropping to her knees and examining the plants for the robustness of their roots.

Arthur kneeled beside her. "I remember ye once told me avens is the most blessed of all the herbs."

"It is, and not as common around these parts as it is to the south. I must harvest these at once, though the roots are better dug up in spring, I do not think it is too late. I'll have ye know, there's no better solution for preventing a wound from going putrid than the oil of avens."

Arthur removed a crisp linen kerchief from his sporran and spread it on the ground. "Then ye're not too angry with me for rowing the boat beyond the bay?"

"I suppose I'll allow such mischief to pass this once." She opened her palm. "May I have the use of your dirk?"

"To dig in the dirt?" He pulled the weapon from its scabbard and offered her the hilt. "Ye'll dull the blade."

"I'll sharpen it for ye."

"No need, I suppose. I've a new squire starting after the fete."

"Oh?" she asked, carefully running the knife around the plants, doing her best not to damage the roots. "And who might that be?"

"Fingal's son Gregor reckons he wants to be a soldier."

With flicks of her wrist, Rhona loosened the dirt. "But he's only ten years of age."

"Och, it will teach him a wee bit of responsibility if nothing else. I reckon he'll be like any lad his age. The excitement will soon wear off, and he'll be back in his da's shop, carrying wood for the fire."

"'Tis nice of ye to give him a go." She carefully lifted the clump of avens and placed it on the kerchief. "I won't harvest all of these in hopes they'll come back stronger in spring."

Arthur tied the ends of the kerchief, making a pouch. After he set it aside, she returned his dirk. He grasped the hilt and slowly slid the knife into the scabbard while he stared into her eyes. "Thank ye for coming with me."

"Thank ye for showing me the avens." All too self-aware, Rhona dropped her gaze and started to rise, but he caught her hand.

"Ye ken we've been in this very spot before."

She nodded. Rhona remembered every meeting they'd had. For years, she dreamed of him. Even after she realized he wasn't coming back. Even after she'd married Ivor, Arthur had not been far from her thoughts, though she'd cursed herself for it. "I wish ye wouldn't remind me."

"Forgive me. Memories of our time together are ever present in my mind, especially having ye so near."

"Is that so?" she asked. "I reckon your return to Argyll is what spurred your memory, else ye would not have left so abruptly. Of course, my life went on without ye. I married, I was planning to start a family. I could not afford to have ye in my thoughts." *Even though he plagued them all the same.*

"I...ah...my father—" Arthur spread his palms as if he had much to say but either could not find the words or felt them futile.

Not wishing to probe any further, Rhona pushed to her feet and stooped to grab the kerchief of avens. "We cannot pretend the years have not whiled away, sir. Do ye think ye can return and expect me to welcome ye with open arms? Too many things have changed. And you—you took up arms with a man who is an enemy of Clan MacDougall."

Arthur stood. "I do not deny the bad blood between the Bruce and your clan, though I hope the wounds of the past will ease in time. For now, I ask ye to look at *me* as a man, and not as an enemy. I am not and never will be your adversary. I want the people of Dunstaffnage to prosper. Think on it, lass. You yourself delivered the missive from the Lord of Lorn to Robert the Bruce. Your granduncle handed over the castle and, in that act, he established a truce between king and clan. All I ask is that you see fit to grant me a truce as well."

By the rood, her heart could have melted. If only their romance actually had a chance to blossom. There he was, Arthur Campbell, standing as a gallant knight insisting they were not adversaries. If he ever discovered her ruse, as well as Gran's meddling, he'd eat his words. Rhona rubbed a hand across her mouth while too many warring thoughts tore her insides apart.

He took that very hand, bowed over it, and applied a well-practiced kiss. "What say ye to a truce, m'lady?"

It was such a simple request. He hadn't asked to court her. He hadn't tried to kiss her again. He simply wanted to cast aside any angst between them. "Very well," she said, though her voice seemed miles away. "A truce."

❧ 13 ❧

The following day, Rhona sat with Gran on a plaid and enjoyed their nooning of bannocks and cheese while the men participated in the Highland games. Thus far, the rain had remained at bay, though by the looks of the clouds coming in from the west, it wouldn't be much longer before the skies opened.

"Oh, look there," Rhona exclaimed, her voice cracking as she pointed to the starting line of a dozen or more shirtless Highlanders, their brechans belted low on their hips. "Sir Arthur has opted to participate in the footrace." Good Lord, her blood stirred. Aye, the man had been shirtless in the cottage, albeit with a hole in his chest and a bruise the size of two fists. She had admired him then, but now she could not drag her gaze away from his muscular form, far more defined and sculpted than any of the others.

Gran seemed not to be affected by the display of brawn as she gave her a dour frown. "He ought to be officiating, just as my brother did when he hosted the games."

"Do you truly believe so? This is the only event of the day he has not officiated. I think he ought to enjoy himself just like everyone else."

The stalwart old lady snorted as she clipped a bite

133

of cheese with her teeth. "Mayhap he's had a change of heart because his brother has decided to join in. As I recall, those two lads were always at odds."

As Rhona recalled, Niall did his best to intimidate his younger brother. If only the elder were the constable of Dunstaffnage, it would be a great deal easier to dislike *him*.

"But my wager is on Fingal," Gran continued.

"Fingal? He's too muscle-bound to be quick."

"And ye reckon Sir Arthur is not? If ye didn't notice when he was in the cottage, the man is honed like the hindquarter of a workhorse."

Yes, of course Rhona had noticed, though Arthur was taller and leaner than the smithy. "Well, then I hope ye are right. It would be nice if Fingal won since Auley's sons are gone—as I recall one of them won last year. There are simply no MacDougall men remaining who are fit enough to take on Sir Arthur and his soldiers."

At the starting line, Niall gave Arthur's shoulder a thwack, making the knight stumble and Rhona sit up a bit taller. Though it seemed the younger might have matured, the elder was still a brute.

She hadn't slept well last eve because he'd given her no choice but to agree to their wee truce. Honestly, Rhona was more worried about how she'd broach the subject with her grandmother, but she had definitely decided it was time to call an end to their tampering. After all, over a month had passed since the Bruce had marched in and laid claim to the castle. And by the way the king was gaining favor, it was likely the constable was there to stay. "Yesterday I made a truce with Sir Arthur."

Gran turned a tad green, her mouth pulling downward and making her look like a harridan. "What kind of truce?"

"'Tis not what ye think. He doesn't ken a thing

about the meddling I've done, or that you've done, for that matter. His request was for us to be on friendlier terms."

"Oh, aye?"

Rhona gave a nod. "I've put some thought to it and have decided 'tis time to stop interfering. Besides, if I continue to free prisoners and close the damper on the bathhouse, I'm likely to be found out sooner or later."

"Humph. I never thought my own granddaughter would tuck her tail and settle. I cannot believe ye've uttered such drivel."

"Think on it, Gran. Your brother is gone, and he's nay coming back. I'm not saying we need to do away with our convictions. I'm just saying we ought to let things settle for a time—especially while Sir Arthur is still trying to find Auley. If he ever discovered I was the one who set the pig farmer and his sons free, I'd be headed to the gallows myself."

"You may have been the one to break into the prison, but if you recall, I'm the one who told ye about the tunnel."

Rhona poured herself a cup of watered wine. "Aye, then we'll both be heading for the gallows if we're not careful."

Gran held up her tankard for Rhona to top up. "Ye ken what I think?"

"I reckon you'll tell me whether I ken or nay."

The old lady gave a knowing look as she sipped. "I think ye are smitten."

Refusing to take the bait, she forcefully shoved the cork into the bottle. "Nay, I'm sensible is all."

"Lass, ye might be able to lie to yourself, but ye cannot fool me."

"Wheesht," Rhona said, growing uncomfortable with the direction of the conversation. "The race is about to start."

The Lord of Garmoran, Arthur's father, held a flag

aloft. "Runners prepare!" He whipped the pennant through the air. "Go!"

"Run, Fingal!" Rhona shouted, even though her eyes were fixed on the man who had a late start after taking an elbow to the center of his scarred chest from his brother.

As Niall stole an early lead, Rhona clenched her fists. *Beat that miserable cur!*

There was no way she could shout for Arthur, but for some silly reason, she desperately wanted him to win. As they rounded the bend marked by red flags, the constable began to close the distance with his brother. Niall jabbed with another elbow but his strike was stopped by Arthur meeting the swing with an upward thrust of his own. The bully faltered for only a heartbeat, but the knight purchased enough time to dart into the lead.

Rhona sprang to her feet. "Faster, Arthur, faster!"

The two brothers were lengths ahead of the rest of the runners. Losing ground, Niall took a swing at Arthur's head.

"No!" Rhona shouted, but the knight leaned forward, well out of his brother's reach. "Well done!" she hollered as Arthur crossed the finish line to the cheers from the crowd. He stopped and planted his hands on his knees, only to have Niall shove him up the backside.

"Do not play into the cur's ire," she whispered behind her clasped hands. Long ago, fists would have flown for certain, with Arthur taking the brunt of it. This time, however, the constable only laughed and clapped his brother on the back.

"Ye're not smitten, aye?" Gran quipped with a snort. "If I just witnessed a reaction of indifference, then I'm nay but a cabbage."

"Och, please. I simply did not want Niall Campbell to be the victor. He's such a blackguard."

The old woman flicked Rhona's shoulder with a playful backhand. "Go on then, fool yourself."

Groaning and looking to the heavens, Rhona was about to argue, when Sir Arthur sauntered toward them, pulling his linen shirt over his head, then wiping his brow with his sleeve. "Good afternoon, ladies."

"Come by to gloat, did ye?" asked Gran.

Rhona scoffed, giving her grandmother a flabbergasted glower. Aye, Lady Mary was a woman who spoke her mind, but how could she be so rude? For the love of Moses, the constable won the race despite the odds. First, his brother had pushed him at the starting line, and then the cur had thrown a few elbows just to keep Arthur from winning. Reverting her attention to the knight, she smiled. "Well done, sir knight. Ye won despite your brother's interference."

"After five and twenty years, a man learns what to expect when competing against Niall, I suppose."

"The knights in St. Andrews must have taught ye well," said Gran without embellishing, but it went without saying that of all the contestants, Arthur stood out like a ram among wethers. He was taller, fitter and, dare Rhona think it, he attracted her eye like none other.

If only someone else attracted her eye. Or no one at all. She was happy living with Gran and tending to the infirm. The townsfolk were her clan and kin and she didn't need anyone else, especially a man.

When an awkward silence swelled through the air, Rhona offered him her cup. "Would ye care for a spot of watered wine?"

"My thanks, this is exactly what I needed," he said, drinking down the contents.

"'Tis good the day has been fine, though it feels as if it will start raining at any moment."

"That it does." Sir Arthur returned the cup and

bowed to Gran. "I would like to invite you two ladies to dine at the high table this eve."

"Your father will be in attendance, I presume?" asked Gran.

"Aye, as will my brother."

The old woman brushed her hands along her skirts. "I'm afraid there are too many stairs for these old legs to manage."

Arthur took her hand and applied a gallant kiss to the back of it. "Och, m'lady, surely we cannot allow the castle steps to pose a hindrance. I shall send a retinue of soldiers with a throne upon which ye can sit whilst they carry you."

The woman's eyes lit up but she shook her head. "They'll drop me for certain."

"I'll see to it they do not." Sir Arthur took Rhona's hand and kissed it as well. "I'm glad that's settled. I'll see ye both in the great hall after the bell has sounded."

"I RECEIVED A MISSIVE FROM THE KING ASKING FOR more men in the north," said Arthur's father, John Campbell, Lord of Garmoran as he stood in the center of the dais awaiting the steward to announce the evening meal.

Though Arthur was keeping an eye on the door of the great hall in anticipation of Mistress Rhona's arrival, hearing of the king's request caught his attention. "Interesting that he didn't send word to Dunstaffnage asking the same."

"I reckon ye have your hands full, son, what with quelling rebellions and preventing scoundrels from escaping your prison."

Arthur took a long drink of ale. Aye, his posting at Dunstaffnage came with its share of problems, but it wasn't anything he couldn't control. Moreover, when the king had departed for the northern Highlands, he'd said he'd be sending for more men. "Perhaps he's allowing me a bit of time. I've written him about the ambush."

"And the prisoners' escape?"

In truth, Arthur was in hopes that the culprits would have been apprehended by now. "I suppose I'll have to add that to my next report."

Da clapped him on the back. "Ye cannot rush these things, son. I say, 'tis good to see Dunstaffnage with a Campbell at the helm."

Arthur raised his tankard. "It is an honor."

Niall sauntered beside them, using a flask to splash a bit of whisky into his ale. "As I recall, there was a Mac-Dougall lass who once captured your heart."

"Mistress Rhona. She'll be dining with us."

"She's married, then?" asked Da.

"Widowed."

"Such a shame." Niall shoved the cork back into his flask and slipped it into his sporran. "I cannot for the life of me remember what I did with the missive ye wrote to her afore ye left for St. Andrews."

Arthur looked between the two men. At the time, his father wasn't supposed to know about the bloody missive. "Exactly what do ye mean?"

"Och, lad." Da clapped him on the shoulder. "Ye cannot think I would allow Niall to deliver a love letter to Lorn's grandniece."

Arthur's knuckles tightened around his tankard's handle. "And why was that? She's a fine woman—would have made a fine wife."

Da tipped up his chin with an aristocratic, priggish purse of his lips. "Mayhap, but she's a MacDougall. I wanted better for ye."

"Better for Niall mayhap. But I'm a second son. Why should it matter whom I married?"

"Why should it matter now?" Da shrugged. "'Tis all

in the past. Ye were destined to become a knight and ye ken as well as I they never would have accepted ye as a squire had ye been wed."

Though his father spoke true, Arthur still burned to discover Rhona had never received his letter. Hell, in her eyes, he well and truly disappeared without a word. No wonder she acted bitterly toward him. He pulled Niall aside and away from the others. "I thought I told ye Rhona would be waiting for me behind the chapel. Ye promised to give her my missive—to explain on my behalf."

"I did not promise anything. I may have said I'd do it to get ye to shut your gob, but I never had any intention of riding all that way."

Arthur balled his fist and raised it. "I ought to thrash ye here and now."

Niall smirked. "Why do ye not? Ye still carry a torch for the wench, I'll wager. Inviting her to the high table, ye cad."

Lowering his fist, Arthur glanced over his shoulder. He was hosting this *ceilidh*. The hall was filled with merrymakers and he had no intention of commencing the evening like a drunken rogue.

"I'm not going to start a row because I'm no longer a wet-eared lad," he replied, splaying his fingers. "Ye are my guest, and I aim to see we both enjoy the evening." He turned away, heading for his father, but Niall grabbed Arthur's arm and yanked him around.

From the corner of his eye, he caught a glimpse his brother's right hook, heading straight for his jaw. Jolting into fighting mode, he ducked, the fist skimming his hair.

Countering with a jab, Arthur slammed an uppercut into his brother's nose. Niall's head snapped back, his knees buckled, and the lout sank to the floorboards.

Before Arthur had a chance to tell his men to stand down, Donal and the king's guard surrounded Niall, their weapons drawn. With blood streaming from his nostrils, Niall batted at them. "Leave me be, ye mongrels."

Arthur inclined his head toward his lieutenant. "'Tis good to see you are on your guard. But this was just a brotherly scrap. It is over now." Arthur pulled a kerchief from inside his leather doublet and handed it to Niall. "Ye shouldn't have tried to take a swing."

The angry oaf snatched the cloth from his fingers and dabbed his nose. "Shut it."

"Ye lads will never change," said Da as if he'd been expecting fists to fly. "Always fighting like a pair of cocks in a henhouse."

Arthur straightened and leveled his gaze with his father's. There were so many words on the tip of his tongue—about Niall's tyranny and mistreatment—about all the times his father turned his back or favored the eldest because he was the heir. But pointing the finger would only make him look like a coward. "'Tis difficult to ignore Niall's right hook."

Da replied, but Arthur didn't hear a word. The doors of the hall opened and four guards entered, carrying Lady Mary on the castle's wooden throne. She looked like a queen sitting tall, but it wasn't Lorn's sister that arrested Arthur's heart. When Rhona stepped out from behind the entourage, even a resounding boom from a slamming portcullis wouldn't have drawn his attention.

No wonder she had been cool toward him. Not only had he led the march into Dunstaffnage to take the castle from her granduncle, but she undoubtedly thought he'd jilted her without a word. It was a wonder the woman had been so kind as to tend his wounds after the ambush. Since his return, Arthur had sensed that Rhona barely tolerated him. Now he knew why.

Arthur gulped as the crowd made way. The beauty wore her striking white tresses plaited and twisted around her ears with a circlet holding them in place. By the gods, it was nice to see her without a veil for a change. She wore a red kirtle, which complemented her complexion like strawberries and cream. The cut was simple as was the fashion, though the scooped neckline was trimmed with gold, adding a wee bit of embellishment. Had she looked forward to coming? Had she thought of him when she'd dressed for dinner?

"Who is that?" mumbled Niall with far too much curiosity and masculine appreciation.

"Not your wife," Arthur grumbled. Niall's wife was expecting their second child and had remained at Innis Chonnel Castle along with his mother. "She's Rhona MacDougall, mind ye."

"Your Rhona?" Niall asked, wiping a stream of blood from his nose.

Arthur wished she were his. "Aye," he hedged. Even though his brother was married, it was best if Niall believed the lass had been spoken for.

Remembering his manners, Arthur padded down the steps of the dais and gave a polite bow. "Welcome, esteemed guests. I have reserved a place beside me at the high table."

His remark earned a fair number of mumbles from the crowd.

"As long as I do not have to sit beside the Lord of Garmoran," said Lady Mary loud enough to be heard up to the gallery.

Arthur didn't bother glancing at his father because the man would be delighted to avoid sitting beside Lorn's sister. "Ye and Mistress Rhona will be on my right and my father and brother on my left."

Lady Mary flicked her hand toward the dais. "Then carry on. I'm famished."

It was a good thing the steward made an appearance and rang the bell, announcing the meal was served and directing everyone to their seats. Arthur had already managed to hit his brother. Lord only knew what other rows might erupt with a hall full of people drinking ale with empty bellies.

As the guards took Lady Mary to the place at the table without a chair, Arthur offered his elbow to Rhona and inclined his lips toward her ear. "Ye are the bonniest woman in the hall this eve."

With the candles flickering in the enormous blackened-iron chandeliers overhead, Rhona's blush seemed to dance upon her cheeks. "And ye are still gifted with a silver tongue."

"I hope ye will not hold it against me." He held the chair for her while the minstrels started into a tune on the gallery—in the same spot where the lass had watched him hear Auley's trial. "I'm ever so glad ye and your grandmother came."

"I suppose we could not have ignored an invitation from our new constable. After all, what would your da think if there were two empty places at the high table?"

Arthur would have quickly filled them with his highest-ranking soldiers, but he need not tell her he'd had a contingency at the ready. He took his seat as the doors from the kitchens opened, filling the hall with the mouthwatering scent of roasted meat and freshly baked bread.

"Mm, it smells delicious," said Rhona, removing her eating knife from her sleeve. "What is the fare?"

"Spit roasted pork, applesauce, partridge pie, and boiled cabbage for certain, though Cook refused to tell me what he planned for the final course."

"Well, 'tis no secret to me. He'll serve us some sort of tart, I'd reckon," said Lady Mary, craning her neck and talking around her granddaughter. "Cook is known throughout the Highlands for his sweet meat and berry tarts."

Arthur sat back to allow a servant to fill his wine

goblet. "Then I will look forward to it with great anticipation."

The food arrived on enormous trenchers with everyone reaching for whatever was nearest and helping themselves. Arthur leaned into Rhona. His knee skimmed her skirts with a welcome soft brush that made fire surge through his blood. "Niall and I came to blows earlier."

"Why am I not surprised?" She covered her chuckle with her palm. "I wondered why his nose was swollen and red. I'll wager it served him right."

Arthur reached for his goblet. "I did not want to hit him, but I—"

"Och, have a look at that!" Da bellowed, jabbing Arthur in the arm, making the ale slosh onto his pewter plate. "I did not ken ye brought in players."

Arthur didn't either, but as sure as he was sitting there, two jugglers skipped through the aisle toward the dais. Doubtless his cleric had made the arrangements. Rhona clapped with the others, her eyes alight. "They're quite good."

"Indeed, they are," he replied while the hall erupted with raucous hoots and hollers. Perhaps now was not the time to apologize.

As the sweets were served, the jugglers performed all manner of acrobatics, climbing atop tables, tossing their balls in the air, leaping high and flipping, and somehow managing to catch their balls as they landed.

"I've never seen such talented jesters," Rhona said as she laughed and gasped. It warmed him to see her happy. She'd been so serious and so guarded ever since he'd been at Dunstaffnage. Mayhap the fete was a good idea, even if just to see her happy.

Arthur didn't bother to watch the players; he couldn't draw his gaze away from the woman beside him. If only she would smile at him that way—just as she once had.

After eating the most delicious plum tart he'd ever tasted, the musicians moved to the far end of the gallery and the tables were pushed aside to make room for dancing. Beside him, Rhona's fingers tapped along with the beat of the drum. Mesmerized, Arthur linked his little finger with hers before he was able to stop himself.

She let out a wee gasp, her eyes round while she held very still.

"May I have the first dance, mistress?" he asked.

The lass slowly drew her hand away. "I'm not fond of dancing."

"But the floor is level."

"Go on and dance with the constable," said Lady Mary. "Och, I cannot remember the last time I saw ye kick up your heels, lass."

"Will ye? Please?" he asked, barely able to take a breath as he waited for her answer.

One look into Arthur's dark and soulful eyes rendered Rhona incapable of saying no. He offered his elbow like a chivalrous knight and she didn't think twice about taking it and, as he escorted her to the dance floor, all heads turned their way.

As she did when she was but sixteen summers, Rhona felt unbearably self-aware, though this time not because she was lame and walked with a limp. Everyone for miles about knew she was a cripple, yet she had her place in the clan and they respected her for it. But her mind roiled with what they might be thinking now. Aye, being Lorn's grandniece, she had dined at the high table many times, however this night she sat beside the constable and his father, who had never seen eye to eye with her granduncle. Might the clansmen and women think she had so easily forgotten that only a few months ago they'd celebrated Midsummer's Eve in this very hall with the Lord of Lorn presiding over the feast?

Or had they accepted the new state of affairs and decided to move on with their lives as Fingal and Sara had done?

Rhona glanced to the onlookers. Their expressions were happy, mayhap a tad curious. And there certainly weren't any scowls. All in all, it appeared as if everyone in attendance was in good spirits and making merry.

The dance floor was already crowded when Arthur left her in the ladies' line and joined the men across. Master Tailor took his place upon the gallery to call the dance. At least some things never changed. As the music for a reel began, the women curtsied while the men bowed. They skipped together and joined elbows, the liveliness of the music making laughter bubble up through her.

Arthur had always been a skillful dancer and he led her through the circles and corners. Rhona hardly miss-stepped and even joined in with the clapping when she wasn't grasping the knight's hands.

Master Tailor called for a tunnel and, standing in their respective lines, the men each touched the tips of their partner's fingers, making an archway while couples sashayed through.

"Are ye ready?" Arthur asked when their turn came.

"Aye," she said, holding his hands and feeling more sure-footed than ever before when dancing. His grip was firm and supportive, yet gentle, his dark eyes focused intently on her while a smile stretched across his face, his teeth shining white.

When they'd nearly made it to the end of the tunnel, Rhona's thick, wooden-soled shoe caught on her hem and sent her stumbling straight into Arthur's chest. He wrapped his arms around her and carried her the rest of the distance. "Are ye harmed?" he whispered in her ear, setting her down while the music ended.

Pain shot up her leg. "I might have twisted my ankle, my blasted lameness."

"Allow me to help ye to a seat."

Shaking her head, Rhona took a few steps. "I ought to be all right if I move around a bit."

Master Tailor had called for a country dance next. "I

don't suppose ye'd like to have another go?" asked Arthur.

"Nay." Rhona walked to the far wall where they'd be out of the way. "I fear my dancing days are over."

"I do not ken about that. Ye did quite well, though in hindsight, it was a wee bit too crowded. Anyone might have stumbled."

"Ye are kind to say so. But if ye recall, I've never been—"

"—fond of dancing," he finished her sentence as if they were kin.

"But ye ought to have fun. There are a great number of lassies here who would be elated to dance with ye." In truth, the men outnumbered the women about three-to-one, though Rhona had been right. What young maid wouldn't want to dance with the dashing constable, the most important man in all of Argyll? The mere thought made her chest burn. Perhaps it was time for her and Gran to take their leave?

She was about to excuse herself when Arthur took her hand and tugged her toward the entry to the donjon. "If ye can spare me a moment, I have something I'd like to show ye."

Rhona tugged back. "Och, I cannot go up to your chambers, sir. It would not be proper."

"Up above to the wall-walk."

"Is it not raining?"

"I ken of a spot where we'll stay dry." He changed directions and pulled her toward the big doors. "And ye're right, for appearances, I'll take you up via a different route."

"But what about Gran and your da?"

Arthur gestured to the dais. "It looks as if my father and brother are deep in conversation with Donal, and Bram is keeping your grandmother company."

"Then quickly. I do not want to be gone too long, else she'll worry," Rhona said, limping out the door.

"And ye should not be walking on a twisted ankle." Within the blink of an eye, Arthur swept her into his arms, ducked into the tower stairwell, and started upward. "Are ye comfortable?"

Comfortable wasn't exactly the first thing that had come to mind. The man smelled like spice and the sea. Her palm had inadvertently pressed against his chest, and his warmth seeped through his shirt while his heart thrummed a steady rhythm. He cradled her with all the gentleness of a lamb, but she was no tiny waif. "Ye cannot carry me all the way to the top of the stairs."

"I can and I will."

She really ought to make him put her down, but giving in to the swooning of her heart, she leaned against his powerful chest and closed her eyes but for a moment. Aye, she might allow herself a modicum of time to revel in his arms, and then she'd be on her way. If only things were different, but life had gone on and her marriage had been arranged to another. Aye, Rhona might be widowed, but she had far too many responsibilities now, especially with Gran getting on in years. Besides, she had too many secrets to harbor from Sir Arthur Campbell. She'd done things that she could not undo, even if she wanted to.

And now Gran had intercepted an important missive, which Rhona couldn't give him even if she'd wanted to since the woman had burned it. The thought made her insides twist. Moreover, a lump swelled in her throat.

This is wrong. Who am I fooling? We cannot pick up where we left off.

"Put me down," she said, pushing against his chest.

But the blasted man tightened his grip. "Nearly there."

"Nay, sir. I demand you set me down this instant. Goodness, I must have lost my senses. I should not have agreed to come up here with ye."

"If ye're worried about appearances, we shall cross to the east tower and return to the great hall through the main doors. Anyone who might notice us will think we've been in the courtyard."

"Ye sound as if ye planned this."

"I'm merely making it up as I go, m'lady." As he stepped out into the open air, he finally set her on her feet. "Here we are."

Though a light drizzle fell, this corner of the walk was a covered dome. Rhona glanced upward. "This is new."

"Aye. The guards can light a brazier in here in winter and step out of the weather for a time, but they can still see the expanse of the Firth of Lorn." Arthur pointed toward the water. "I've also had the trees cleared so there's a better view of the shore from here, though I suppose it goes without saying, there will never be another escape from Dunstaffnage's pit."

Rhona gulped as she looked down to the spot where she'd used the pickaxe to access the tunnel. "Ye can definitely see a great deal more with the trees cleared," she said, her voice sounding a wee bit shrill. "I'll wager 'tis stunning on a clear day."

He took her hand between his warm palms. "Aye."

"Is this what ye wished to show me?"

"It is, but I wanted a moment to speak with ye as well," he said, standing so near, his breath skimmed her forehead.

Rhona closed her eyes and leaned into him. "Oh?"

"Ye recall I mentioned that Niall and I came to blows?"

"Mm-hmm."

"Well, I found out that he did not give ye the letter I wrote afore my da sent me to St. Andrews."

She snapped her head up. "You wrote me a letter?"

"Aye. We were supposed to meet at the chapel, remember? But my father found out that ye had won my heart and made it eminently clear that he had gone to great lengths to secure a place for me as a squire to the Knights Hospitallers. He also insisted there was no room in my life for a woman."

"Is that what your letter said?"

"Nay. I poured out my heart and asked ye to wait for me." Arthur grasped a lock of her hair and ran it between his fingertips. "Though now I ken it was selfish of me to do so."

A cold chill spread across Rhona's skin. He'd sent word? "But why did you not write after ye joined the knights? Seven years passed. It was as if you'd vanished."

"At first I'd hoped to receive your response—to tell me ye returned my love and promised to wait. None came, and then Niall sent word that you had married. There was no use writing when I was convinced ye had forgotten me."

Good Lord, he had truly loved her. He hadn't callously left her standing in the cold outside the chapel waiting for hours. His worthless brother was supposed to give her a missive. "I never forgot ye," she whispered while tears stung her eyes. With all her heart, she wished things had been different. But now she was wrapped up in such a tangled and sticky web, from which she could see no way out. "I, too, was beholden to my duty. Lorn arranged my marriage not long after ye disappeared and I had to marry Ivor whether I wanted to or nay." Though she had not been in love with him, Ivor was a good man and a good husband.

Still holding her hand, Arthur drew her fingers to his lips, his brow furrowing as he kissed them. "Ye must know, not a day has gone by when I haven't thought of you, and now to learn that we both were deceived by my brother, burns like a raging fire in my chest."

Oh, for the love of the angels, Rhona's knees went weak. She'd harbored such animosity toward this man, yet he had done nothing to earn her ire. Aye, he supported Robert the Bruce, but the reasons he'd given for his loyalty had sounded so incredibly sensible. In fact, when he'd explained the opposing point of view, it had been very difficult not to allow herself to be swayed.

And now rumors were mulling about that the Lord of Lorn was considering changing his allegiance. Was this true? Was her fierce loyalty to clan and kin misplaced? Goodness, she hated doubting herself, doubting her values. Even if she had suffered an error of judgment, Rhona still would have freed Auley and his sons.

Arthur's gentle hand caressed her cheek. "Och, I'm so sorry, lass."

Rhona opened her mouth to speak, but the comfort of his touch, his kind smile in the dim light, the swirling of desire deep and low in her belly, rendered her speechless. As she raised her chin, his lips came nearer, parting with his sharp breath, making her body come alive with a want she had not felt in years. Ever so gently, he brushed his mouth across hers. As a sultry sigh slipped from the depths of her soul, he deepened the kiss.

Unable to think, Rhona slid her arms around his waist and held on for dear life as she closed her eyes and melted into him. His hands were on her shoulders, then moved to her back, kneading and feeling ever so heavenly. And as his tongue danced with hers, their bodies molded together as if they'd always been meant to be paired.

As her hips rocked forward, his erection pushed against her. Heaven help her, it felt so inexplicably good. Arthur trailed delightful kisses down her neck and along her bodice while Rhona clung to him. Her breasts filled with fire as he ran his lips across the exposed flesh just above her neckline. And when he took her breast into his palm, she threw back her head and moaned.

It had been so long since she she'd made love. After

Ivor, she thought she could no longer feel passion, but Arthur brought the deep yearning back and raised it to new heights with the force of a hundred horses. She could feel, she could desire, she could fall in love again.

Love?

Gasping, Rhona pushed away. "Nay, nay, nay!"

"Nay?" Arthur asked, his voice filled with disbelief.

"Too many things have changed." She had deceived this man. How could she love him now? What the devil was she thinking? "You do not want me. I tell ye true, I am ruined for ye."

"But you are here now, and in my eyes, you are sweeter and bonnier than ever before; I lo—"

"Nay!" Needing to put an end this madness, she dashed out into the rain and headed for the east tower. "I cannot fall in love with ye again!"

❧ 15 ❧

The days following the fete were busy with all the problems that came with controlling a large fortress. Arthur was determined to keep his men in fighting shape and trained with them every morning. Daily, he followed a rigorous routine of sparring, and joined Donal's sorties at least three times per week. Arthur also listened to supplications on Tuesday and Thursday afternoons, and those meetings always incited a flurry of activity necessary to address the issues that had been brought to his attention.

Needing a bit of respite, on Sunday morn after the mass for the soldiers had ended, Arthur took Gregor into the hills to gather a basket of heather.

"I did no' think squires dallied about picking flowers," grumbled the lad as he yanked on a sprig, his fingers slipping upward and destroying half of the delicate blooms.

"Mayhap that's because ye've never been a squire afore." Arthur pointed to a bush with his *sgian dubh*. "All knights, as well as squires, must ken how to pick flowers, and ye do not go breaking off the stems and smashing the buds with your fingers."

He demonstrated. "Ye gently push away the buds

and reveal the stock, then with a flick of your knife, cut it away and leave the plant to flourish."

"Och, but what's the use of cutting them anyway? They're only going to shrivel up and die."

The lad had evidently not been born a natural charmer. "We cut them for the womenfolk and to make our chambers smell sweet. Does your mother have an appreciation for flowers?"

"Aye, she does, I reckon."

"Then whilst we're here, cut a posy for her."

Gregor stood for a moment, drumming his fingers on his chin. "Mayhap she might make an apple tart if I bring her flowers."

Arthur placed another sprig into the basket. "See? Never forget people repay kindness with kindness, even parents."

The lad took his knife and managed to snip a clump without destroying half the blooms. "But I'd rather be in the stables with the horses."

"Not polishing my armor?"

"Och, nay. That's boring."

"Not every task is fun. 'Tis why they call it work rather than play."

Gregor cut another. "This doesn't seem like work."

"So, have ye decided ye enjoy gathering flowers?"

"Nay. It seems like women's work, no' a man's."

"Mayhap one day ye'll think back on our flower-picking and realize it is worthwhile."

"Are ye planning to take those flowers to your ma?"

Though it was a good idea, Arthur had another woman in mind. For the past sennight, the words "I cannot fall in love with ye again!" repeated over and over in his mind. Spoken with exasperation as she had fled, those words had seemed so final.

Why couldn't Rhona fall in love with him again? Only moments before, the lass had eagerly embraced him. She'd returned his kisses with the same fervor and passion they'd shared long ago. Clearly, desire lurked in Rhona's heart, but something grave had turned her against him. Was it the state of the kingdom? Or was she still pining for her husband?

Aye, the woman was kin to Lorn, but if His Lordship had two licks of sense, he'd soon pledge his fealty to Robert and put the past behind him. True, the wounds from their recent battles might still be too raw but, sooner or later, the king intended to unite the kingdom, and the Lord of Lorn ought to have a place in parliament, else his title would be forfeited.

Was the rift between king and clan the sole reason for her rejection? Arthur intended to find out. He was not accustomed to walking away from anything and he wasn't about to start. He'd decided before and he stood by his convictions. He would persevere.

Perhaps I'm pushing too hard. I should not have kissed the lass.

"Sir?"

Blinking away his thoughts, Arthur straightened. "Aye?"

"Your ma? Are ye taking her the heather?"

Realizing he hadn't responded, Arthur replied, "Nay. I'm taking them to Mistress Rhona."

"The healer? She's awfully bonny. Are ye planning to ask her to marry ye?"

Most definitely. "I am not. She has been kind to me and I want to give her a gift to brighten her cottage."

"If I were you, I'd ask her to marry me."

"I'm not certain she would agree."

"Why no'? Ye're a knight and the most important man in the village." Gregor threw up his hands with an exaggerated shrug. "Women are curious."

"Aye, they are." Before the lad probed any further, Arthur picked up the basket. "I think we've gathered enough flowers. Besides, ye have your evening chores to do."

Gregor held up the little bouquet he'd prepared for his mother. "Mayhap me ma will grant me a holiday."

Arthur patted the boy's shoulder. "Now ye're dreaming, lad."

PROUD OF HER DAY'S WORK, RHONA WIPED HER hands on her apron. "We have five and forty vials of avens oil, thanks to the yield by the shore."

"We'll still need to use it sparingly," said Gran, picking up a vile and holding it to the candlelight. "These wee beauties are worth their weight in silver."

Rhona collected four, cradling them between her fingers, and carefully placed them on the shelf just as a knock came at the door. It was a firm rap and, by the way the butterflies took to flight in her stomach, the caller was the one person she had been avoiding. Her face burned as she ignored the noise and continued stacking all the vials on the shelf.

"Do ye expect me to answer that?" asked Gran.

"Och..." Rhona huffed out a groan. "I'll do it."

After she moved to the door, she stood for a moment, wringing her hands. *I'm no innocent maid to be trifled with. I'll see what he wants and send him on his way.*

But as soon as she opened the door, her thoughts were forgotten. The man wore a finely woven brechan, a shiny leather doublet, and his hair was brushed away from his face, curling to his shoulders. Sir Arthur raised a basket of fragrant heather and grinned. Heaven's stars, his smile was enough to make her swoon, but somehow the flowers made him more masculine and more attractive to her soul.

When she said nothing, he inclined the basket toward her. "I thought you and your grandmother could use a bit of heather to brighten your cottage. The violet of the blooms is ever so vibrant this year."

She took the handle. "They're lovely, thank ye."

"I see ye have not been struck by any arrows of late," called Gran from the table.

"Nay, m'lady. It seems things are settling." He looked around Rhona. "I hope ye are well."

"Aye, I've recovered from the *ceilidh*, and having ye keep me up all hours."

Would Gran never stop? "Thank ye for your kindness," Rhona said, moving to shut the door.

Arthur thrust out his palm and stopped it. "'Tis a fine afternoon. I've brought along a couple of mounts and was hoping ye might ride with me."

"Ah..." Rhona glanced over her shoulder, trying to think of an excuse.

"Go on and have a wee bit of fun," said Gran.

Good heavens, the woman never made a lick of sense. One minute she was stealing the constable's missives or spewing saucy remarks at him, and the next she was telling Rhona to have fun.

She glanced down at her apron, stained after ladling the avens oil into the vials. "I'm hardly fit to be seen out of doors."

"I'm not taking ye to a gathering, lass." He threw a thumb over his shoulder in the direction of the tethered horses. "In fact, when I was returning from the hills, I noticed the grouse are active in the wood. I thought we might go on a wee hunt."

Honestly, since he'd brought a horse for her to ride, the notion of having an afternoon in the fresh air sounded tempting. "Give me a moment to don a clean apron, and I'll join ye anon."

"Very well."

As he released the door, Rhona made sure it was closed, then faced her grandmother. "Why the blazes do ye encourage him?"

The meddler looked up from her embroidery, eyes wide as if she had no idea to what Rhona had been re-

ferring. "If ye did not want to go riding, ye should have said so."

Slipping her dirty apron over her head, Rhona huffed. "That is not the point. Ye ken what I mean. By the way ye give the constable sass, it is obvious you do not care for the man."

"'Tisn't Sir Arthur I dislike. 'Tis his lord and master."

"But ye dislike all the knight stands for."

"Perhaps. But as a man, ye must admit he's a fine specimen."

"Specimen?" Rhona snorted. "He's no root to be boiled and poured into a vial."

"Nay, but he's still young. Young minds are pliable like clay."

"Mayhap a bairn's mind, but Sir Arthur is fully grown and more set in his ways than ye believe. He would never turn away from King Robert."

"Perhaps not, but with the right woman at his side, she would have a great deal of influence over Argyll."

Rhona gaped so widely, her chin practically dropped all the way to her chest. "Good heavens, I cannot believe ye just said such a thing."

Gran pointed to the basket of heather. "He obviously has eyes for ye."

"But you never have a good word to say to him."

"Hmm," mumbled the old woman, shoving her needle through the linen.

Groaning, Rhona pulled on a clean apron, then tiptoed over to her grandmother's chair and gave the top of her head a kiss. "Try not to intercept any missives whilst I'm away," she whispered.

"Och, I do believe ye are becoming a curmudgeon."

"Remember I've done my share of meddling. And as I said before, I reckon we'd best mind our own affairs for a time."

"Because ye are smitten with him."

"Nay, because I prefer to keep my head attached to my neck." Rhona patted her grandmother's arm. "We shan't be gone long. Have a wee nap and I'll be back afore ye know it."

Outside, Arthur was running a comb through his horse's mane.

"Haven't you a groom to do that for ye?"

The knight rubbed his palm along the steed's neck. "Aye, but grooming builds the bond between horse and rider."

Rhona walked to the gelding he'd brought for her to ride and patted his shoulder. "This is a fine-looking beast."

"He's sound as a stone foundation." Arthur laced his fingers together, making a cradle. "How long has it been since you last rode?"

She grasped the reins and placed her knee into his makeshift step, and then he hoisted her onto the back of the horse as if she weighed no more than a bushel of oats. "I ride one of the farrier's horses whenever I need to travel farther than a few miles to help someone— though 'tisn't often. Gran and I have no need to keep one."

After she settled into the saddle, Arthur moved his hand to her knee. "Afore we set out, I want to apologize. I did not take ye to the wall-walk..." He glanced over his shoulder and lowered his voice. "For a wee kiss. I took you up there to show ye the work the men have done. I ken ye oft visited the castle when Lorn was...*ah*...in residence."

She laid the reins over the horse's neck to turn the gelding away and tapped her heels. "No apology is necessary." If only the man knew she hadn't been able to think of much else since that night. A hundred times she'd kicked herself for running, and a hundred times she'd insisted it was for the best. The problem was, the more she saw of Arthur Campbell, the more muddled

her convictions. When he'd first entered Dunstaffnage and announced that His Grace, Robert the Bruce had laid claim to the fortress for the Kingdom of Scotland, Rhona had stood firm and faced him as though her life were about to be smote. At the time, she had been ready to fight, though she had not expected Arthur to be named constable. Neither had she expected him to behave civilly, courteously, politely...or *fairly*.

Her mind running \, she kicked her heels and demanded a canter straight through the village and toward the path leading to the hills.

Not surprisingly, Arthur caught up in no time and reined his horse beside hers. "I didn't ken ye wanted to race for the mountains."

"Forgive me." She slowed her horse to a walk. "It feels good to ride for a change."

"I'm glad of it. Mayhap we can go riding from time to time."

She scraped her teeth over her bottom lip. Agreeing would encourage him. Agreeing would mean that they would be seeing more of each other. And Rhona didn't want that.

Do I?

Of course not!

Not after the damper in the bathhouse. Not after the vinegar. And especially not after Auley.

Och, I'm such a mutton-heid!

"The days are growing shorter," Arthur said, taking the turn to the Cruachan Trail.

"Aye," Rhona mumbled, wishing she had not agreed to this excursion.

"Ye seem tense. Is there something troubling ye, lass?"

"Me?" Her shoulders shook with a nervous laugh while she tried to think of something to say other than the fact that she thought about kissing him day and night. For the love of Moses, her dreams did not even escape the braw knight. "Nay. Of course, I always worry about leaving Gran. She doesn't move around as well as she used to."

"Though she does well enough for a person of her advanced years. And ye leave her alone when ye set out for your visitations, do ye not?"

"I do."

"Did she enjoy the *ceilidh*?" he asked, changing the subject.

"She enjoyed all the attention from the soldiers who carried her up all the way into the castle on a chair. My heavens, she'll be talking about that for the rest of her days."

"I'm glad. Though she still sees fit to rouse me at every turn."

"Och, she's Lorn's sister. If she didn't ply ye with a bit of vinegar, she'd feel as if she were betraying her kin." Rhona shrank, tightening her grip on her reins. Why did she say "vinegar"? There were so many other words that would have done. "Um...I hope my grandmother doesn't annoy ye overmuch."

"Nay, her grousing makes me laugh."

"Good."

"I thought we'd take the path up through the crags."

"Oh? 'Tis longer."

"Are ye in a hurry?"

"Not exactly."

"Very well, follow me. Besides, the heather is bonnier up there." He glanced at her. "Ye do like heather?"

"Aye, and I do appreciate the blooms ye brought."

Together they rode for a time. On a horse and away from the castle and all the soldiers, Arthur seemed so much more at ease. Sometimes when Rhona was among people, she felt as if she had to keep the conversation going, but at the moment, it was as if simple talk wasn't necessary between them. Just being together was comfortable, as if they were two old friends who didn't need mindless prattle.

But we are old friends, are we not?

She ought to admit to that. Mayhap when he'd first arrived it was easier to be angry with him because she'd thought he'd abandoned her. Yet, she should have known it was his father who had sent him away. And Niall had not delivered Arthur's missive, the brute.

What would have happened if she had received the letter? Rhona doubted her granduncle would have allowed her to wait for Arthur. Regardless of her wishes, her marriage would have been arranged come what may. Then she would have married Ivor while pining for another all the more.

What a messy web life weaves.

As the trail narrowed, Arthur took the lead and started to hum. Rhona smiled, the tune she knew well, and after he finished a verse, she sang the chorus, "Hey o, my bonnie o."

Arthur flashed a toothy smile over his shoulder, and sang aloud, "There bade a lord in the North Country..."

"Hey o, my bonnie o."

"He had twa dochters, ane fair, ane mean. And the swan swims sae bonnie o. A young man came a wooin' them..."

Rhona echoed, "Hey o, my bonnie o."

Arthur belted at the top of his lungs the entire song about a man who errs and chooses the youngest daughter to marry rather than the eldest but, in the end, the older girl weds a king and gets her due.

By the time the song finished, their singing had grown so loud and animated that any grouse that may have been about had been duly warned.

Rhona drew in a deep breath of sweet Highland air and laughed from her belly. "I cannot believe ye remembered all thirteen verses."

"I've no idea where it came from. I do not believe

I've sung that song since..." He pulled his horse to a stop, his gaze meeting hers. If she'd thought his eyes dark, they were doubly so now, as she realized that most likely the last time he sang "The Twa Sisters" was when they'd slipped away from their families at *ceilidh* in Achnacloich along Loch Etive. They'd sung and danced among the standing stones, and that was where they'd shared their first kiss.

By the shock on his face, it was clear he hadn't intended to sing that very song. Rhona glanced up the slope. "Ye were right about the heather. It is like a blanket of lavender up here, though I fear we've most likely frightened the grouse away."

"I reckon I ken where to find them...unless ye want to head back?"

When she shrugged noncommittally, he dismounted. "We'll hobble the horses here, and we'll go the rest of the way on foot."

Rhona started to dismount, but within the blink of an eye, Arthur moved beside her, placing a hand on her waist. "Allow me to help."

"I can do it."

"I ken," he said, his dark eyes twinkling with sunlight. "But I'd be no gentleman if I stood back and watched."

Rhona did her best to convince herself to slow her sudden rapid pulse as she leaned forward, placing her hands on his shoulders. His grip on her waist was firm. As he slowly lowered her to the ground, he leaned forward, touching his lips to her ear, and sang in a deep bass, "And the swan swims, sae bonnie o..."

A shiver of tingles coursed through her entire body. "Hey o, my bonnie o," she breathlessly chimed.

Grinning, he stared into her eyes for a moment while all the yearning she'd endured over the past week swirled in her breast. His tongue slipped over his bottom lip before he released her and took a step away.

"I made myself promise not to kiss ye, no matter how much I wish to do so."

No kissing? Rhona rubbed the back of her neck and glanced away. She ought to be relieved, but she'd been all but certain he was about to kiss her. Should she ask why?

Nay, ye dolt.

She had only pushed him away and fled the last time they'd kissed. She untied the bow and quiver of arrows from her saddle. "Since we came up here to hunt, we'd best set to it, had we not?"

❧ 16 ❧

"I'll carry those along with mine," Arthur said, easing the bow and arrows from Rhona's grasp and putting them over his shoulder, along with a satchel. "Are ye up to a wee climb?"

She glanced to the trail leading up the slope, the hillside covered with purple heather shimmering with the breeze. "'Tis so bonny, ye could not keep me away."

Taking the lead, he grinned to himself. It actually had been Gregor who'd spotted the covey of grouse this morn. At the time, Arthur had realized a hunt was an excellent idea for a Sunday afternoon jaunt. "We'll have to keep our voices down from here on out."

"No serenade?" she teased.

"Mayhap we should forget about your healing and my post as constable and travel about like minstrels."

"Aye, if we want to rid the Highlands of people."

He glanced her way, feigning a pained expression. "I thought ye liked my voice."

"Yours is pleasant enough, but I sound like a squawking hen."

"Nay." Arthur stopped and faced her. "Ye sound like a lark, ye do."

The lass thrust her fists onto her saucy hips and waggled her shoulders. "Squawk, squawk, squawk."

Trying not to laugh, he focused on her face. "Wheesht, mind ye."

She dropped her hands to her sides and thrust out her chest like a foot soldier ready for inspection. "Aye, sir."

The path was rocky and Arthur oft glanced behind to ensure Rhona wasn't having too much difficulty. She did walk a great deal, but that was mostly in town where the roads were smooth. In truth, she moved around so well, it was easy to forget her lameness. But now they were in the hills, she was struggling a bit. Moreover, her skirts kept snagging on the brush.

"Not much farther," he said, offering his hand. "Allow me to help."

She glanced to his palm and met his gaze with a challenging icy-blue stare. "I can manage, thank ye."

Arthur knew that look. One of the things he'd always admired about Rhona was her spirit, and if the lass wanted to follow without help, he'd not force the issue. After some grunting and mumbled curses on her part, they arrived near the top of the crag. He slapped his hand on an enormous boulder. "We can use this outcropping as a hide," he whispered.

Rhona pulled a twig from her skirts and tossed it aside. "My weapons, please."

After loading their bows with arrows, they crept to the spot Gregor had shown him where all but head and shoulders were hidden by the stony ridge. Arthur pointed downward just as a pair of birds came into view.

He took aim, but Rhona nudged him with her elbow as she pushed back her veil, slid her bow and arrow over the rock, and drew back the string to her cheek. He froze in place as he watched her concentrate. Her gaze narrowed while a delicate pink tongue slipped to the corner of her mouth. If only he could frame this moment. The hunting goddess was magnificently formed and entirely focused on her task.

Before his next blink, she released her arrow with the twang of the bow. And then her mouth dropped open as she hit her mark.

At once, the second grouse took to flight, sounding the alarm. Birds of all varieties soared above the trees. Arthur laughed aloud. "With shooting like that, ye ought to join the ranks of my men."

"No thank ye, kindly. I don't reckon I'd blend in well with your bedraggled lot of soldiers."

"Bedraggled?" he asked, clapping a hand to his chest as if she'd wounded him.

She shoved her bow over her shoulder. "Come, let us fetch the bird afore the buzzards do."

Arthur sidled around the rock. "I'll get it. Ye stay here."

"Have ye lost your sense of adventure?" Giving him a gentle shove, she skittered ahead of him, while her veil dropped to the ground. "The wee beasty down there is mine. I'm not about to sit idle up here whilst ye gather the spoils of the hunt."

Arthur picked up the veil, stuffed it into his doublet, and followed, much preferring this view, with her white hair swaying to and fro, brushing those saucy hips. "Let no man ever fault ye for being milk-livered."

"After ye play midwife to a few women giving birth, the idea of having a single thread of milk-liveredness vanishes, never to be seen again."

"Are ye not afraid of anything?"

"Nay."

Arthur reflected back to the godawful passageway someone had traversed to help Auley and his sons escape. "What about a tunnel filled with spiderwebs?"

As the lass turned and gaped, the ground gave way beneath her feet with a shower of stones and debris. As she fell, Arthur lunged for her hand, but she slipped away from his grasp, tumbling down the slope.

"Aaaaaaaaah!" Rhona cried while he bounded after her.

Flinging out her hands, she grappled for a clump of heather and abruptly stopped.

"Rhona!" Arthur dropped beside her, digging in his heels, the ground crumbling beneath his feet as well. "Are you hurt, lass?"

She looked at her palms and hissed. "Nothing a bit of avens oil won't fix."

"Let me see," he said, sitting beside her and examining her hands. Her palms were scraped with spots of blood coming through the dirt.

Arthur reached for his kerchief, just as she let out a sharp gasp. "Och, nay!"

"What is it?"

Rhona clapped a hand over her mouth. "My shoe. It has lost its sole and I think I've twisted my ankle as well."

Sure enough, the wooden platform of her special boot was about two yards down the hill. She poked her ruined boot out from under her skirts and looked at her foot. There was no sole on it whatsoever. "Oh no, I'm never going to make it back to the horses with bare toes."

She was right. There were thorns, thistles, and thousands of rocks between here and there. "Not to worry." He took her hand and dabbed at the scrapes. "I'll carry ye."

"Ye cannot tote me that far."

He eyed the lass with a stubborn expression of his own. "I can and I will. Now tell me, ye've twisted your ankle and scuffed your hands, what else is ailing ye?"

Rhona shifted her backside a bit, and he imagined it was sore as well. "Nothing else."

"Very well, we'd best head back," he said, pulling her into his arms.

"Wait a moment. Ye aren't planning to leave without the bird are ye?"

Arthur glanced down the hill to the fallen grouse. Above, the buzzards had begun circling and it wouldn't be long before they tried to steal him. "I suppose we mustn't leave without your quarry. One shot and ye hit the mark clean through." He straightened. "Stay here. I'll be but a moment."

"Would ye fetch the sole to my boot as well? The cobbler will be able to make use of it to make another."

"Your wish is my command, m'lady," he said, hastening downward, collecting both the sole and the bird and placing them in a satchel. As he returned to Rhona's side, he pushed the bag to his back.

To his surprise, the willful lass obeyed him and hadn't budged, although she was injured. "I ought to at least try to walk."

Now that was more like the Rhona he knew. It might pain her to not only walk with a twisted ankle, but to do so without a shoe and with one leg shorter than the other would cause her undue misery. "Nay. Ye ought to allow me to carry ye and pretend I'm a hero."

Those lovely white eyebrows arched. "Why do ye say pretend?"

He gathered her into his arms and looked up the crag. "Because I reckon ye'd rather have any other man in all of Argyll carry ye off this mountain."

"I wouldn't say that."

Good Lord, had his ears deceived him? Aye, he'd brought her flowers, but she'd nearly closed the door in his face for the third time since his arrival at Dunstaffnage. And he didn't have any illusions that wooing this woman would be effortless. Nor had it escaped his notice that her sharp-tongued grandmother had prodded Rhona into coming along on this mishappen adventure, which perplexed him to no end. But at the moment, he'd heard her sure enough and he was completely unable to hide the smile stretching his lips.

Arthur's heart soared and the weight of the woman in his arms turned featherlight. "What *would* ye say?" he asked, his voice a tad unsure.

"Well...I'm glad ye're not Gregor, 'cause I weigh more than he does."

Blast. Perhaps he had read too much into her comment. But presently, the lass who filled his dreams was in his arms with her soft hip pressed against his belly. She leaned into him, her scent more alluring than the entire mountain of heather. "I'm just glad..."

His mouth went dry. "Aye?"

"I'm glad I was with you," she whispered.

By the stars, if he hadn't promised not to kiss her, he would set her down and plunder that sweet mouth this very instant. He'd kiss the woman and worship her as if the sun shone only for Rhona MacDougall. "I'm glad of it as well."

AT THE MOMENT, RHONA FELT AS IF SHE WERE IN A dream, cradled in Arthur's arms. It was ever so difficult to think of anything aside from how much she had enjoyed being with him this day, as if she were a damsel and he a dashing knight who had rescued her from untoward peril and she'd swooned in his embrace. His face showed not a hint of strain as he held her tight to his chest. He smelled like leather and spice with a whiff of apple-blossom soap.

And by the rood, he was tenacious. Even after she'd pushed him away at the *ceilidh* when they were atop the wall-walk, he'd still shown up at her door a sennight later with a basket overflowing with her favorite flowers. And she'd been so wrong about him. He hadn't left for St. Andrews without attempting to say goodbye.

If only they had a chance to be together. But she must treasure these fleeting moments together and lock them away in her heart. It was ever so hard not to fret over the future. And she still must not risk growing too fond of him. Perhaps given time, if she stopped her meddling, she might be able to let her guard down. Could she hope? But what of Gran? The woman was unpredictable. What if Her Ladyship intercepted more missives? Especially letters from the king.

Hope? Who am I fooling but myself?

Moments like these were but whispers on the wind. Still, she closed her eyes and let herself revel in Arthur's comfort, his strength. Being with him made her want to lock the past away and only look ahead.

Could she?

Aye, with Arthur at her side, she might start anew.

But what if he discovers I'm his culprit?

"Here we are," he said as he stopped beside his horse. "Ye'd best ride with me."

Though in her heart she wanted nothing more than to be close to him, to feel their bodies sway in tandem as the horse ambled back to the village, Rhona shook her head. "I didn't fall on my head, mind ye. I'm perfectly able to sit on a horse."

"Is that so? With a bare foot in an iron stirrup?" Demonstrating a herculean show of strength, Arthur hefted her onto his mount. "What if the gelding should spook?"

She moved her leg over the horse's withers and arranged her skirts so they covered down to her ankles. "I used to ride my pony bareback as well as barefooted when I was a wee lass."

"Aye, but not through the wood with rough footing." He stooped to release the hobbles on both beasts and affixed a lead line to the gelding's bit. He then mounted behind her, reached around, and took up the reins. "Thank ye for humoring me. I'd never forgive myself if ye had another fall."

"I reckon you put me on your horse because ye..." Good Lord, when she was a lass of sixteen, she would have finished the sentence, but doing so now would be too brash.

His breath skimmed her ear, making a shiver course all the way down to her knees. "Because I what?" he asked, his voice like silk.

"Ye wanted to," she whispered, praying he didn't hear her, but hoping he did. His upper arms tightened around her and she dared twist enough to look him in the eye.

His tongue swept over his bottom lip as his gaze lowered to her mouth. "Mayhap ye are right."

Quickly snapping her eyes forward, Rhona busied herself with running her fingers through the horse's mane. Though she sensed Arthur was about to say something more, he did not. Instead, he remained silent, his presence enveloping her, making her tingle with awareness. She wanted to turn and wrap her arms around his neck and kiss him—show him exactly what was in her heart.

If only.

But rather than bare her soul, she also sat silent, reveling in the warmth of his chest against her back, every so often glimpsing the turrets of Dunstaffnage standing proud against the blue waters of the Firth of Lorn.

As guilt from her actions over the past several weeks began to make her chest grow tight, she wrapped the horse's mane hair around her knuckles and closed her fist. Bless it, she had freed Auley because it was the right thing to do. Mayhap Arthur didn't know the man well, but no matter what, Rhona could never sit idle and allow an injustice, even though Auley had fired upon the retinue. Besides, no one had died. If only she had seen the man first, she could have told him of her granduncle's orders to stand down.

About halfway to the village, Arthur shifted the reins to one hand, then pulled something from his doublet. "I nearly forgot. Ye lost this during the hunt."

He draped her veil across her arms. "Oh, my heavens, my head has been uncovered all this time."

After shaking it out, she raised it to her head, but before she could secure the veil in place, he caught her wrist. "I prefer it off."

As his lips skimmed her ear, she drew in a quick inhalation. "What will they think if we ride into the village not only double, but with my head bare?"

"Ye can put it on afore we arrive." He lifted a lock of her hair and let it lazily slide from his palm. "Your tresses have always astounded me—so soft, so long, so very fair."

Rhona shivered with delight as his voice grew deeper with his every word. "'Tis my grandmother's color."

"Aye. But it is as if ye were kissed by the fairies. Aside from you pair, I've never seen tresses this color. I wish..."

A wee gasp slipped through her lips. Did she want to know what he was about to say? "What do ye wish for?" she whispered despite herself.

"I cannot say."

"That's hardly fair. I revealed what I was thinking afore."

"Perhaps, but my thought should not be heard by anyone's ears." He shifted his hands on the reins. "Do ye ever have thoughts that aren't meant to be uttered aloud?"

Only every other thought Rhona had since they'd set out was something she couldn't put into words, else she'd be facing the gallows. "At times, aye, I do," she said, trying to sound innocent.

"One day I'd like to tell ye. Just not now."

She twisted around and gave him a good once-over. Heaven's stars, the man's eyes were blacker than coal and filled with hunger. Rhona knew such a look, and it made a yearning coil right down to the depths of her nether parts—in the very place where longing resided—in the very place it should not stir.

His eyes trailed up to the top of her head. "We'll be riding out of the forest in a moment if ye want to don your veil."

"Thank you," she said, quickly affixing the head-cover in place. Where had the time gone? It seemed as if only moments ago they were high up in the mountains.

All too soon, Arthur reined the horses to a stop out-side the cottage. "I'll carry ye inside."

"Nay, Gran will have one of her spells if ye do. Be-sides, I may have one shorter leg, but I'm fully capable of walking without my boot."

"If ye insist," he said, helping her to dismount. As she turned toward the door, he grasped her elbow. "Ye'd best try your ankle afore I let go."

She took a few steps, then eased her arm away from his hand. "'Tis a wee bit tender, but nothing I haven't dealt with in the past. Twisted ankles are a hazard for a lame lass. Ye'd be surprised how easy it is to turn an ankle wearing a stilt on one's foot."

"I'm sure it isn't easy but ye manage well." He pulled the satchel from around his back. "May I see ye inside?"

"Aye." Rising up on her toes, Rhona kissed his cheek and could have sworn the hardened constable blushed.

One corner of his mouth curved up. "What was that for?"

"I reckon a bit of thanks is in order."

"Any time ye want to repay a favor, ye are more than welcome to shower me with kisses."

"One kiss, mind ye," she said before she opened the

175

door to find Gran bent forward, slumbering in her chair.

Rhona turned to Arthur and raised a finger to her lips, then tiptoed across the floor. "Gran," she whispered. "I'm home."

The old lady slowly opened her eyes, then jolted. "How dare ye sneak up on me like that? Good gracious, ye'll give me one of my spells for certain."

"Forgive me," Rhona said, gesturing to the constable. "Sir Arthur is here and we've just returned from our hunting excursion."

"And ye came back empty-handed?"

"Nay," said Arthur, pulling the grouse out of his satchel and holding it up. "Mistress Rhona nabbed a beauty with a single arrow."

Gran planted her hands on the armrests and sat straighter. "Of course she did. She's my granddaughter."

Rhona reached for her quarry. "I'll pluck and clean the bird, then put it on to boil."

"Nay." Arthur shifted the grouse away from her grasp. "I'll take the wee beasty out back and clean it whilst you prepare the pot."

"Very well," she said, watching him go.

"Ye're limping more than usual," said Gran as she picked up her needle and thread.

Rhona moved to the hearth and added a block of peat to the fire. "My boot lost its sole. I've an old pair I can wear whilst the cobbler fixes this one."

"Ye're awfully hard on shoes."

"I rather like to think they're hard on me," she mumbled as she looked in the water pail. Curses, it was empty. She'd need to go out back to the well to refill it.

"Will the constable be staying for dinner?"

Rhona chewed her bottom lip. They hadn't discussed it, though the grouse would take at least two hours to cook, and that was if she managed to keep the fire ablaze. "I need to fetch some water. I'll ask him."

"Mayhap it would be best if he did not stay."

"Why is that?"

"Och, ye've been out with him all afternoon. Ye do not want to make the man think he's won your heart now, do ye?"

"Perhaps ye're right." Rhona picked up the bucket and headed for the door, painfully aware nothing good would come from encouraging him overmuch, no matter how much Arthur Campbell stirred her blood.

Gran chuckled as if she were scheming. "There's nothing wrong with a wee bit of meddling now and again."

"Speaking of that..." Rhona lowered her voice. "I said it afore, and I still believe we've done enough."

"Are ye losing your nerve?" Gran chided.

"Nay. All I'm saying is we might let matters rest for the time being." How could she put it to make it sound reasonable to this stalwart matriarch of Clan Mac-Dougall? "I say, we are under Sir Arthur's protection. And for the most part, he has been reasonable. And until your brother returns, we must...*endure*."

Gran stabbed her needle through the air. "Not only are ye turning softhearted, ye're smitten."

Aye, Rhona was a little, but she wasn't a fool. "If ye recall, ye're the one who encouraged me to go riding with the man."

"Humph." After making a few stitches, Gran looked up. "Very well. We shall cease for a time, especially since my laggard brother hasn't seen fit to write."

Rhona breathed a sigh as a weight lifted from her shoulders. She put on her spare shoes before she headed to the well, stepping a bit lighter. Thank heavens Gran had seen reason.

❦ 17 ❦

After Arthur removed his shirt and doublet so he wouldn't soil them while cleaning the grouse, he plucked the feathers and set them aside for Rhona. But once he cut into the bird to clean its innards, a wind got up, and damned if the blasted feathers didn't adhere themselves to the blood on his hands and forearms. He not only looked like he'd been tarred and feathered, any passersby would think he'd never cleaned a bird before.

Of course, this was when Rhona chose to come around the corner swinging a bucket. The woman stopped and gaped. Her gaze first focused on his hands, then slowly slid to his chest while she tapped the corner of her mouth with her tongue. "Och, 'tis usually best to clean the bird afore ye don a shirt of feathers."

He held out his palms. "Is that what ye call it? So much for saving the feathers for ye. I'm afraid these are ruined and the rest have been scattered by a gust of wind."

The lass still hadn't looked him in the eye. "Do ye always strip bare when ye clean a bird?"

Good God, if only they were in a bedchamber. The way she looked at him made him so incredibly hard. Arthur had gone far to too long without a woman and stealing kisses from Rhona MacDougall only served to give him an insatiable appetite. Ever since the fete, his every other thought had been of her—of how he wanted to slowly peel off her clothing while kissing every inch of skin as he exposed it.

He moaned aloud, then tried to pretend he hadn't by clearing his throat.

"Are ye well?"

"Aye." He returned his attention to the grouse before he did something totally daft like pulling her into his arms and kissing her while smudging blood and feathers all over her apron and kirtle.

She held up the pail. "I need to fetch some water for boiling the grouse."

"I can do that for ye."

"No need. I usually make two or three trips to the well every day. 'Tisn't as if I'm an invalid." She kicked out her foot. "And I've donned my old boot to wear until I can have another made."

"I'm glad ye have a spare."

"As am I." She chuckled as she headed away.

Arthur quickly finished the job and followed Rhona to the well. "I'd be grateful if ye'd pour a bit of water over my hands."

Again, her gaze slid to his chest while her lips parted, emitting the slightest of gasps. By the grace of God, he liked having her eyes upon him and the way her pupils grew larger. She raised the bucket and started a stream.

"Ye've had practice," he said, rubbing his hands clean.

"Aye, everyone kens me to be the bucket-wielding widow."

He chuckled as she set the pail down, picked up the hem of her apron, and set to drying his hands. Her touch was firm, yet gentle, the linen, soft and soothing. "Ye've had a difficult time of it over the years, have ye not?" he asked, his tone gentle.

His hands were dry, yet she continued to rub the cloth over them and up his forearms. "Things haven't been all that bad. Ivor and I were only married a year, and he's been gone so long, his memory is fading. I suppose it was difficult at first, but now I have Gran to look after and my patients, of course."

"And you enjoy your work?"

Rhona's apron fell away as she gripped his hands. "I do. Being a healer gives me a sense of purpose."

"Just being yourself is purpose enough for me."

She took a step nearer and raised her chin. "Ye oughtn't remove your shirt when visiting a... um...widow."

"Forgive—"

Within a heartbeat, she wrapped her arms around him and fused her lips to his in a passionate, burning, demanding kiss, expressing more emotion than she had during the entire day of conversation. Her tongue swirled with his in a bone-melting, fire-igniting dance. A kiss that promised to lead to so much more with frantic caressing. The discarding of clothes. The erotic sensation of flesh brushing flesh, of taut nipples, of heady, steamy, moist—

Dear God, Arthur's knees nearly buckled as she pressed her body against his. Her breasts molded to his chest, her mons connected with his cock, making him harder and more ravenous than he'd ever been in his life.

His heart soared as he moaned into her mouth, wanting this moment to last an eternity, every inch of his flesh craving more. Arthur swirled his hands around her back, keeping her close, pressing himself against her supple body, his very flesh afire. Gradually, he slid his hands downward and sank his fingers into the soft roundness of her bottom and urged her even closer.

As he trailed kisses to her ear, he growled deep and

low, "I've dreamed of this..." Of kissing and so much more.

"Forgive me," Rhona sighed, her head dropping back. "I should not have kissed ye."

"Never say that. Kissing you makes me forget who I am. What I've done. When I kiss ye, I am the only man in the world and you the only woman." Arthur brushed his lips across hers. "I never want to stop."

"But I'm not the same lass ye fell in love with over that fanciful summer. Nor are ye the same lad. We both have our crosses to bear."

He moved his palms to her shoulders and took a step back. "What are ye saying?"

"I know not." Shaking her head, Rhona hid her face in her palms. "Whenever we are together, I am always so confused."

"Are you muddled because of the rift between Lorn and the Bruce?"

"Aye," she said, her voice uncertain. "Ye ken I must be faithful to my granduncle and to my clan."

"Hmm." He pressed his lips to her forehead and closed his eyes tightly. By the gods, he wanted her more than life's breath, but she needed to want him with equal fervor and without a rift tearing apart her heart. The lass was too conflicted and until she reconciled her loyalties, she would not love him as much as he loved her. No matter how much he wanted to bend his knee and ask the question to make her his, he mustn't push her. "I've been away from my post for long enough. I must be heading back."

As he released her, she stepped away. "Now?"

He bowed. "My thanks for an enjoyable afternoon spent in your company, mistress. Mayhap we can sing another round of 'The Twa Sisters' again soon."

With that, he straightened and walked away. It took a will of iron, but Arthur did not look back.

SPARRING IN THE COURTYARD DURING THE MORNING training session, Arthur advanced on Donal with light-ning-fast strikes of his sword. He gnashed his teeth and hacked downward as the lieutenant raised his targe in the nick of time. Arthur sidestepped as Donal's shield shattered, wooden shards flying.

"Bloody oath, sir, ye're fighting like a demon possessed."

Lowering his sword, Arthur stopped dead in his tracks. "Are ye turning milk-livered, soldier?"

"God, no." The lieutenant raised his blade. "If ye want to spar like ye're in the midst of hell, then be my guest, but do no' expect me to go easy on ye."

Arthur circled. "If ye dare, I'll kick your arse all the way to the loch and douse ye."

Donal lunged. "I reckon ye have a gnarly hair up your arse."

Shifting aside, Arthur deflected the blade with an upward strike. With the lieutenant's recoil, he took ad-vantage and went on the attack, violently thrusting and hacking as if he were truly being driven by a demon. Though Rhona MacDougall mightn't be a demon, there was no doubting she was a vixen. Heaven help him, he had wanted to ravish the woman with every bloody, miserable fiber of his body. When she'd kissed him, she'd turned him into a stark raving lunatic and his blood had not yet cooled.

If Arthur had not taken his leave, her skirts would have been up over her hips and he would have plunged into her right there in the light of day, against the well, on the grass, or in a bloody bramble for all he cared. Damnation, he may have walked away, but his erection hadn't eased. Hell, he was so hard, the only way he knew to relieve the tension was to spar as if the devil himself were after his soul.

Aye, Arthur wanted Rhona clear to his bones, but he wasn't going to take her like a harlot. She'd surprised him with the kiss in the garden, when only a sennight prior, she'd told him never to kiss her again. The internal battle she fought between loyalty to kin and loyalty to her heart had to be sorted out before she could truly give her heart to him. And once he was sure she loved him, he would take her to bed and worship the woman as if she were the only female alive.

Donal's sword clashed with Arthur's and iron screeched as the two blades slid together, meeting at their hilts. Baring his teeth, the lieutenant growled. "No one douses my arse in the loch, no' even you."

Arthur returned the sneer, his eyes blazing. "Is that—?"

Atop the wall-walk, the ram's horn sounded. All heads shifted upward while a sentry waved and pointed to the firth. "A fleet of *birlinns* is sailing from the south!"

"How many?" Arthur demanded.

"Five."

"And the colors?"

"They look to be MacDonalds."

"It could be a ruse," said Donal.

The man was right. Not only was Arthur not expecting a visit of any sort, this was war. "Dispatch the archers to the wall. Close the gate. No one leaves until we are certain they are truly Angus MacDonald's men."

Arthur hastened for the tower and climbed the winding stairs, taking them two at a time.

"It may be a ploy by Lorn," said Donal, on his heels.

"Mayhap." When he stepped out onto the wall-walk, he spotted the *birlinns* straightaway, their sails billowing with the MacDonald crest depicting a ship.

Bram, the old sergeant-at-arms met them. "The archers are in place. I've ordered the braziers lit and we're at the ready to shower them with lighted arrows."

"Excellent," said Arthur. "Order the men to prepare."

"Bowmen, ready your arrows!" bellowed Bram.

Arthur leaned through a crenel, squinting for a better look. As the ships lowered their sails, crewmen in each boat took up oars, though not a single ship was manned by more than a half-dozen sailors. Odd, often Scottish *birlinns* heading into battle carried a score of men. Moreover, if they'd come for a fight, they were sorely outnumbered.

"Is that Fairhair standing in the bow of the lead boat?" asked Donal.

Arthur slapped his palm on the stone wall. "By God, it is!" No man in all the Highlands sported such a wild mane of blond locks as those belonging to Angus Og MacDonald.

"Shall I have the archers stand down, sir?" asked Bram.

"Douse the arrows but remain in place until they've disembarked."

"Aye, sir."

Arthur beckoned Donal. "Come with me."

The lieutenant marched forward. "Perhaps I should greet them. It could still be a trap."

"Very courageous of ye to volunteer, but I would not be the constable appointed by Robert the Bruce if I cowered in my bedchamber."

Arthur led the way to the pier, arriving in time to catch a rope from the first boat. "Fairhair, are the waters about Dunyvaig rid of English marauders?"

The big Highlander hopped over the side of his boat, landing on the pier with a thud. "Och, by the number of patrols we spot every sennight, I reckon the bastards do no' ken north from south."

Islay grasped his forearm in greeting. "Then what brings ye up here?" Arthur asked.

"Did ye not receive a missive from Robert?"

"The king?"

"Aye, the bloody king of Scots. He's expecting ye to fill my boats with able fighting men." Islay leaned in and lowered his voice. "He's hell-bent on taking Urquhart."

Arthur did his best not to show his surprise. "No missives came, but I've men ready. When do we sail?"

"Good God, man, ye're staying here." Angus pulled a letter out from inside his doublet. "Read this. The Bruce believes a solid force must remain at Dunstaffnage with ye at the helm."

Arthur shook open the vellum and read. Sure enough, Islay's letter was written nearly a month ago, making it clear the king had dispatched another to Arthur. Though it wasn't entirely unheard of for letters to go missing, he couldn't shake the creeping feeling that this was yet another attempt to subvert his authority.

He returned the missive. "Are ye hungry, friend?"

Islay rubbed his belly. "Always."

Arthur turned to Donal. "Take the men to the great hall and tell Cook we've thirty more soldiers to feed. Have him send up a trencher to my solar as well. I need to have a word with His Lordship."

Islay eyed him. "I didn't reckon assuming control of this keep would be easy."

"Come, we've much to discuss." Arthur led the way through the hall and into the donjon. Once they reached his solar, he gestured to a chair. "Would ye care for a dram of whisky?"

"Don't mind if I do," said Islay, taking a seat at the table. "What else has gone awry aside from missing messengers?"

At the sideboard, Arthur poured two cups and set one in front of his friend. "What makes ye think I've more problems than a letter or two going astray?"

"I've two keeps to run and there are always problems." Islay held up his cup and swirled the whisky. "Besides, people are resistant to change. Especially Highlanders."

"Ye're not wrong there." Arthur slid into his chair at the head of the table. "I reckon it all started with someone closing the damper on the bathhouse the first night of my arrival. That trickery seems to have stopped for the time being, but we have a scoundrel in our midst and I intend to catch him and then make an example of the fiend."

"Aye?" asked His Lordship, sipping thoughtfully.

Arthur told him about the vinegar in the wine and ale, Auley and his sons' attack, and their subsequent escape, which had obviously been orchestrated by a local band of Lorn's miscreants.

Angus took another drink of his whisky and let out a long breath. "Word is Alexander MacDougall stayed in Carlisle as a guest of the Lord Warden, though I've no idea if he's still there."

"Is that so?" Arthur smoothed his fingers down his beard. "I've sent a spy to the borders to see if he can find out where Auley landed. But if the bastard made it to England, he's lost to me."

"Mayhap, but at least ye can rest assured he'll not be firing arrows at your sorties from there."

"I suppose we shall see what my man uncovers. Hopefully the swine farmer isn't recruiting an army to march on Dunstaffnage. Meanwhile, I'm not taking any chances. I've been riding out with more numbers in my sorties of late."

"Then the king is right to keep ye here. Are you certain ye have enough men to hold the fortress should an attack come?"

"Though recruiting has been slow, word has spread of the Bruce's victories and fighting men are joining us near every day. And if the king wants Urquhart Castle, I reckon he ought to take her."

"Aye, and when he does, he'll have control of the Highlands."

"Thank the gods." Arthur raised his cup. "Then he'll have the numbers needed to move south. I can bloody taste victory."

"Hear! Hear!" Islay took a drink and wiped his mouth with the back of his hand. "Ye ken what ye ought to do?"

"What?"

"Make the lot of the local folk pledge their fealty to you and to the king."

Arthur drummed his fingers against his cup. "I like the idea. We'll do it straightaway. With the Lord of Islay standing beside the constable of Dunstaffnage and an army behind us in a show of might."

"Now ye're talking like the fearsome knight I've come to know."

While the conversation moved on, Arthur's unease grew. Someone had intercepted a missive from the king, and he'd be a fool to believe the letter wasn't taken by the same knaves who'd been plaguing him since he arrived. And this was the last straw, dammit. He was not a bloody fool and it was high time he proved it.

⚜ 18 ⚜

"I reckon the bairn will come afore Samhain," Rhona said as Sara walked her to the door.

"Och, the wee one cannot come soon enough, truth be told. I feel as if I've been heavy with child for years and years."

Rhona's shoulders shook with her laugh. "Mayhap that is because ye have been."

"Thanks to Fingal, I suppose." Sara rested her hand on the latch. "And how about you, my dearest? Ye've been widowed for at least four years now. I reckon 'tis time ye thought about marriage again."

"Aye?" Rhona could naught but shake her head. "A lass needs a suitor if she intends to wed."

"I've seen ye speaking to the constable now and again."

"Sir Arthur?" she asked, trying to sound indifferent, but her breath whooshed out of her as if she'd been startled from behind.

Sara opened the door and followed her outside. "And why no'? He's a fine-looking man and a knight to boot."

"But he's the Bruce's vassal."

"True, but Fingal says the king is here to stay. No' only that, he believes in an independent Scotland where all are free from tyranny. I for one think the man has a point. Moreover, 'tis time for the folks living in the shadow of Dunstaffnage to move on."

"I only wish it were that easy," Rhona mumbled more to herself than anything, while a retinue of soldiers led by the knight himself rode into the village square. A cleric walked beside Arthur's horse, ringing a bell.

"Come one, come all!"

Sara tugged Rhona's elbow. "It looks as if the Sir Arthur's cleric has come to make an announcement— let's hear what is to be said. Mayhap he has news about the boats that sailed in yesterday. Fingal told me 'twas the Lord of Islay, Angus Og MacDonald."

Rhona gulped. She'd put the contents of the missive Gran had intercepted, out of her mind—but the bare truth of the matter was, His Lordship was due to arrive to collect men and take them northward to meet up with the Bruce—soldiers who Arthur was supposed to recruit, train, and prepare for the journey.

As a crowd gathered, she hastened to the square with Sara, though by the way her chest tightened, she would have preferred to run for the cottage and bar the door.

At least a dozen horsemen seated on warhorses stood in an arc in the square while a force of pike-wielding foot soldiers gathered behind them. A formidable knight in full armor sat a mount beside Sir Arthur. Behind the nose guard of his helm, a pair of hawkish blue eyes scanned across the crowd. With long blond hair picked up by the breeze, she reckoned it was Fairhair for certain, the Lord of Islay and sworn enemy of her granduncle. Must every MacDougall enemy come to Dunstaffnage to underscore Lorn's demise? By the rood, Rhona had nothing against the unification of the kingdom, but clan feuds had endured over centuries, regardless of who sat on the throne of Scotland.

The cleric climbed up to the platform and moved in front of the stocks and pillory, unrolling a scroll. "Hear ye one and all, young and old. The people of Argyll are hereby notified that anyone caught tampering with messages intended for Sir Arthur or anyone in the king's service shall be considered a traitor of Scotland and will suffer the fate of a traitor. This decree also encompasses tampering with the king's property as well as aiding and abetting convicted criminals. Every man and woman who has reached their majority will on the morrow come to the great hall, place their hand on the psalter, and pledge fealty to King Robert and to his constable, Sir Arthur Campbell. Anyone who ignores this order will be locked in the stocks and held until they submit."

Rhona's gaze trailed to Arthur, the cur. Curse him, he kept his hard stare straight ahead and didn't once look at her. She should have expected this. In fact, she was somewhat surprised it hadn't happened sooner.

As the cleric rerolled his vellum, the constable cued his horse forward. "Let it be known my quarrel is not with the good people of Dunstaffnage and Argyll. But I cannot abide the interception of my confidential missives, *especially* those from the king. Nor can I abide anyone who breaks into my gaol and frees a man who willfully fired upon me and my retinue of king's soldiers. Pledge your fealty on the morrow and we will all continue to live in harmony and peace."

"But why has Islay sailed here with an fleet of ships?" asked Fingal from across the square.

Arthur regarded the smithy, narrowing his gaze as if choosing his words carefully. "His Lordship is here to collect conscripts for the king."

Low murmurs rumbled through the crowd. It was obvious Rhona wasn't the only one disgruntled by the news. At least Fairhair would not be staying, which was a relief.

"Goodness," whispered Sara. "Who about the village would have been so bold as to seize missives from the king to Sir Arthur?"

Rhona shrugged. "'Tisn't surprising now, is it?"

"I suppose no..."

With a hard stare, Arthur bowed his head her way before he reined his horse around and led the retinue back across the bridge leading to the enormous fortress. The crowd disbanded, but Rhona didn't budge. She stood rooted, watching the constable ride away. She had been such a fool to encourage his attentions. Good glory, she had thrown herself at the man. Thank the stars, he'd walked away, what with his threats of the stocks and worse.

Traitor? Arthur sees the person who freed Auley as a traitor. He'll never understand that the man was just acting as a loyal servant of my granduncle.

She moved her hand to her throat, imagining what it would be like if the constable were to put a noose around it.

WITH MORE EFFORT THAN USUAL, RHONA MADE HER way up the stairs and into Dunstaffnage's great hall. Thank goodness the cobbler had started on fashioning a new boot, because the leather of the old was so worn and stretched, her ankle wobbled with every step.

All day, she'd watched the townsfolk parade through the gates, and had purposely bided her time. She didn't like being required to pledge an oath of fealty. It made her feel like a traitor to her clan.

And what point was Arthur trying to make? Surely anyone who wanted to cause him consternation wouldn't be dissuaded by taking an oath.

Rhona bit her lip. Only days ago, she'd decided it was nigh time to stop her meddling. But then Arthur had to go and run roughshod over the village with his ridiculous proclamation. And to add insult to injury, he'd done it with Angus Og MacDonald by his side, the fiend.

As she crossed under the portcullis, she glanced over her shoulder to the village. There were still a few outliers on their way in from their crofts, but she'd be one of the last, which she hoped sent a message that she wasn't at all happy with this state of affairs.

Only a handful of people milled about the great hall when she stepped through the doors.

Bram greeted her with a polite bow. "Mistress Rhona, 'tis good to see ye."

"I wish I could say 'tis good to be here."

"Och, Sir Arthur is only doing what he can to encourage peace."

She gave him a sharp poke in the arm. "Goodness, Bram, are ye a MacDougall or nay?"

"I'll always be a clansman, madam. That said, ye must ken I'll also always serve within these walls."

"Which poses a conundrum, it seems."

"Aye. We've no' but to make the best of it." He gestured toward the dais. "Go on, there's no wait at the moment. Ye picked a good time."

"Wonderful," she said, releasing a pent-up breath and limping forward. Why was it when her ire got the best of her, her lameness seemed to worsen?

Arthur sat in her granduncle's enormous chair, his hands braced on the armrests, his knees wide, and his feet planted firm, as if he were lord of the land. The constable was flanked by two pikemen while the cleric stood off to the side, holding a psalter.

"Good afternoon, Mistress Rhona," Arthur said as if they were merely passing acquaintances. "Thank ye for coming. Your presence here means a great deal to me as it surely does to the townsfolk."

She pursed her lips and gave a curt nod, trying to

convince herself that his words had been uttered with halfhearted enthusiasm. Though he didn't sound half-hearted. He sounded sincere and warm, curse him and the throne he sat upon.

"Step up onto the dais, please," said the cleric, his black robes billowing as he gestured for her to move beside him.

Rhona refused to look Arthur in the eyes as she did as told.

"Place your hand on the psalter and repeat after me."

The leather felt cool beneath her palm and she fixated on her hand, telling herself she was doing this to ensure she allayed all suspicion that she might be to blame for any of the tampering.

The cleric cleared his throat. "I hereby pledge my fealty to King Robert the Bruce and to his servant Sir Arthur Campbell."

Rhona repeated verbatim, her lips taut and her speech clipped.

"And I promise to uphold the laws of Scotland as well as adhere to the decrees and proclamations made by the constable in the best interests of Dunstaffnage and her surrounding lands."

Rhona repeated this as well, though adding, "As long as said decrees and proclamations are in the interests of those *residing* in the surrounding lands."

The cleric stiffened, his gaze shooting to Arthur.

"I believe Mistress Rhona wishes for there to be mutual harmony between the king's men and the townsfolk, and I heartily agree," said Sir Arthur, once again attempting to sound as if he were sincere, as well as aloof, and had not passionately kissed her only two days prior.

Rhona gave a hasty curtsey and started for the steps —and some fresh air. Presently, the atmosphere in the hall was both stale and stifling and it made her feel a bit ill.

"I beg your pardon, mistress," the knight called after her.

Rhona stopped, looking at the faces of the few folk who had straggled in. *Would he not just let it be done?*

"Where is your grandmother?"

Holy hellfire, Sir Arthur didn't expect Gran to climb the stairs just to engage in this sham? How quickly he forgot that he'd sent a retinue of soldiers to carry her on her chair for the feast. "As ye may recall, she is too infirm to manage the stairs," she said over her shoulder.

Arthur rapped his knuckles on the table. "Then we shall take the psalter to her."

"I'm sure that isn't necessary. She's too old to cause a man as big and as strong as you consternation."

"On that I must disagree. I believe Lady Mary, Lorn's sister, is quite capable of causing mischief...unless she *refuses* to pledge her fealty."

"Of course not." Rhona clenched her fists, imagining her grandmother suffering the humiliation and agony of being locked in the pillory. "If ye bring the psalter, I'm certain she'll take the oath."

"Excellent," said Arthur. "Tell your Lady Mary we shall be along as soon as we've finished here."

Rhona gave a nod and hastened out the door. Once she reached the courtyard, she stood against the wall and pressed a hand to her chest, taking a number of deep, reviving breaths. By the saints, she had been a complete fool to allow herself to feel anything for that man. She must have utterly lost her head when she'd thrown herself into his arms.

Aye, Arthur had charmed her when they went on the hunt—singing and carrying on as if they hadn't a care. Furthermore, the man had carried her for a good mile. After all, he was a hulking beast and in her moment of weakness, she had seen herself as a damsel... thought herself capable of loving him.

But she could not. No, no, no. She could never allow her traitorous heart to fall in love. How could she live a lie? She didn't love him. She must not!

Well, perhaps she had fancied herself in love at one time, but too many things had happened since that summer long ago. There was now an insurmountable divide between them and, even if she were discovered, she would not apologize for her actions. Auley did not deserve to die. His sons did not deserve to be tortured to death. Gran may have intercepted the missive, but Rhona had known of the contents, yet she had not relayed the information to Sir Arthur. Her heart might be conflicted, but her actions prevailed. She was a Mac-Dougall and would always be a MacDougall.

Rhona started for the gate but as she neared the bathhouse, she noticed there wasn't a single soldier in sight on the wall-walk. After glancing over her shoulder, she slipped behind the building and closed the blessed damper. Then she brushed off her hands and gave it a satisfactory nod.

"Enjoy a cold bath this night, Sir Arthur."

Rhona tiptoed to the edge of the building and glanced out. When a pair of guards deep in conversation strode past, she quickly plastered herself against the wall and waited until their footsteps echoed inside the tower stairwell. Holding her breath, she peered out again. Without a soul in sight, she slipped into the courtyard and hastened toward the gate.

"Mistress Rhona," said Bram, moving in beside her, seeming to materialize from nowhere. "Have ye a moment?"

She glanced up. He might not have seen her the last time, but now she was sure he'd followed her. "I'm afraid I must hurry away home. Sir Arthur and the cleric are taking the psalter to Gran so that an old woman of five and seventy can pledge fealty to King Robert."

"Och, it won't take but a moment." He grasped her elbow with a firm hand and tugged.

Rhona tried to wrench her arm away, but the sergeant-at-arms held fast...and then he led her back behind the bathhouse.

Holy hellfire, a lead stone dropped to the pit of her stomach.

He shoved open the damper. "I had my suspicions, but now I ken 'tis you."

She huffed out a sigh, thrusting her fists onto her hips, trying to appear unruffled. "Oh, please, I've only caused a wee bit of mischief."

"Och, lass, ye're no' fooling me. Who else would ken about the old tunnel? Hell, I didn't even know about it until Auley and the lads escaped. And I kent it was ye with the vinegar for certain." He tucked one of his thumbs into his belt. "Tell me, what happened to the missive? Did ye ken the Lord of Islay was coming to collect reinforcements?"

Rhona clapped a hand over her mouth. She might be able to withhold the truth from the king's men, but Bram was as good as kin. "Why should ye care if I've meddled or nay?"

"Jesu, lass. Do ye no' understand? Lorn's only hope to save the lordship and keep at least a portion of his lands is to admit his errors and yield to Robert the Bruce as king. And do no' try to tell me any different. Dunstaffnage is now owned by the Scottish crown, and we are beholden to whoever sits on the throne, as well as the man the king appoints to govern."

Feeling a bit faint, Rhona shifted her hand to her forehead. She'd told herself to stop interfering and now she'd been caught. "Will ye turn me in?"

"Good God, gel, ye are the closest thing I have to a daughter." Bram shook his finger beneath her nose.

"But let this be a warning to ye. I ken you have a good head on your shoulders. Stop this nonsense at once. Ye are capable of doing a great deal of good. Ye're a fine healer, and the townsfolk love ye."

She nodded. "I reckon ye're right. 'Tis time to mind my own affairs. Ye ken if it weren't for Gran, I would have boarded my granduncle's ship, sailed to England, and left this place behind me."

Bram pulled her into a fatherly embrace and cradled her head to his chest. "Nay, ye're a Highlander through to the bone. The only place ye'd be truly happy is here. The village of Dunstaffnage is your home. 'Tis my home, too, where it will always be."

ARTHUR STOOD BESIDE RHONA AS LADY MARY TOOK the oath, though the old woman did so as if she were about to blow steam out her ears. He had tried to allay doubt, but the fury that seemed to be roiling beneath Rhona's skin, coupled with the same unpleasantness from her grandmother, made prickles fire across his nape.

As the cleric tucked the psalter under his arm, Lady Mary eyed Arthur. "Where is the MacDonald scourge?"

Arthur frowned. Even if the woman was Lorn's sister, he didn't like anyone insulting a friend—and a brave soldier at that. Angus Og MacDonald had not only been instrumental in the Battle of Loudon Hill, he had harbored the king during a winter when he was pursued relentlessly by his enemies. Of course, Arthur was well aware of the centuries-old feud between the clans. "The *esteemed* Lord of Islay set sail this morn."

"Good. I'll sleep better this night knowing that man is not within my brother's keep."

"I beg your pardon, but your brother surrendered to

Robert the Bruce, and said keep is now the property of the crown."

Lady Mary snatched her embroidery. "Humph."

Arthur patted the cleric on the shoulder and dismissed him before turning to Rhona. "Would ye walk with me for a bit?"

She rubbed her shoulder and looked toward the hearth. As a matter of fact, she hadn't met his gaze the entire day. "I need to tend to the evening meal."

"I won't keep ye. Mayhap come with me whilst I fetch a bucket of water for your hearth...please."

Huffing, she grabbed the pail and headed for the door.

Arthur bowed to Lady Mary and followed Rhona out. The lass practically sprinted for the well, and he hastened his step to catch her. "I wanted to thank ye."

"For what?"

"As kin to Lorn, it mustn't have been easy to pledge your fealty this day."

"I suppose I didn't really have a choice, did I?"

"Ye always have a choice, lass. Though I would have been sorely disappointed had ye not come to the hall. But..."

She stopped beside the well and looked into the black abyss. "What is it ye want to say, sir?"

"I sense your displeasure."

"I haven't the convenience of being displeased."

"If that's true, then ye have an unusual way of showing it."

"Och, if ye must know, I do not appreciate being threatened and bullied into pledging an oath of fealty, and I doubt anyone within ten miles of Dunstaffnage would think any differently."

"Is that so? What would ye have me do? Stand on the battlements and invite every MacDougall in Argyll to skewer my heart with arrows?"

She put the bucket on the hook and dropped it into

the well with a resulting splash. "I'd have ye leave me be, that's what I'd have you do."

"You wound me." Arthur clutched at his chest as if she'd cut him. "Whatever has happened since we were last standing in this very spot together? In each other's arms, mind ye?"

"I-I was wrong. I must have lost my senses for a moment." She grappled for the rope, and he leaned in and pulled up the bucket. "I never should have gone hunting with ye."

"Did ye not find the afternoon enjoyable?"

"It doesn't matter."

"Why the hell not?" he barked, a bit more curtly than he ought to have done.

"Because too many things have happened since ye went away to St. Andrews. So much so, we cannot start anew. We are separated by an expanse wider than the Firth of Lorn."

"How can ye say that? In my heart, I truly believe destiny has brought us together at long last." He placed his hand on her shoulder, feeling her tense beneath his fingers. "I care deeply for ye, lass. Please do not push me away."

"I must," she whispered, still staring into the well.

He lowered his hand to his side. "Would ye do me the favor of looking me in the eyes and saying that?"

She pressed the heels of her hands against her temples and groaned before she faced him with an expression of utter torture. "You must understand, I cannot have feelings for ye."

"Ye cannot or will not?"

"Does it matter?"

"Aye, it does to me."

"I *cannot*." She grabbed the bucket's handle and started away. "Now please leave me be."

❧ 19 ❧

For the first time since he'd arrived at Dunstaffnage, Arthur did not follow his routine. He directed the sortie to ride off without him, giving the excuse that he must attend to the king's affairs. But the truth was, he just did not have the motivation to mount his horse and face the townsfolk and the crofters this day.

Until now, he'd been certain that he would be able to win Rhona's heart, but the woman had slayed him with her bitter tongue, insisting an insurmountable divide existed between them. Why was she so resistant? And he'd worked so diligently to crack through her hardened shell. She'd melted in his arms. Hell, she had been the one to initiate their last kiss. Even a dead man would have sensed the strength of her ardor.

Had the blasted request for fealty really set her off? For the love of God, he'd be no kind of man if he didn't take a stand. The bloody Lord of Islay had come with boats to take men to the north that Arthur had no idea had been requested. Perhaps Donal was right, he should have imprisoned the entire town until the culprit confessed.

Perhaps they were all in cahoots together, blast the lot of them.

He poured himself a dram of whisky and stared at

it. God's bones, it was too early to be in his cups, but damned if he didn't want a drink. He wanted to drown himself in the flagon and not wake for a fortnight.

A knock came at the door.

"I am occupied," he bellowed, taking the cup and tossing back the fiery brew.

"Forgive me sir," came Clyde's voice. "I thought ye might want to ken I've returned from the borders."

"Clyde?" Bloody hell, why did he not say so sooner? "Come in, ye hellion."

The old manservant cracked open the door. "Hellion, sir? If this is no' a good time..."

"Bring your arse in here and take a chair. Would ye join me in a dram?"

"But 'tis not yet noon, sir." The man looked to the flagon and licked his lips.

"Ye cannot tell me ye have never imbibed in spirit afore noon afore. I ken where ye've been, sir."

"Well, no' for some time, mind ye."

Arthur retrieved a cup from the sideboard, poured, and pushed it toward Clyde. "What news? God's stones, I hope it is good."

"Hmm," the manservant said, opting to take a sip.

"Well?"

"Most of the information I collected came from Carlisle."

Arthur slid into his chair and rubbed his palms together. "As was expected."

"Aye. The Lord of Lorn stayed at the castle for a time but has moved on to London."

"Not surprising. Did ye find Auley?"

"Not exactly, sir." Grunting, Clyde slid the cup aside. "I did, however, find an inn where he had stayed with his lads."

"And ye did not follow him?"

"Not to London, sir."

"Och, bloody London." Arthur knew full well following Lorn to the big English city would be an exercise in futility. "What else? Surely you must have something more."

"Well, a barmaid gave me a tidbit of information I reckoned ye'd find interesting." Clyde looked at the cup and licked his lips, then frowned. "I say, sir, the whisky is fine, but I no longer have a thirst for it."

"I understand, and do not feel as if ye must finish it. But come, man. What is this news?"

"Ah, yes," Clyde said, scratching his beard. "It seems Ricky, Auley's youngest, boasted to a serving wench that it was a wee crippled woman who helped his kin escape the deathly clutches of Robert the Bruce."

Arthur's stomach squelched. A sweat broke out across his skin. "My God."

"I seem to recall there was a lass who walked with a wee bit of a limp in the great hall when we first arrived. Was she not kin of the Lord of Lorn?"

Unable to look the man in the eye, Arthur gulped. "His grandniece. Her grandmother is His Lordship's sister." He could not bring himself to tell Clyde she was the lass he'd pined for when he was a squire.

"I see."

"And ye are sure of your source?" Arthur asked, praying he wasn't.

Clyde nodded. "As certain as I can be. After all, the wench told me the young fella had bragged about escaping from the Bruce, but I figured ye are the king's knight, and assigned to carry out Robert's bidding. And I'd reckon Ricky embellished the truth to impress the woman."

Fie.

Arthur sat rooted in his chair while boiling blood pulsed through his veins. For the love of all that was holy, he should have suspected Rhona from the outset. He had doubted her for certain, but he was too bloody blinded by his own ardor to see through her ruse. She had been seen nearby every time the damper had been closed. She had been in the brewhouse the day the ale and wine were laced with vinegar. Her grandmother might very well be the only person remaining in the village who was old enough to remember the tunnel—not to mention, Lady Mary had grown up within the castle walls.

He'd been so bloody daft. So bloody gullible. No wonder Rhona insisted there was an irreconcilable divide between them.

What had she done with his missive? And the messenger? Was the man still alive? God on the cross, had she sent Auley on the ambush? So blind with rage, he couldn't think straight. If she were involved with the ambush, then why did she not poison him when he was unconscious in her cottage? She had the means to do so, for certain.

"Are ye unwell, sir? Ye're looking awfully pale."

Arthur blinked. "I ken the lass. She and I were…" He still couldn't say it. "Who else kens it was Rhona?"

"No one, sir. I came straight here."

"Let us keep it that way for a time. At least until I've had an opportunity to confront the woman myself."

"Very well, sir."

Arthur pushed his chair away from the table and stood. "If you'll excuse me, I need some air."

UNABLE TO FORM A COHERENT THOUGHT, ARTHUR took his mount and rode into the hills. Except the heather reminded him of Rhona. The grouse flitting about the clearing in the forest reminded him of Rhona. Hell, the bloody outline of the fortress reminded him of Rhona.

He'd been elated to take this posting because he wasn't only going to be near his home, he'd be able to see her. And then when he'd discovered she'd been widowed, he was certain he had a chance to win the lass.

She'd kissed him. She'd turned to sweet cream butter in his arms. But all along, she'd been keeping secrets and conspiring against him. There was a divide between them. It was bloody greater than the Firth of Lorn. The expanse was as large as the endless sea.

He trusted her.

He loved her.

Worse, now he must act. By law, she was a traitor to the crown and that one fact ripped his heart out and cast it to the wolves. Aye, she was a MacDougall, but she was the first to know Lorn had surrendered. That meant his clan surrendered and the king had won. Did she not realize Robert the Bruce intended to bring freedom to all, to unite the kingdom, and to rid Scotland of tyranny?

But the woman did not back down. She did not accept her granduncle's fate. And she'd stabbed Arthur in the heart.

What was he do to with her? The thought of condemning the woman to the gallows made him wretch. Beautiful Rhona, gifted Rhona, the lass everyone looked to for healing. How could he preside over a trial and order the woman he loved to be burned at the stake? Or hanged by the neck until dead? Or tied to a post at low tide and drowned as the water rose?

The sun had traversed to the western sky by the time he returned to the castle and left his mount with the groom.

"Sir, I thought ye had decided to remain in for the day," said Donal as Arthur passed through the courtyard.

"I had a change of heart," Arthur replied, not ready to share the news. "Send the sergeant-at-arms to my solar. I need a word with him forthwith."

"Straightaway, sir."

When Bram's footsteps echoed from the stairwell, Arthur opened the door. "Ye'd better hasten your pace, soldier," he barked.

"Ye wanted to see me, sir?" asked the silver-haired guard as he stepped inside. Hell, if the man had any clue of what was coming, he was either the best player in Scotland, or he knew nothing.

Arthur banked on the player. He shut the door and crossed his arms, not taking a chair or offering one. "Tell me what ye ken of the tunnel."

"The tunnel to the prison, sir?"

Arthur threw out his palms and stared the man in the eyes. "Do ye ken of another?"

"Nay."

"Well? Did ye ken it was there?"

Bram scratched his beard. "I told ye true when I said Auley's escape was the first I'd learned of it."

Arthur crossed his arms. "Is that so?"

"Aye."

"And ye never suspected anything was behind those rusted old bars?"

By the furrow in the man's brow, he was utterly dumbstruck. "I thought it was a wall, just like everyone else."

Arthur paced, clasping his hands behind his back. "Ye were Lorn's man. Can ye honestly say ye haven't had thoughts of retribution since he surrendered the castle to the king?"

"Och, just yesterday I said it to Mistress Rhona, and I'll repeat it now...though I may be loyal to Clan Mac-Dougall, I am also a soldier, and I serve the master of this castle, where my bread is buttered. If that means I owe fealty to ye and to Robert the Bruce, then so be it."

"Not exactly the strongest declaration of loyalty I've ever heard, but I do believe ye speak true."

"Thank ye, sir. My word is my oath."

"As is mine." Arthur again paced. "What do ye ken of Mistress Rhona?"

"The healer, sir?" The sergeant-at-arms shifted his feet as his eyes widened. "The lass has always been dear to me. I do believe she was the Lord of Lorn's favorite."

"That stands to reason."

"Sir?"

"Come, you were the one who told me you left her alone in the brewhouse. She tampered with the wine and ale, did she not?"

Bram's face turned scarlet as he drew in an enormous breath. "Ah..."

"Tell me the truth, or I'll have ye flayed."

"Aye, sir. I believe she did."

"Only believe?"

"If ye must know, she's the one who has been closing the bathhouse damper." Bram's shoulders fell. "I caught her in the act only yesterday—made her promise no' to do it again."

"Fie!" Arthur cursed, slamming his fist against the wall. Though he knew it to be true, he desperately wanted Bram to assert her innocence.

Presently, the only two people who knew about Rhona's guilts were the sergeant-at-arms who used to be Lorn's man, and his manservant. "I'm sending you and Clyde to fetch the woman and bring her here."

"Shall I arrest her, sir?"

Dear God, he wanted to avoid a spectacle at least until he had a chance to speak to the woman and allow her to explain herself. He owed her that at least. "Tell Mistress Rhona she has been summoned and if she refuses, you may use whatever force is necessary to see that she is standing in this solar within the hour."

❧ 20 ❧

At the cottage, there had been something in Bram's expression that made Rhona uneasy and the feeling had only grown worse while they walked in silence. The last time Bram had summoned her on behalf of Sir Arthur, he'd been alone. This time he brought an old curmudgeon named Clyde, a man she didn't know, and the lout continued to leer at her as if she were Satan's bride.

As they strode through the courtyard, Donal stepped in front of Clyde and tipped up his chin. "Ye cannot fool me, old man."

"Mind your own affairs," Clyde growled, stepping around the lieutenant while exchanging glances with Bram. The two of them shared an unspoken exchange for certain, and whatever it was made the hairs on the back of her neck stand on end.

They directly cut through the great hall and into the stairwell of the donjon. Odd, this was the first time she didn't think of the enormous tower as being her grand-uncle's home.

When they arrived at the solar, Arthur stood with his back to them, his hands planted on the hearth's mantel, his head dropped forward.

"Mistress Rhona," Bram announced.

As she stepped into the chamber, the sergeant-at-arms started to close the door behind her.

"Clyde. Bram. Remain where you are," Arthur bellowed over his shoulder as if he were shouting orders from the battlements.

Rhona's back shot straight as a pike. "I insist ye tell me what this is about forthwith, sir."

The constable spun around, his eyes narrowed and honed on her, reflecting more malice than she'd ever imagined him capable.

Within a heartbeat, her flesh turned icy cold. *Oh, help. He knows.*

"Take a seat," the man seethed through straight white teeth.

She glanced at the other two. Both of them stood flush against the wall and neither of them met her gaze, not even Bram. Gulping, she slid into a chair, not because Arthur commanded her to do so, but if she remained standing, her knees just might buckle out from under her.

Folding her hands atop the table, Rhona stared at her fingers. *This is the end. My judgment day has come.*

"I see ye've met my manservant, Clyde."

"Manservant?" she asked. The fellow seemed more like a headsman.

"Among other things. He once served in the Order of St. John." Though Rhona didn't look directly at Arthur, she watched him pace out of the corner of her eye. "Did ye honestly believe I would sit idle whilst Auley and his ill-begotten sons made me out to look like a bloody fool?"

Rhona's knuckles turned white while Arthur's tone grew thunderous.

"Well, did ye?" he shouted, standing over her.

Unable to speak, she shook her head.

"God on the bloody cross, woman, ye have made a mockery of me."

"I-I didn't—"

"What's that? If ye have something to say, speak up."

"I did not intend for ye to look foolish. I only wanted to do what was right."

"And since when did ye become judge and jury of Argyll?"

Rhona said nothing while her mouth went dry.

"Do ye deny breaking into the king's gaol and setting Auley and his sons free? Do ye deny subverting justice to be delivered to the men who shot me with a crossbow bolt to the heart, intending to cause a mortal wound?"

When he put it thus, the ambush did sound rather awful. "But your injuries were not overly serious," she whispered in her defense, as well as Auley's.

"I cannot believe ye just said such a thing! Would you rather see me dead? What am I to do with ye? By rights, I should order ye to the gallows this very day." Arthur slammed his fist on the table beside Rhona, making her practically jump out of her skin. "Have ye no regard for me whatsoever?"

She shrank. Yes, she cared for him—too much so. But she had already told him they could never be together. And now he knew why.

"Do ye want to be labeled a traitor of Scotland?"

Rhona shook her head. Never in all her days had she thought of herself as a traitor. Every one of her actions had been out of loyalty.

Arthur slapped the hilt of the dirk attached to his belt. "Would it make ye happy if I pulled my dirk and plunged it into my own bleeding heart?"

"Nay," she croaked, barely able to make a sound.

"I cannot believe I was so utterly daft." He paced behind her. "When the king granted me the constableship of Dunstaffnage, I was elated because I'd be able to see ye. My gullible heart leapt simply by the mere fact

I'd be able to bid ye good day from time to time. And then when I discovered ye'd been widowed, I vowed to win your heart."

Arthur bent down, moving his lips close to her ear. "But ye have no bloody heart."

Rhona shut her eyes and cringed. He was right. Her heart was but a stone.

Arthur stood motionless for a time, hovering beside her while silence swelled, making the air so thick, Rhona's skin prickled with sweat. What should she say? An apology hardly seemed appropriate. If only he would pronounce her sentence and be done with it.

"Excuse me, sir, if I might be allowed to speak," said Bram, still standing against the wall beside Clyde.

The constable threw out his hands. "By all means."

"Ah…it may be a bit untoward…"

"Damnation! Out with it, man!"

Bram spread his palms to his sides. "Very well. Ever since you arrived at Dunstaffnage, I've had the occasion to observe ye pair, and I've reckoned ye are very well suited for one another."

"I beg your pardon?" asked Arthur, thrusting an accusing finger at Rhona. "It appears this woman did not only deceive *me*."

"Och," The sergeant-at-arms continued. "As far as the incident with Auley is concerned, I believe she did not try so much to be deceitful as to try to help a man who, up until the castle was claimed as a royal stronghold, had been a good servant, had lived a good life."

"So, what is your point?" asked Arthur, throwing out his hands.

"What I mean to say is, after watching ye, I ken the *fondness* isn't merely one-sided. And if I might be so bold as to add, when a woman marries, she joins her husband's clan."

Rhona clutched her hands over her heart. "Ye cannot be serious, Bram."

"Absolutely not," Arthur agreed.

"Tie her to the bloody stake and burn her!" echoed a voice from outside.

"Mercy!" a woman cried, sounding quite a lot like Sara.

"Her bloody grandmother is to blame!"

"Send them both to the stake!"

"Nay," yelled a man. "Mistress Rhona is the best healer in the Highlands. We need her."

"What the devil?" Arthur marched to the window and pulled back the fur, making the uproarious shouts from the courtyard all the louder. "There's a bloody mob out there."

The constable looked between the two men. "I thought I told ye to keep mum!"

"I did, sir," said Clyde. "But when we walked Mistress Rhona to the great hall, Donal stopped us...said something about not being able to fool him."

"Bloody hell!" Arthur cursed. "That man is a damned good soldier, but he has no clue as to when to hold his tongue."

"It was bound to come out sooner or later, sir," said Clyde as if the riot below were but a mere inconvenience.

"Well, we cannot allow this to grow any worse than it already has." Arthur grasped Rhona's elbow and tugged none to gently. "Come."

"What are ye going to do?" she asked, her voice shaking.

"The only thing I can do," he growled, pulling her into the corridor.

"Ye're hurting my arm," she said, trying not to stumble because he was walking so fast.

"Forgive me," he snapped, moving his grip to her hand and squeezing it every bit as tightly.

But Rhona hardly noticed the pain. He was dragging her to the courtyard to face her accusers. Most likely, she wouldn't see out this day. She wouldn't see another sunrise. She would never again feel the rain on her face or hold a newborn babe after toiling for hours alongside a mother in labor.

She had lived a good life and would be sorry for nothing.

"Silence!" Arthur hollered as he pulled her outside.

"Wheesht!" bellowed Donal, climbing the stairs and flailing his arms. "Wheesht!"

Arthur tugged her into the center of the crowd. "I do not ken what the lot of you think ye may know, but I hereby inform ye it is wrong. I've summoned Mistress Rhona here for one purpose only and that is—"

"To send her to the gallows!" shouted a soldier.

"Nay!" Arthur glared at the man, wrapping his arm around Rhona's shoulder and crushing her against his side.

She glanced up at his face. His eyes were ablaze with ire, his lips white. What the devil was he on about?

"Mistress Rhona and I are to be married!"

R hona sat at the high table in the great hall and stared at her trencher of food.

She was married.

Arthur had refused to allow her a mere day to grow accustomed to the idea, or even to don a clean gown. As soon as the announcement had been made, the priest was summoned and they'd proceeded directly from the courtyard to the chapel in the wood that very afternoon. There she'd taken her vows, standing in a kirtle, apron, and her old boots, without so much as a posy in her hands. To her astonishment, Arthur took a ring with a lovey pink stone out of his sporran and slid it onto her finger.

He'd also sent someone to fetch Gran, though as soon as the ceremony was over, the woman hadn't said a word of congratulations and insisted on returning to the cottage with a maid Arthur immediately appointed to see to her care.

Of course, the townsfolk had all borne witness to their vows. Now their voices echoed throughout the great hall in merriment while a hollow bubble stretched throughout Rhona's chest. She might be content with the turn of events if Arthur seemed even the slightest bit pleased, but he sat beside her as quiet as she, not touching his food. Though he'd had more than one tankard of ale. The man had taken a few nips from his flask as well. That he wasn't happy with the state of affairs was an understatement.

"Are ye no' hungry, m'lady?" asked a servant, filling her goblet with wine.

Rhona didn't respond until she realized the lad was speaking to her. Aye, she *had* married a knight, which meant she was no longer Mistress Rhona, but Lady Campbell. Bram and Arthur had referred to her thus as well but she hadn't given it a second thought at the time. "Ah...no. I don't seem to have an appetite this eve."

After giving him a forced smile, she took a sip of wine. As soon as the ruby liquid hit her stomach, it made her head swim. Perhaps she was hungry after all. Rhona stabbed a bit of mutton with her eating knife and clipped a bite with her teeth, though swallowing proved to be a chore. Perhaps she ought to stick with wine. After all, the numbing effects might be what she needed to survive this moment.

She sipped again and licked her lips, chancing a glance at Arthur. He hadn't moved aside from his elbow, bending as he mechanically shifted the tankard to and from his lips.

He was as numb as she for certain. Worse, he'd seen her actions as a personal affront to his honor—an embarrassment, yet he'd gone ahead and married her.

Why?

Why didn't he just send her to the gallows and have it done with?

But Rhona knew the reason. He loved her. At least he *had* loved her. But from his viewpoint, she'd shunned his love and made a mockery of it.

The servant had refilled her goblet when a fiddle began to play—one of the soldiers. The crowd cleared the floor, clapping their hands and urging the newly wedded couple to dance.

Rhona shook her head. "Oh no. There's no need."

Arthur, too, held up his palms. "The lot of ye enjoy yourselves."

Gregor dashed onto the dais and gave a quick bow. "I beg your pardon, sir, but me ma says no one is allowed to dance until the married couple has had their turn."

The knight rested his tankard on the board while the lad performed a wee jig. "Did ye no' tell me soldiers must ken how to dance with the lassies?"

"I did." Pursing his lips, Arthur pushed back his chair and stood, offering his hand to Rhona. "It seems we've no choice."

She placed her fingers in his palm. "I suppose we cannot disappoint Gregor, especially if he has been practicing."

"I have been, m'lady. Every day with me sister."

Rhona's world may have crumbled into a heap, but she wasn't about to disappoint Gregor. After all, he was a MacDougall, and that made him as close as kin.

Arthur escorted her down the dais steps and inclined his lips to her ear. "Please try to appear as if ye are not about to be led to your doom this night."

"Why, I do believe those are the first words ye've spoken to me since we took our vows." She smiled serenely. "I will play my part if ye play yours."

"An easy country dance, not a reel," Arthur said to the fiddler.

Though Rhona was relieved not to be skipping about in her old boots with the worn leather, the fiddler seemed to take Arthur's directive to heart and chose a tune with sad tones, sounding far more like a funeral march than a wedding celebration. But it mattered not. Together, the miserable couple plodded through the dance without looking at each other. Well, Rhona didn't dare glance up at Arthur's eyes, so she didn't have any idea if he'd bothered to look at her or not.

As the fiddler drew out the final note, Rhona sighed and dipped into a curtsey. At least that was over. Now the others were free to make merry.

Except they were all clapping their hands and crowding her and Arthur.

"'Tis time to go above stairs!" shouted Master Tailor. He might be the village's self-appointed caller, but Rhona was fairly certain, he had presently exceeded the limits of his responsibilities.

Mortified, she shot a panicked glance at Arthur. "I don't believe I've enjoyed enough of your fine company."

"Och," exclaimed Donal, clapping Arthur on the shoulder. "The men and I made certain your chamber is right prepared for your wedding night, sir. Ye'd best go on above stairs."

Were they all colluding together? Rhona looked to the smiling, expectant faces as the crowd urged them toward the entry to the donjon.

Good Lord, until this moment, she'd almost assumed she'd be spending the night below the tower, locked in a cell. Or perhaps sent back to the cottage where she could crawl into bed with Gran.

Aye, Rhona had spent a year married to Ivor. She knew exactly what to expect, and the deed had never been terribly enjoyable. She'd felt inklings of pleasure now and again, but Ivor had always been so fast, she'd barely had a chance to...well...prepare herself.

Though Rhona felt relieved not to be sleeping below in her gaol cell or back with Gran, the idea of stripping to her shift and lying beneath Arthur—

AS THEY CLIMBED ABOVE STAIRS, THE TORCHES HAD been lit in the wall sconces. Arthur shouldn't have found this unusual because the servants always lit the torches at dusk, but presently the route to his bedchamber seemed brighter, and not in a brighter-happier way. Rather, it was too bloody bright. In the hall he'd done his best to feign good cheer, else Donal and the others would ken what had truly transpired in his solar.

Indeed, Arthur had done his best to make it appear to the men that he had summoned Rhona to the castle to propose marriage. Not only that, he wanted them to believe his heart was so full of love, waiting a moment longer to marry the lass would have been impossible.

Rhona followed closely behind as he passed the floor to his solar and continued upward. Every night since he'd arrived, he dreamed about the day when he brought her to his bedchamber as his wife. But now he felt as if she'd cut open his chest and ripped out his heart. Aye, he'd just married a woman he'd been madly in love with, but who didn't give a rat's arse about him, and that changed everything.

Dear God, his feet felt as if they were weighed down by five-stone bricks as he climbed each step. The progress was torture. And it wasn't as if he'd married a virgin. Rhona knew full well what to expect on her wedding night and, by the way she'd stared at her trencher throughout the meal, she wasn't thrilled about the prospect. If only he could drown himself in a vat of ale.

He stepped out into the passageway and pushed open the door. "Have ye been in the lord and lady's chamber afore?"

"Nay," she said, moving inside before she stopped and drew a hand over her mouth.

The entire chamber had been lit with dozens of candles everywhere. And near the hearth was a table and two chairs that hadn't been there when he'd left this morn. Atop it was a feast with two goblets, a flagon of wine, stewed apples, bread, small slices of cheese, grapes, and Lord knew what else.

"It seems Cook worked faster than ever before."

"He did well to feed the lot of us."

"I told him to clean out the larder and serve whatever he could manage at such short notice."

"I'll wager he wasn't happy."

"Didn't seem to be at the time, though he must have forgiven me." The door closed behind Arthur. He didn't make any move to walk farther inside, for every moment in this woman's presence was torture. "I shall send for your things on the morrow."

She nodded and rubbed the back of her neck.

"And you'll need a lady's maid."

"Och, I've done for myself and Gran for years. I can manage."

"I beg to differ. Ye are now Lady Campbell, and you will have a lady's maid."

The corners of her mouth tightened. Did she not realize things would be a great deal easier for her now that they had been wed? "And my work?" she asked.

He tried to smile. "There's no need. I shall provide for you." This is what he'd wanted all of his life. If only he could feel anything other than remorse.

"I beg to differ," she argued, those pale blue eyes flashing with ire. "I'm the only healer for miles. The clansmen and women rely on me."

The last thing Arthur wanted to do was argue. Aye, he knew she was needed, but he hadn't thought about it, or much of anything beyond keeping her neck out of a noose. "I'm certain there are many things we must discuss."

"Aye," she clipped.

"Well, then..." He looked to the table and heaved a sigh. "Until the morrow, m'lady."

With that, he gave a stilted bow and stepped out the door. Except, he hadn't thought about where he might go. The hums of laughter wafted up through the stairwell. Hell, if he went anywhere this night, someone would see him. And then they'd know something was amiss. He paced for a time. Damnation, he wasn't about to go back into his chamber.

What was she doing now?

Blowing out all the candles?

Using his comb to brush out her silken white tresses?

Removing her kirtle?

He placed his palm against the door and listened until he heard a woeful sob that twisted around his heart like a tourniquet.

She's crying.

❧ 22 ❧

Rhona's eyes flashed open when someone slipped into the chamber. She peered through the dim room while a woman made her way to the hearth and stirred the fire before lighting a candle.

"Gillie, is that you?" she asked, rubbing her eyes. She'd known the cobbler's daughter most of her life.

"Aye, m'lady. Good morn."

Rhona sat up and looked toward the window, but since it was covered with a fur, no daylight shone inside. "What is the hour?"

"'Tis mid-morn."

Truly? Rhona never slept late, but then again, it had been nearly dawn when she'd finally drifted off. It was amazing she'd slept at all, after the day she'd had.

She pushed the hair away from her face. "What are ye doing here?"

Gillie was about four years younger, and usually helped her father in his shop. "I'm your new lady's maid."

"Oh, please. I do not need a maid."

"But ye're a lady now. Of course ye need a maid." The lass held up a shiny new pair of boots. "I brought these for you and I'm to tell ye the men have been sent to the cottage to collect your things."

"Already?" Rhona asked, swinging her legs over the side of the bed and stretching. At least the feather mattress in the enormous four-poster had been far more comfortable than the lumpy old bed she shared with Gran.

Gillie gestured to the table where the food from last eve had been replaced with a steaming bowl of oats. Evidently, the lass hadn't been the first to enter the bedchamber. "Ye'd best break your fast. Sir Arthur wants to see ye in his solar straightaway."

Realizing she was famished, Rhona moved to the table and picked up the spoon.

"Isn't it romantic?" The lass pulled a boar's-hair brush from a basket. "The constable could no' even wait for ye to change your kirtle afore he took his marriage vows."

Rhona shoveled the oats in her mouth as fast as she could swallow. If only she could tell Gillie exactly how unromantic their race to the altar had been. And how pathetic their first night of wedded bliss.

Where had Arthur slept?

To be honest, she didn't care. At least, that's what she told herself as she went through the motions of donning the apron and kirtle she'd worn the day before with Gillie's unneeded help. Though Rhona would have preferred to set out on her rounds with her medicine bundle, her *meddlesome* new maid walked with her to the solar and left Rhona standing outside the door where she hesitated before she knocked.

"Come," barked Arthur. Evidently his mood hadn't improved since last eve.

"Good morn," she managed rather flatly as she popped her head inside.

"Is it?" he asked, gesturing to a chair. His hair, though usually tidy, looked as if it hadn't been combed and the dark shadows beneath his eyes were a testament to lack of sleep. "I trust you are happy with Gillie."

"Aye, if you feel a lady's maid is necessary."

"I do." He ran his fingers around the bronze brooch at his shoulder. "Ye ken ye are part of Clan Campbell now."

She nodded.

"That said, I cannot allow ye to leave the fortress without a guard. I've assigned Clyde to the task, and I'll say he—"

Rhona's spine shot straight. "I beg your pardon? I have always been able to come and go."

"That may well be, but it is no longer safe."

"But nary a soul would dare lift a finger to harm me...unless..." Her heart squeezed. "Unless ye no longer trust me."

The shift of Arthur's eyes revealed the truth. "First of all, we are in the midst of war, and as the wife of one of the king's knights, there is a need to be cautious. On the topic of trust, I believe it goes without saying, we have established no precedent for the basis of trust."

Rhona wanted to scream. Never in all her days had she been deceitful. At least not until Arthur Campbell returned to Argyll, and then she'd only done what she felt was right. She clenched her fists beneath the table.

"As I was saying, I have appointed Clyde to be your personal guard."

"Clyde?" she scoffed. "He's older than the hills. Should I be abducted, do you honestly believe he'd provide any protection whatsoever?"

"The man is far more capable than you might imagine. I trust him with my life."

Rhona pushed back the chair and stood. "Well then, I hope he is prepared to leave anon, because I not only need to oversee the collection of my things from the cottage, there are clansmen and women who need healing."

A knock came at the door while Arthur smiled. "Och, that would be Clyde now."

FULLY AWARE THAT THE COBBLER'S DAUGHTER WAS renowned for being a gossip, after three days, Arthur decided to pay his bedchamber a visit to ensure rumors didn't start. He tapped on the door before popping his head inside, finding the lady's maid brushing Rhona's tresses. "Forgive me, I didn't realize Gillie was still within." It was a small fib, but necessary for his ruse.

"I was just finishing," said the maid, placing the brush on the table.

Arthur clasped his hands behind his back and rocked onto his heels while Gillie finished. By the stars, his wife's hair was stunning, as if it were kissed by a snow fairy. It was longer than he remembered, hanging past her buttocks. He arrested a low growl in his throat. Aye, he'd like to sink his fingers into her wee bottom, but, on the other hand, he had made a pledge to himself not to act on his carnal urges until she gave some indication of an interest on her part.

"Is there anything else ye'll be needing, m'lady?" Gillie asked.

From her perch on the stool, Rhona glanced back to Arthur as if she were surprised to see him. "Nay, thank ye. Have a good night."

Arthur forced a smile while the maid took her leave and his wife stood and faced him. "Ah...is all well?" she asked.

Not really. Nothing had been well since Clyde returned from the borders. And it didn't help matters that Arthur had a stiff neck from sleeping on the floor —or not sleeping. The only thing bothering him more than the pain in his neck was lack of sleep. "Aye," he replied.

Rhona glanced to the door. "Um, I...ah." She tapped her lips with her fingers.

"Is there something on your mind?" Lord knew there was plenty on his mind.

He glanced to the bed.

Longingly.

She followed his gaze. "Is there somewhere else ye would prefer me to sleep?"

"Why would ye ask such a thing?"

"Ah...um..." There she went again, wanting to say something, but either unwilling or unable to form the words.

"Hmm?" he urged.

"Clearly ye haven't had a decent night's sleep since our wedding day. And I assumed..."

He arched his eyebrows. "Go on."

"Ye might want to sleep in *your* bed."

God strike him dead, the enormous four-poster looked damned inviting. Arthur licked his lips and waited. If only she would say something to make him feel wanted. But she just stood there, wringing her hands, a blush filling her cheeks as if she were a maiden who'd never been alone in a bedchamber with a man before.

He sauntered to the door, opened it and peered into the passageway. Fortunately, Gillie was long gone. Before he stepped out, he bowed to his wife. "Sleep well."

"But—"

He didn't wait to hear her objection. Besides, the wounds were too raw. In fact, the wounds might never heal.

Arthur slid down the wall, released the brechan from his shoulder, and bunched it up to make a pillow. Why he'd spent three sleepless nights in a row, he had no idea. He was a soldier and a squire before that. He'd slept in far more uncomfortable places than the corridor floor of this donjon. Hell, fighting this blessed war he'd slept in a rocky trench in the rain for an entire sennight.

Sleep did come this night, though it was interrupted all to soon when something kicked him in the spine and flopped across him with a clatter.

"Ow!" Rhona said, grappling for a candlestick and candle. "What are you doing out here?"

He rubbed his back. "I was sleeping."

She scooted away, looking at the wick as if she expected its flame to flicker back to life. "I can see that, but why?"

Somehow all the reasons he arrested on the tip of his tongue seemed deficient...mayhap a tad pitiful. "The question is, are ye hurt?" he asked.

She blew on the palm of her hand. "Not terribly."

"Where are ye off to?" he asked, praying she wasn't trying to sneak out of the castle in some mad plot against him.

She shoved the candle into the holder. "I was hoping to slip into the kitchens for a wee bite to eat. I didn't care overmuch for this evening's mutton, and now I'm a wee bit hungry."

Arthur let out a long breath, now noticing she was wearing a robe cinched around her waist. He took the candle and lit it from a wall sconce, then offered his elbow. "Come, let us go see what we might find."

Because many of the men slept in the great hall, to avoid their scrutiny, Arthur led her down to the cellars and then up into the kitchens. He set the candle on the board and turned full circle. In truth, he'd steered clear of the kitchens since his arrival. "I didn't realize this chamber was so large."

Rhona chuckled, lifting lids on jars. "It has to be big to feed all the soldiers ye have milling about." She opened a wooden box, making the hinges squeak. "Here we are."

"A bit of bread?"

She set the loaf on the table, found the butter and a pot of honey, then took a seat and gestured to the bench across. "I think this will do."

Arthur spotted a jug, picked it up and sniffed. "Would ye care for a spot of milk?"

"Is it fresh?"

He poured a bit into a cup and sipped. "Aye, and creamy."

"Sounds delicious," she said, buttering the bread.

After grabbing another cup, he slid into the seat and poured for them both. "Ye look comfortable with a knife in your hand."

She set it aside and drizzled honey over the treat. "Why would I not be? I've been laboring over a hearth ever since I moved in with Gran."

"Interesting that."

"Why?" she asked, pushing a plate across the table.

Arthur picked up his bread and took a bite. "Well, first of all, she's the daughter of a lord, and secondly, she married a knight. I'm surprised she did not retain any servants. What happened after her husband passed? Did her children not provide for her?"

"The wars claimed both her sons." Rhona shrugged, tucking a lock of hair behind her ear. "What coin she has, she wanted to keep, and I'm perfectly able to run the cottage—or *was*."

"So independent, are ye not?"

"Mayhap. But I like to think I'm practical."

"Still, it is an interesting point of view coming from the daughter of a knight. Ye grew up with servants."

"Aye, but my mother saw to it I learned to cook. And Gran saw to it I learned the healing arts."

"Indeed."

"Are you of the opinion that now that I am the wife of a knight, I should spend my days embroidering?"

"Nay."

"But ye brought in Gillie to be my lady's maid."

"Aye, but that's different." He licked his lips and took a sip of milk. "Mm, I say, milk goes very well with honey and bread."

"I'm glad ye like it."

"Truly?" he asked, suddenly not interested in the food. He studied her face for a moment, wishing things were different between them.

Rhona smiled, the flickering candlelight turning her skin golden.

Making Arthur's breath catch.

By the stars, no matter what she may have done, he could gaze upon her for days and never grow bored.

"What is it?" she asked.

"Hm?"

"Ye're looking at me with an odd stare." She wiped a hand back and forth across her mouth. "Do I have milk above my lip?"

"Nay."

Rhona leaned forward, almost close enough for him to kiss her. "I ken..." Rocking back, she swatted her hand through the air. "Never mind."

"Oh, no. No, no, no." Arthur shook his finger. "I reckon 'tis time we start finishing our sentences."

She took in a deep breath and huffed. "Very well. I ken ye are angry with me. Ye may never deign to forgive me. But—"

"Och, lass—"

"I beg your pardon! If ye want me to finish my sentence, then ye must not interrupt."

Arthur clamped his lips together and gave her a nod.

"We are married. I am living in your bedchamber, and ye are sleeping on the floor in the passageway, which cannot be comfortable."

When he opened his mouth to speak, she held up her palm and shook her head. "Ah, ah, ah."

Arthur drew an imaginary line across his lips.

"The bed is plenty large enough for the two of us to

sleep. Ye may not want to consummate our marriage, but if it is appearances ye want to keep up, which I assume it is, then I reckon ye ought to sleep on your side. I'll stick to mine. Moreover, those dark circles beneath your eyes might just go away."

This time when Arthur opened his mouth, he was at a loss for words.

Had she just extended an olive branch?

If so, how the devil was he supposed to lie in the same bed with the only woman he'd ever loved, the woman he'd dreamed about ever since his eighteenth summer, and actually sleep?

❧ 23 ❧

W hen Rhona awoke, she slid her hand across the bed linens just as she had done every morning for the past sennight. Again, Arthur's spot was cold. When had he slipped out, and why did she never wake?

Thus far, it had been quieter living with the knight than it ever had been living with Gran. Since the night when they'd fancied a snack in the kitchens, he had agreed to sleep in the bedchamber, but he often came in very late and was never there when Rhona awoke. All in all, in the past week, they'd hardly seen each other.

There had been no kissing, no touching, and very little talking. Aside from their jaunt for their late-night snack, when Arthur had engaged in conversation almost normally, he acted as if she wasn't there for the most part. And Rhona didn't care to be ignored in the least. She didn't care to be in a loveless marriage either.

Once she'd eaten and dressed, she collected her medicine basket and headed for the gates. Predictably, Clyde fell in step beside her. "Good morn, m'lady."

"Is it?" she asked.

The man chuckled. "Any day is good when my belly is full and there are no battles to fight."

Rhona couldn't fault him for his positive outlook. Perhaps she ought to give it a try. After all, Arthur had chosen to marry her rather than send her to the gallows. Though being his wife was a bit lonely, he hadn't mistreated her.

"Where to today?" asked Clyde as they strode through the gateway.

"I need to check on little Benny's cough and call in to see Sara, of course. Then I'd best stop by Gran's cottage."

"Brave one ye are to take her vinegar."

"Och, she's not all that bad."

"So say you."

Rhona stopped on the bridge over the moat where, to the right, lay the Firth of Lorn and, to the left, the waters of Loch Etive lapped the shore. The sun flickered silver on the waves of the loch, reminding her of the wee boat trip she and Arthur had taken during the fete. He had found the avens plants, which had yielded enough salve and tincture to last the winter.

Beside her, Clyde leaned forward and rested his elbows atop the stone wall. "Ye look deep in thought, m'lady."

"Hmm." She glanced his way. There were so many unanswered questions about what Arthur had been up to after he'd left for St. Andrews. Aye, he'd gone off to be trained as a knight, but he'd changed a great deal in his time away as well. "How did ye meet Sir Arthur?"

"Ye might say he pulled me out of the gutter."

"He?" By the way Arthur had explained it, she would have thought their meeting would have started the other way around. "But was he not a lowly squire at the time?"

"Squire, aye. Lowly, never."

"Ye ken what I mean. Tell me more. What happened and why were ye in the gutter?"

The old fellow drummed his fingers on the masonry. "I'm not proud of it, mind ye, but after returning from crusade, I lost myself in a barrel of whisky. Turned into a right drunkard, I did."

"Such a shame. I understand war can ruin a man." Rhona crossed to the other side of the bridge and gazed out to the Firth of Lorn, where a fishing boat lazily drifted from where it was moored in the distance. "How did ye overcome it?"

"Sir Arthur literally pulled me out of the mud, sobered me up, and refused to allow me to drink another drop of spirit."

"When he was but a squire? And ye obeyed him?"

"Let us just say, he made it impossible for me to drink," the old man chuckled. "I tried, but as time passed, my head cleared, and thanks to him, I discovered a new purpose."

She regarded him over her shoulder. "Which was?"

"The lad, of course. He was bent on earning his knighthood, and about as skilled with a sword as...as your grandmother."

"So ye took him under your wing?"

"More or less...taught him how to survive in a world of cutthroats and knaves. Sir Arthur saved my life and for that I will serve him until the day I die."

She started off and beckoned him. "He's fortunate to have ye."

"He's a good man."

Her throat thickened. Aye, she believed her husband to have a good heart, but she had no idea how to win it. "Have ye been knighted?"

Clyde shrugged. "They took away my spurs when I fell into the bottle."

"Can they do that?" she asked, skirting around a puddle.

"Aye, the Order can do anything they please."

"Have ye ever been married?"

"My word, ye ask a great many questions."

"Have ye?"

231

"Nay."

Arriving at the first cottage on her list, Rhona knocked, not happy at the coughing coming from within.

Benny's mother opened the door. "Och, Rhona, I'm glad to see ye."

She stepped inside while Clyde followed. "How is the lad?"

"Ready..." The little boy coughed twice. "To rise from this bed and play with my puppy."

"I'll wager you'll take very good care of him, too." Rhona moved to the bedside and placed her palm on his forehead. "Hmm. Ye're not as warm today. 'Tis a good sign."

"But he's been coughing a great deal," said his mother.

Benny pointed toward the hearth. "That's on account of the smoke from the fire."

Rhona checked for swelling under the jaw and along the throat and found none. "Are ye giving him the feverfew tincture thrice per day as I instructed?"

"Aye, m'lady."

"And it tastes awful," said Benny, sticking out his tongue.

"I'll tell ye what." Rhona mussed the boy's hair. "Come morn, if your forehead is still cool to the touch, I'll let ye venture outside, cough or nay."

The lad's eyes widened. "I can?"

"Do ye really think it is wise?" asked his mother.

Rhona stood, but continued to look at Benny. "Ye may go out as long as ye promise not to overdo, which means no running. Ye can throw a stick for your puppy, but no dashing after him. Can ye do that for me?"

"Aye. I'll do anything."

"Good, then take your tincture without complaint." Rhona turned to the worried parent. "Watch him and see if being in the fresh air helps. He may have a point with the smoke. Some wee ones are more sensitive to it than others, especially when recovering from the croup."

"And what do I do if he grows worse?"

"Send for me, of course. And make certain ye give him willow bark tea straightaway if his fever returns." She patted the woman's arm. "And do not worry. 'Tis a very good thing his fever is down and I reckon the cough will improve given time as well."

Benny's mom walked Rhona to the door where Clyde waited, standing as still as a statue. "His cough has been ever so worrisome, I do no' ken what I would have done without ye."

"I do what I can, but as I always say, our health is in the good Lord's hands. We oft don't know what brings on a bout of the croup like Benny's. We can only treat it with the remedies we have available and pray for the best."

Together, Rhona and Clyde made their way through the village. "Ye're a very good healer," he said.

Rhona shrugged. "I try, though it is frustrating not to be able to do more."

"Mayhap, but ye also have a way with people. The lad might just improve because ye gave him leave to do what he wants. Ye gave him a wee bit of hope and playing with a puppy will make him feel better as well."

If only puppies cured all of her patients. "And what if it doesn't?"

"I'll wager it will." Clyde grasped her elbow and led her around a pile of horse droppings. "As do you, m'lady."

"Aye," she agreed. In truth, that had been her strategy. There was nothing like a bit of hope to improve one's spirits, no matter what their age. But that's not what was on her mind at the moment. "Earlier, ye told me about how Arthur pulled ye out of the gutter, and then ye became his mentor."

Clyde frowned. "I suppose that was the way of it."

"What was my husband like back then?"

"I'd reckon ye'd ken as well as anyone."

She stopped and looked the man in the eye. "Why?"

The old guard leaned in and pointed at her heart. "He never stopped talking about ye. At least until..."

"Until?"

"He received word from his brother that ye had wed." Groaning, Clyde looked to the skies. "Good Lord, I reckon I was the one preventing him from losing himself in the bottle at the time. Och, those were dark days, for certain."

There was something about knowing Arthur had pined for her that warmed Rhona's heart. She'd pined for him a great deal as well. "What pulled him out of it? After all, he became a knight, as well as a favored soldier of Robert the Bruce."

"The discipline."

"Discipline?"

Clyde offered his elbow as they continued on toward Sara's cottage. "An education at St. Andrews is very demanding, even if your spirits are low. Arthur was pushed at every turn. Aye, he was crushed by the news of your marriage, but after he finished feeling sorry for himself, he did the only thing he could have done."

"Which was?" she asked.

"Excel. At *everything*. The man became a beast, training day and night, and nary a soul could best him."

Rhona couldn't disagree with Clyde. Arthur had become a formidable man in his own right and she admired him for it. "And I'll wager ye had something to do with that."

"Mayhap. But Arthur found it within his soul to rise above and persevere. Not every man is capable of such a transformation."

"Nay..." she mused, thinking of the many patients she'd

cared for, who, unlike Benny, felt sorry for themselves and ended up succumbing to ailments they might have overcome if they had decided to endure and conquer.

They visited Sara who was irritable and ready for her bairn to be born. From there, they went on to visit Gran, who seemed to be perfectly happy with her new housemaid and didn't appear to miss Rhona at all.

"She never chides me about venturing outside without my cane," the old lady said, while the maid emphatically shook her head.

Rhona played along, saying she reckoned Gran's hip was improving, though she knew full well it was not. When they left the cottage, dark grey clouds swirled in the sky and a gale whipped the waters into white-capped waves. As she and Clyde hastened to the castle, the heavens opened with a torrential downpour and, by the time they stepped inside, she was soaked to the bone.

DRIPPING WET AND CLENCHING HIS TEETH TO KEEP them from chattering, Arthur marched across the great hall as he headed for the donjon.

"A messenger has arrived with a missive from the king," said Bram, falling in step beside him and thrusting the letter into his hands.

Arthur examined the seal and looked toward the stairs. He ought to take this to his solar, but he was too bloody cold. Instead, he put his back to the wall so no one could peer over his shoulder, slid his finger under the wax, opened the missive, and read.

The news made him smile so wide, his lip split. "This is a day for celebration."

"Aye, sir?" asked Bram.

Arthur clapped the sergeant-at-arms on the shoulder. "The king has taken Urquhart Castle. At last, he has the Highlands fully under his banner."

"That is good news, indeed."

"Open a cask of whisky for the men and see to it they drink to the king's success." He started off but stopped. "Please inform Clyde that I need a bath."

"Straightaway, sir."

Buoyed by the news, Arthur took two steps at a time as he hastened above stairs. As he walked, he pulled off his brooch and let his brechan fall away from his shoulder. He untied the laces of his shirt and pulled it over his head while water dripped onto the floor along the way.

Whistling a ditty, he opened the door to his bed-chamber. But that's as far as he managed to go. Stopping frozen in his tracks, it was all he could do to keep his knees from buckling beneath him.

"Ack!" Rhona squeaked, crossing her arms and dipping lower into the water of the large tub.

Arthur managed to blink. "Ah...forgive me." He stared for a moment longer before his mind started working. "I didn't realize ye were bathing. I'll take my leave."

He shuffled backwards, but before he was out the door, Rhona lowered her arms and sat straighter. "Wait."

Lord strike him dead, the woman's breasts posed a vision like nothing he'd ever before seen. Arthur's mouth grew dry. Any cold he may have felt was completely replaced by hot, burning desire. He took one giant step into the chamber and let the door whoosh closed behind him.

"I'm wet," he blurted like a simpleton.

"I can see that." She cupped a handful of water and let it trickle from her palm. "I, too, was caught in the storm."

"Aye?" he asked, his voice gravelly. The past several

nights, sleeping beside her had been pure torture. He wanted, needed, craved Rhona from the depths of his soul. Hell, gazing upon her bare flesh was enough to make him forget why he'd stayed away in the first place.

Does she want me?

She gestured beside her. "This is an awfully large basin."

Arthur nodded. She wasn't wrong. The Lord of Lorn could have entertained a harem in it.

"And the water is warm," she added with a half-lidded gaze.

He gulped. "Is it?"

"Why not join me?"

It took but a flick of his fingers to release his belt, sending his brechan to the floorboards.

The lass's mouth fell open as her gaze trailed from his face, to his abdominals, to his erect member. Arthur knew he had a reason for his abstinence, but at the moment, he couldn't form a coherent thought.

He stepped into the tub and slid downward with a sigh. "Och, that warms the bones."

Rhona blushed, as if she'd suddenly gone bashful. "Clyde told me about how ye pulled him out of the gutter."

"Oh?"

"Aye."

"What else did the old fellow say?" Arthur asked, tucking a lock of her hair behind her ear.

"He mentioned ye turned into a curmudgeon after I, um...married Ivor."

The mention of her former husband caused his gut to twist, but only a little. "The news was a devastating blow. Beforehand, I always dreamed of the day I would return and marry ye."

"Ye may have married me. However..." Rhona scooped a handful of water into her hand and let it dribble back to the bath. "I'll wager our wedding was nothing like ye dreamed."

Arthur didn't really care if the wedding had been grand or not, but he desperately wanted his bride to love him. "Nay."

"Ye ken, I had no choice but to marry Ivor."

Arthur nodded.

"Not only was I of marriageable age, ye were gone without a word, and since Lorn was my guardian, he granted my hand to..."

Grasping Rhona's fingers, Arthur drew them to his lips and kissed. "None of that matters now."

"Doesn't it? I felt ye needed to be aware—ye ken I did not receive your missive."

"Aye." He trailed kisses up her arm. But there was one thing he needed to say before he allowed himself to go further and act upon the desire burning like a raging brush fire on the inside. "I received a wee bit of news afore I came up."

She met his gaze and raised her brow in question.

"The Bruce has taken Urquhart."

"Oh my." Rhona traced a finger down the center of his chest. "The Highlands are well and truly under his control."

"They are," he croaked, gooseflesh rising beneath her touch.

She stilled her hand, her expression resolute. "Then my granduncle will have no choice but to join him now."

Arthur's heart took to flight. Almost. He had one more question. "How does that make ye feel?"

"Mayhap a wee bit foolish. But more than anything, I am relieved to hear it."

He narrowed his gaze. "Truly?"

"Arthur, ye must know I've always cared deeply for ye, but I had a duty to clan and kin. If Lorn joins Robert, then the feud is over."

Her words touched him and made him think. What would he have done if the roles had been reversed?

In one move, Rhona straddled him, slid her arms around his shoulders, and nuzzled into his neck. "'Tis time we agreed to an accord of our own, husband."

❧ 24 ❧

R hona may have never seduced a man before, but she had enough experience in the marriage bed to know how to please one. Except at the moment, she wasn't even in a bed and she had brazenly thrown her leg across her husband's lap and sealed her lips atop his. By Arthur's guttural moan, he told her that he liked what she was doing. Her body was afire, the intense yearning in her nether parts consuming her like nothing she'd ever experienced.

For the first time in her life, she released her inhibitions and rubbed her cleft along his member. His very long, very hard member.

"If ye keep doing that, I'll spill."

"Would that be such a bad thing?" she asked, swirling her hips.

He nibbled her neck. "Aye. I want our first joining to be something ye'll never forget. Something shatteringly good."

"Good for the woman?" She rubbed again, the intensity of the need inside her growing. "I've never heard of such a thing."

Arthur pulled his head back and looked her in the eye. "Do not tell me ye have never come."

"Come?"

"Ye ken, come to completion with your insides quivering." He moved his fingers between her legs and stroked the exact place where she needed him, making her gasp. Ivor had never stroked her there. "Here, and..." Sliding his finger inside her, he swirled it. "And a violent quivering of the walls. Right. Here."

A shiver coursed throughout her body. "I-I do not think I have."

He brushed his lips along her neck, bringing on a shiver. "Well, that must be remedied."

With his words, he cupped his hands on her bottom and stood, the water whooshing from their bare skin and splashing back into the tub.

"What are ye doing?" she asked, clinging to him.

"Something I should have tended to on our wedding night," he said, grabbing the drying cloths as he carried her to the bed.

Arthur dried her back before he laid her down. Rhona watched as he dried himself with languid strokes, across his arms, his chest...his member. Heaven help her, she wanted her hands upon him.

"Do ye like to see me naked, wife?" he asked as he gently swirled the cloth across her chest and around her breasts. In truth, she'd never seen Ivor naked, not really, nor had she so wantonly allowed him to touch her as Arthur was doing now in full candlelight.

She again raked her gaze down his body. "Aye," she replied, feeling no inhibitions whatsoever—as she'd done before. In fact, this intimacy with Arthur could not be compared to anything from her past. As the realization dawned, she resolved only to think of this man and to do everything in her power to please him.

"Are ye cold?"

Though gooseflesh rose across her skin, the last thing on Rhona's mind was the chilly air.

Arthur made quick work of wiping away the remaining water droplets, then climbed beside her, his lips fusing with hers while Rhona's hands slid to his back, stopping when she felt a puckered scar. "What happened here?"

"'Tis nothing," he growled.

"Did your mail not protect you from such a blow?"

"Armor may save a man's life, but it doesn't mean he won't be injured in battle."

Rhona traced her finger along the jagged line. She'd seen enough scars to know this wasn't a trifling injury. "What happened?"

"'Twas during the Battle of Turnberry. I was fighting two at once. A third flanked me. Thanks to the Black Douglas, the third hadn't a chance to best me."

She shuddered. "How awful, the wars."

He smoothed his knuckle over her cheek and grasped a lock of hair. Raising it to his nose, he inhaled and closed his eyes. "Awful, aye. But right now, I'm not thinking about awful. I'm thinking about kissing you."

Rhona arched up and kissed him while he climbed between her legs, coaxing her back down to the bed. His lips worked magic, finding every wanton place on her body. He nibbled his way downward, his wicked tongue teasing her nipple while she sank her fingers into his powerful shoulders. Rhona gasped as he moved lower, kissing her navel, making the flame deep inside her loins rage.

She drove her fingers into his thick onyx locks. "Och, I thought ye went to St. Andrews to be a knight."

"Mmm? I did," he mumbled, his lips tickling the sensitive skin right above the nest of hair at her apex.

"I reckon ye learned how to wield a devilish tongue rather than a lethal sword," she teased, nearly breathless.

Arthur's roguish chuckle rumbled, vibrating in her womb. "Close your eyes and allow yourself to feel." Rhona released a stuttering breath as he combed his fingers through her curls, his touch nearly driving her to madness. And then he slid his finger into her most sacred parting, as he'd done in the bath. "For the past seven years, I've been dreaming of kissing ye here."

"Kiss?" Rhona tried to sit up, but her head was spinning too much to do so.

His deep black eyes grew even darker as he grazed his teeth over his bottom lip. He held her gaze as he inched downward, coaxing her legs wider with his shoulders.

And then he did something Ivor never would have dreamed of trying. Merciful heaven, it took but one lap of Arthur's tongue to render her completely and wholly at his mercy. "Och, ye wicked devil, ye have bewitched me."

The man's deep rolling chuckle vibrated through her. His tongue swirled and licked while his lips closed over her, and by the grace of God, he sucked.

Stars darted through her vision as she arched and bucked against him. Higher and higher the tension mounted, filling her with such want, she would shatter if he stopped. While his mouth was still upon her, he slid his finger into her core, driving her mad. Rhona tossed her head from side to side. "Oh, my, oh, my!"

Insatiable need completely controlled her and sent her to a place where she was positive she'd burst...until all at once her entire body went taut, hanging upon the precipice of pure ecstasy. A cry caught in the back of her throat. With her next gasp, the world splintered into pulsing bursts of rapture.

Unable to move, Rhona lay prostrate on the bed. Who knew a woman could be so utterly pleasured? "How did ye ken that would happen?"

Arthur slipped up beside her, pressing his member into her hip. "'Tis part of the training to become a knight."

"Truly?"

"Mayhap I fibbed a tad." He kissed her lips. "But

when we take an oath of chivalry, let us just say it means taking care of women in every way."

"I don't think I want to know any more about that." At least, she did not want to think about Arthur being with any woman other than her.

He laughed and nuzzled into her hair. "I dream of bathing in these tresses."

She coaxed him atop her and spread her legs while his manhood slid to the place she wanted it. "And I dream of having ye here."

"Ye do?"

She nodded. Arthur covered her mouth, kissing like a man starved. When he came up for air, his dark eyes were filled with desire. "I want ye more than life itself."

As Rhona rolled her hips, the coil of hot desire pulsed through her once more. But this time she needed him inside her. "Then take me as your wife."

"I want it to be good for ye. Are ye ready so soon after..."

She arched enough to catch the tip of his member at her entrance. "Ever so ready."

"I'm dangerously close to spilling my seed."

"We have a lifetime ahead of us." Aye, she prayed it was true. Their union was tenuous, but they had taken their vows in a house of God. Rhona prayed their marriage would grow from this moment forward as she grasped his shaft and guided him inside.

He thrust deep and pulled back. His breathing sped with every plunge. He filled and stretched her, rubbing the spot that might again send her to the stars. Rhona bucked against him, sighing uncontrollably. The spiciness of his scent enveloped her. His cock filled her. Every inch of skin craved more until once again she froze at the pinnacle of ecstasy. In one earth-shattering burst, she pulsed around him. "Arthur, oh Arthur. I love you!"

With a roar, he thrust deep and held himself inside

as he released. Rhona watched in amazement as his body shook as if his seed burst from his very soul. And when he opened his eyes he grinned, his white teeth gleaming. "Do ye really?"

"Love ye?"

"Aye."

She cupped his cheek. If only she were better at revealing her heart. "I always have, sir knight, and I always will."

THE ICE ENCASING ARTHUR'S HEART CRACKED. HELL, it not only cracked, it shattered and melted. Rhona loved him. At least he hadn't misjudged that. He wanted to proclaim his love with every fiber of his body, but his wounds were still too raw. No matter how much he desired to instantly forgive her for her misdeeds, a wee voice in his head commanded him to bide his time.

Nonetheless, he did not want this moment to pass. "Ye ken how I feel about you," he whispered into her neck, praying those words were enough for now.

Her arms tightened around him. "Aye."

He rolled to the side to ease his weight from atop her. "Do ye ken how fine ye are to me?"

The sparkle in Rhona's eyes touched his soul as did her sweet smile. "I'd wager nearly as fine as ye are to me." She ran her fingers through his hair. "You were my first love, and even when you left and broke my heart, I still pined for ye. You always look upon me like no other man. Ye do not see a cripple with hair too white and eyes too pale. I ken ye like what ye see, and it fills me with warmth to be wanted."

"I do want you. More than anything. I want you."

She kissed him and whispered, "Mayhap in time ye'll find it in your heart to forgive me."

Arthur's mouth grew dry. Dear God, he wanted to

forgive her of everything, especially when she lay naked in his arms.

The door creaked open at the most inopportune time. "Oh my!" squeaked Gillie. "Forgive me. I thought Her Ladyship would need to dress for the evening meal."

As Rhona curled into him and hid under the bed-clothes, Arthur chuckled. "I think I'd rather take our meal up here this eve. Please arrange for a trencher to be brought up."

"Aye, sir. Is there anything else ye'll be needing?"

"A ewer of wine ought to suffice. Thank you."

When the maid closed the door, Arthur raised Rhona's chin with the crook of his finger. "Are ye bashful, lass?"

"That was mortifying. Here we are in bed together and at this time of day."

"I'm glad of it. For one, it will allay any rumors, and for two, 'tis about time we were caught. After all, we are newly wed."

"Well, I reckon we ought to have the foresight to bolt the door in the future."

"If you wish." He sat up and pulled the blanket from the foot of the bed and held it up. "What say you to a fireside feast?"

"That sounds perfect," she said, rolling into the blanket and covering herself before she pattered across the floor and slipped her shift over her head.

Arthur belted his brechan low across his hips and set to arranging the coverlet and pillows in front of the hearth.

Rhona donned her kirtle and tied the laces. As she looked up, her gaze meandered to his chest and her saucy tongue slipped to the corner of her mouth. "Are ye planning to put on your shirt?"

He shrugged. "Would ye prefer it if I did?"

"Not necessarily."

The corners of his mouth turned up with a devilish grin. "Who knew ye were a wanton?"

She batted her eyelashes. "Me?"

He pulled her into his arms and tickled her ribs. "I'll wager you did not even ken ye were a wanton."

Squealing, she writhed against him. "In a single day ye have corrupted me, sir knight. I blame you entirely."

"So it is my fault?"

"Absolutely."

"Then I am glad of it."

The food arrived and, after the servants took their leave, Arthur made certain to bolt the door. He fully intended to spend the evening enjoying his wife. For the first time since Clyde returned, Arthur allowed himself to feel and simply be with Rhona without judgment clouding his mind. They took turns nourishing each other, all the while sipping wine. The fire was warm, the bedding on the floor was cozy and they were alone in their own wee world.

Once their hunger was satiated, he tugged open the lace on her kirtle and urged her to slip it and her shift over her head. As he sealed his lips atop hers, Rhona's fingers fumbled for his belt and released it.

Arthur was hard and ready, but this time, he wanted to linger. He rested her against the pillows and gazed into her eyes, a wicked grin spreading across his lips. "I want ye to lie perfectly still. I can touch you, but you cannot touch me."

Ignoring his command, she traced her finger down the center of his chest, making his cock so rigid, it tapped his stomach. "Is it a game you wish to play?"

"Aye," he croaked, kissing her fingers and placing them at her side. "But ye mustn't touch me again."

"Will I be able to go next?"

"I hope ye will wish to."

She smiled. "When will it be my turn?"

"After you have been completely and utterly ravished."

Rhona reached for him but drew her hand away before her fingers brushed his flesh. "And who is to determine that, you or me??"

"'Tis only fair for you to be the judge, is it not?"

Kneeling, he braced his hands on either side of her head and kissed each of her eyes. His lips caressed her supple cheeks until he meandered downward and found her mouth. Arthur didn't try to stop Rhona from returning his kiss, and a bit of seed dribbled from his cock as she hungrily swirled her tongue with his.

But he had only started on this journey. He plied her milky-white skin with feathery kisses along her neck and down each arm, licking each finger as he watched her writhe. When he at last reached her breasts, her nipples stood proud for him. And as he lingered, her whimper drove him to the edge of madness.

Taking in a reviving breath, he moved down to her navel. Then he passed very near the apex of her sex while he kissed his way down her shapely thighs, her calves, and toyed with the sensitive arches of her feet.

Rhona grasped the coverlet in her fists. "Pleeeease."

"Do ye want more?" he asked.

She nodded and reached for him. "Now."

He grinned, enjoying this game ever so much. "Ye mustn't touch me wife."

As she groaned, he shouldered between her legs for the second time that night. It thrilled him to no end that she had never been pleasured with a man's mouth. He dipped his gaze to her womanhood and inhaled the most heavenly scent—floral concoction, nearly sending him to the stars. "Ye are divine."

He lapped his tongue along her sensitive flesh.

"Again," she demanded, rocking her hips.

Arthur slid his tongue in and out of her and then sealed his mouth over the wee button that would drive her over the edge. Rhona's eyes grew dark as she curled up, crying out. With an enormous sigh, she dropped back to the cushions and thrust her hips, circling in tandem with his merciless kisses.

As she gasped, her flesh erupted into a sea of tremors. Arthur slowly eased the intensity of his ministrations while Rhona shivered, her entire body experiencing a series of involuntary shudders. Only then did he slide up beside her.

She blessed him with a satiated smile as she smoothed the hair away from his face. "Ye were right, I am completely ravished." And then her grin widened with a wicked flash in her eyes. "Now 'tis your turn."

Arthur obeyed and rolled to his back, his cock jutting from his loins like a tree limb. If she dared touch it, he'd spill for certain.

Rhona kneeled beside him, her hands on her exquisitely curved hips, her gaze raking over his body as if deciding where to start. Fingers twitching, Arthur forced himself not to reach out and trace his hand along the arc of her waist. Obey the rules of the game he must, lest he lose.

He steeled himself to endure her blissful torture while she straddled his legs. God strike him dead, for everything holy, the woman's hands did not caress his flesh, but she cupped her breasts and pushed them together. Arthur tapped his top lip with his tongue, imagining burying his face in her exquisite bosom.

"Do you like to see me touch myself?" she whispered.

"Aye," he growled hoarsely.

Her gaze dipped to his loins. "I want to watch you stroke it."

He moved his hand, his fingers aching to give him release.

She grasped his wrist and guided it back to the floor. "But nay this time," she teased, smiling like a vixen.

Rhona devoured his mouth, then moved southward with the same fervor. She toyed with his nipples while his cock throbbed with need. She moved down, down, down, until she licked the inside of his thigh. God's stones, would she be so bold as to take him into her mouth? How charmed was he to have a wife so brazen? The woman's deft tongue flicked kisses around his manhood but did not touch it.

"Open," she demanded, sliding between his legs. Arthur arched and gasped as she tickled his balls with her tongue and then suckled them. Never in his life had any woman turned his cods into tight, raging fireballs.

At last, Rhona swirled her tongue along his shaft without grasping it.

"God save me," he groaned.

And then she completely benumbed his mind by gripping the root of his manhood with her hand and sliding her mouth over the sensitive tip. Moaning, Arthur's eyes rolled back. Trying not to come, he clenched his bum cheeks, and gnashed his teeth. "I can take this no longer!"

He grasped her shoulders and pulled her atop him. "You are the victor," he said, sliding inside her.

Rhona arched her back and rode him. "I like winning."

Arthur's heart raced as he kept hold of her hips and urged her to thrust harder and faster. When a shocking gasp came from the depths of her throat, stars crossed his vision with the most powerful climax of his life. It transported him to paradise and filled him with the love he'd forever carried in his heart.

When his breathing finally slowed, he wrapped his arms around her and kissed her as if their souls were entwined. "When we are alone, nothing matters but us."

R hona settled into a routine of passionate nights with her husband, though Arthur was still mostly absent during the days, and never in their bed when she awoke in the morning. She knew it would take him time to admit his love for her, but she fully intended to earn it. And once she did, she vowed never again to forsake such a gift.

Tonight, they sat in front of the fire while Arthur read from a book of sonnets—a very rare and valuable book from his days in St. Andrews.

"My lady!" came a child's voice from beyond the door. "Me ma's bairn is coming!"

Rhona immediately sprang to her feet, dashed across the floor, and threw open the door. "How far apart are her pains?"

Twisting his mouth, Gregor spread his palms to his sides. "Da just said to fetch ye. Ma's sweating something awful. She's screaming, too. I don't remember it being like this with the last babe."

Rhona hastened to swing her cloak across her shoulders and looked to Arthur. "Please fetch Clyde. There's no time to lose."

Arthur was already at the door. "I'll go with you."

She picked up her medicine basket and started out. "Are ye certain? It could be a long night."

A tic twitched at the corner of his eye. "I'll go."

Rhona had not a moment to argue as they rushed to the cottage. As soon as the door opened, Sara cried out with a hideous wail. Making her way to the bedside, Rhona brushed past the children, their cheeks wet with tears as they clung to each other and wept.

Fingal's eyes were wild and frantic as he reached for Rhona's basket and set it on the table. "Thank the good Lord ye are here. The pains came on faster than ever before."

Rhona ran her hand over her friend's sweaty forehead. "How are ye, love?"

"'Tis bad. The bairn doesn't feel as if it has moved low enough but my pains are fierce."

"May I have a wee peek?"

After Sara nodded, Rhona took a candle and peered beneath the bedclothes. "Oh my."

"What is it?" demanded Fingal.

"The babe is in a breech presentation," she said as the wee ones cried all the louder, making her head pound. In an instant, she made a decision and grasped the smithy's meaty hands. "Take the children to Lady Mary's and bed down there for the night."

"Gregor," barked Fingal as a bead of sweat drained from his temple into his beard. "Ye heard Her Ladyship. Go!"

"You, as well." Rhona grasped the man's elbow and urged him toward the door. "I'll send for ye as soon as the babe is here, but ye must go take care of your wee ones now. This is no place for ye at the moment."

Arthur beckoned him. "Come, I'll go with ye."

"Nay," Rhona released Fingal and grabbed her husband's wrist. "You will stay and you will help."

The big knight's face went stark white. "Very well," he mumbled.

Fingal hastened to the bed and gave Sara a kiss before he took the children away.

Rhona returned her attention to the patient. "Thank heavens he didn't give me an argument."

Sara half chuckled, half cried. "He kens how awful it can be. This is our sixth, mind ye." The words hadn't completely escaped her lips as her face turned ashen, followed by a harrowing scream.

"Quickly." Rhona beckoned Arthur. "I need your help to turn the babe."

"Are ye jesting?" he asked, moving beside her.

"We must try. And Sara, no matter what, do not push, do ye hear me?"

Rhona had Arthur push downward while she tried to move the unborn, but as Sara grew weaker and her breathing labored, the bairn would not budge. "'Tis no use," she said, snatching a razor-sharp dagger from her basket and running the blade through a candle's flame. "Please see to it there's water on the boil and plenty of cloths at the ready."

"The cloths are on the washstand," Sara managed to grind out through clenched teeth.

Hiding the knife behind her skirts, Rhona moved to the bedside. "Do not push until I say it is time. Do ye understand?"

Sara nodded. "Please." She panted. "Help."

"Now lie back and bring up your knees."

"Eeee!"

Rhona glanced to Arthur before she made the cut. He may have fought in dozens of battles, but he looked as if he were turning as green as the moss on the thatched roof. And if she knew anything about midwifery, it was best to keep her helper occupied. "Set the cloths at the foot of the bed." She looked to Sara. "This might hurt a wee bit, but it will keep ye from tearing."

"Haste!"

Rhona bit down on her lip as she deftly made the cut.

"Och, Lord have mercy!" Sara cried.

"Hold her hand," Rhona shouted as she slipped her fingers inside, grasping the wee bottom. Careful not to apply too much pressure, she gave the slightest of tugs while Sara's breathing became more and more labored.

"She's fading," Arthur said. "What can I do?"

"Keep hold of her hand and wipe the sweat from her brow."

"Eee! The. Pain. I. Have to. Push!"

"Aye, push." Rhona tugged a wee bit harder with the force of Sara's pushing and bloodcurdling screams.

ARTHUR HAD SEEN MEN CUT OPEN, BUT THE TORTURE and agony suffered by Sara this night surpassed anything he'd witnessed on the battlefield. The linens were soiled with so much blood. The woman was on death's door. And Rhona, God bless her, was as stoic and solid as a soldier.

"He's coming!" Rhona shouted. "Keep pushing!"

Sara's eyes rolled back as she gasped for air, her body completely spent.

Arthur squeezed her hand. "You can do it. I ken ye can."

Crying and holding on for dear life, Sara curled up, squeezed her eyes shut, and bore down. "Arrrrrrghaaaaah!"

Rhona tugged the babe away. "I have him."

Sara collapsed to the pillow.

Rhona grasped the blood-covered babe by the feet and slapped his bottom. "Fetch the string and shears from my basket."

Arthur's heart lurched as a cry pealed out.

"Now!" his wife ordered.

Arthur did as told, acting on Rhona's every request as she tied off and cut the umbilical, cleansed the bairn in the warm water and swaddled him, and then rested the lad in his mother's arms.

"'Tis a miracle," he said, awed by his wife's caring nature, and the skill with which she had efficiently carried out each task.

"Aye, but it isn't over yet. I need to stitch the cut. Whilst I take care of that, you must help the babe to suckle."

Arthur gaped.

She jabbed him in the shoulder with the heel of her hand. "Do it, I say!"

Sara, barely conscious, winced as Rhona set to stitching.

Arthur gestured to the tie closing her shift. "May I?"

"I'll do it."

But the mere act of tugging on the string sapped the woman of her remaining strength.

Rhona looked up. "Put another pillow under her head; then move the lad to her teat. The bairn will ken what to do from there."

All he could do was obey. Never in his life had he felt so out of place, yet so proud to be married to this woman who was capable of bringing a life into this world even when the odds were stacked against it.

By the time Rhona sent him to fetch Fingal and the children, it was dawn. But Sara had sipped some water, and some color had returned to her face while the babe slept in her arms. They left the family together, the wee ones all clamoring to see their new brother.

As they made their way back to the castle, Arthur held Rhona's hand. "You are an astonishing woman."

She snorted and looked to the skies. "I do what I can. But mark me, 'tis a miracle we did not lose them both."

He stopped and braced his palms on her shoulders.

"Mother and child are alive this morn because of you, my love."

"I'd like to think I helped."

"Well, I know it is true."

"Thank ye for staying with me. I could not have done as well without you." She bit her lip and glanced away. "I've been doing some thinking, and I ken I owe ye not only an apology, but I owe ye my life."

"Och, ye owe me nothing. I, too, have been doing some thinking. I tried to imagine myself in your shoes, and I believe I understand your fierce loyalty. But more than that, I clearly realize that you have a heart the size of the North Sea. Ye love your clan and kin, and there's nothing ye wouldn't do for a sick or injured man or woman, be them friend or foe."

She smiled. "I cannot turn my back when someone is in need."

"No, you cannot, and I love ye all the more for it."

Rhona's eyes grew wide while her mouth formed an O. "L-love me?"

"Aye." He brushed his lips across hers. "I've loved ye ever since I first set eyes on ye. One innocent smile from you, and ye owned my heart for the rest of eternity."

❦ 26 ❦

TWO WEEKS LATER

Before the Samhain festivities began, Arthur accompanied Rhona through the village while she made her rounds. Not because his wife needed an escort, as she was now free to come and go as she pleased, but because he'd offered to do so this morning, and she was only too happy to have him with her.

They checked on Benny, who had made a complete recovery. Next, they visited Sara, who was now up and about while Fingal had returned to his duties at the smithy shack. Gregor was thrilled to return to the castle and continue as Arthur's squire, if only to escape the overcrowded one-room cottage. The new bairn was thriving and healthy with ten fingers and ten toes and a gummy wail loud enough to shake the rafters.

As the sun began to set, they called into Gran's cottage. Arthur looked on while Rhona crossed the floor and gave the old woman a kiss. "Goodness, the place is looking tidy."

"Thanks to my maid," Lady Mary replied in her usual saucy manner. "She's far better at housekeeping than you, my dear."

Rhona glanced at Arthur over her shoulder and gave a very slight shake of her head. Some things never changed, especially when it came to her grandmother.

257

"Mayhap because I was always out visiting the sick and infirm."

"Aye, there's that." Gran waggled her eyebrows at Arthur. "Ye might be interested to ken my brother sent me a letter at long last."

"Is that so?" he asked, stepping nearer.

"Aye and it may please ye to ken you are for once in my good graces, lad, because not only have you married my granddaughter, the Lord of Lorn has made amends with Robert the Bruce and will be in attendance at parliament in St. Andrews, God willing."

Though Arthur had received a letter from the king stating the same and clarifying that Dunstaffnage would remain in the possession of the crown, he wasn't about to deflate Lady Mary's good spirits by letting her know he'd already been informed. "I say, that is wonderful news."

"I kent Granduncle Alexander would come to his senses," said Rhona, though her shoulders shook as she laughed.

"What is it?" Arthur asked.

"I was just reflecting back to the day I stood in the great hall as the clan's spokeswoman. When you barreled through those enormous double doors claiming Dunstaffnage for the king of Scots, I made a silent vow to never look to the Bruce as my sovereign. At least not until my granduncle pledged his fealty."

Arthur took her hand and thumbed her wedding ring with the pink stone. "And now he has."

"Aye, but in hindsight, I cannot believe I was so stubborn. Especially given all the unity and peace Robert is trying to bring to the kingdom."

Lady Mary picked up her knitting. "Stubbornness is a MacDougall trait. We're all obstinate, but in time we come to our senses."

Arthur shook his head and regarded the woman. Had she just admitted to being wrong? "I'm glad to be in your good graces once again, m'lady. This evening, expect my guards to arrive and carry you to the castle for the celebrations."

"Och, I'm too old."

"Nay!" Rhona exclaimed. "You will have a place of honor at the high table. And I'll entertain no arguments."

AS THE SUN DIPPED BELOW THE WESTERN HORIZON and the sky took on striated hews of orange, pink and violet, Rhona stood beside Arthur in the outer bailey. He held a torch aloft. Before them was a fire pit filled with kindling and logs, prepared for the evening's celebration. Down below in the village, no smoke billowed from the cottage chimneys, as all flames had been snuffed to commence the Samhain festival of fire.

"Good people of Dunstaffnage," Arthur said, his voice strong and assured as he addressed the crowd. "Together we have brought in a bountiful harvest that will keep our larders full through the season of winter and shorter days. With this torch, I light the fires of winter. As we celebrate the fortune of an abundant yield, this fire will continue to burn, and when ye head for home's hearth this night, light your torches and bring Samhain's fire to warm your cottages and bless them with our good fortune!"

When a cheer swelled through the air, Rhona placed her hand over Arthur's and together they lit the fire, celebrating the ancient Celtic tradition of welcoming the harvest and marking the midpoint between the autumnal equinox and the winter solstice. Once the timbers were ablaze and crackling, Arthur tossed the torch into the flames, then wrapped his arm around her shoulders and pulled her close.

"I feel as if I am the luckiest man in all of Christendom."

"And why is that?" she asked, though she, too, felt as if good fortune had blessed her as well.

He faced her, his hands sliding around her waist. "Because I am married to the only woman I have ever loved. And though the kingdom may not yet be at peace, this corner of the Highlands is our haven."

Rhona gazed into her husband's eyes. As always, they were dark and intense, but she loved how they focused only on her and filled with love. "I cannot believe I am so happy."

He dipped his chin and kissed her, right there in front of everyone. And as the cheers became hoots and hollers, he deepened the kiss, sealing their bond forever.

As he touched his forehead to hers, she chuckled. "If ye keep kissing me like that, we'll have to retire above stairs afore the feast has begun."

He took her hand and kissed it, too. "A private feast for the pair of us sounds far more tempting, lass."

She gave him a playful wink. "Perhaps we ought to at least make an appearance. After all, Gran is already seated at the high table."

"If you insist." He straightened the pink stone on her ring and kissed it as well. "When I purchased this from Fingal, my only intention at the time was to put it on your finger when we took our vows."

Rhona smiled at the way the stone caught the flickers of firelight. "I'm ever so glad ye did, and now that I know it was made by our very own smithy, I like it all the more. I look upon the stone every day and it reminds me of you, of your kindness, of how you never gave up hope for me even after I had behaved like a naughty renegade."

"Och, someone needed to rein you in." He pressed

his lips to her temple. "Even if ye are a stubborn Mac-Dougall."

"Campbell," Rhona replied, rising onto her toes and kissing his cheek. "Ye ken, I love you more now than ever."

"And I you," he said, taking her hand and leading her into the great hall to enjoy the feast and the evening's celebrations. At least until they could slip above stairs for an intimate gathering of their own.

I had a lot of fun writing *Highland Beast*, and hope you enjoyed the story as well. I was able to visit Dunstaffnage castle on one of my many trips to Scotland, and there I discovered the castle had gone through many changes over the centuries. The ruins that now stand on the promontory between Loch Etive and the Firth of Lorn are quite different from what the fortress would have looked like in the fourteenth century. Fortunately, I used an artist's rendering of the medieval fortress to help me with some of the descriptions.

As with all my stories, I try to weave the fiction around actual events. After Robert the Bruce defeated the MacDougall army in the Battle of the Pass of Brander, he laid claim to Dunstaffnage Castle and appointed Arthur Campbell as constable. Alexander MacDougall, Lord of Lorn, fled to England where he remained until making amends with the king, though Dunstaffnage remained the property of the crown. In time, Dunollie, the small keep mentioned in the story, became the MacDougall seat.

Though it's not known who Arthur married, he is responsible for starting the Clan Arthur line. Since we know nothing of his wife, Rhona's story is entirely fictional. I must admit, it wasn't easy for me to write a character who was fiercely loyal, but whose loyalties were so terribly misplaced. I'm only happy that Arthur chose to marry her rather than send her to the gallows. And though she may have thought him a beast at one time, he proved his heart was as big as the Highlands.

Also of note, in 2019 I stayed in Stonehaven Scotland where I attended a concert given by Aberdeenshire folksinger, Iona Fyfe. I purchased one of her albums, which has become a favorite. At the concert she sang "The Twa Sisters", the folksong that Arthur and Rhona enjoyed when they went on their hunting expedition. If you would like to learn more about Iona's music, her website is https://ionafyfe.com/.

ALSO BY AMY JARECKI

The MacGalloways

A Duke by Scot

The King's Outlaws

Highland Warlord

Highland Raider

Highland Beast 3

Highland Defender

The Valiant Highlander

The Fearless Highlander

The Highlander's Iron Will

Highland Force:

Captured by the Pirate Laird

The Highland Henchman

Beauty and the Barbarian

Return of the Highland Laird

Guardian of Scotland

Rise of a Legend

In the Kingdom's Name

The Time Traveler's Destiny

Highland Dynasty

Knight in Highland Armor

A Highland Knight's Desire

A Highland Knight to Remember

Highland Knight of Rapture

Highland Knight of Dreams

Devilish Dukes

The Duke's Fallen Angel

The Duke's Untamed Desire

ICE

Hunt for Evil

Body Shot

Mach One

Celtic Fire

Rescued by the Celtic Warrior

Deceived by the Celtic Spy

Lords of the Highlands series:

The Highland Duke

The Highland Commander

The Highland Guardian

The Highland Chieftain

The Highland Renegade

The Highland Earl

The Highland Rogue

The Highland Laird

The Chihuahua Affair

Virtue: A Cruise Dancer Romance

Boy Man Chief

Time Warriors

ABOUT THE AUTHOR

Known for her action-packed, passionate historical romances, Amy Jarecki has received reader and critical praise throughout her writing career. She won the prestigious 2018 RT Reviewers' Choice award for *The Highland Duke* and the 2016 RONE award from InD'tale Magazine for Best Time Travel for her novel *Rise of a Legend*. In addition, she hit Amazon's Top 100 Bestseller List, the Apple, Barnes & Noble, and Bookscan Bestseller lists, in addition to earning the designation as an Amazon All Star Author. Readers also chose her Scottish historical romance, *A Highland Knight's Desire,* as the winning title through Amazon's Kindle Scout Program. Amy holds an MBA from Heriot-Watt University in Edinburgh, Scotland and now resides in Southwest Utah with her husband where she writes immersive historical romances. Learn more on Amy's website. Or sign up to receive Amy's newsletter.

Ingram Content Group UK Ltd.
Milton Keynes UK
UKHW041255260723
425821UK00004B/81

9 781648 391064